HARBOR

2023 edition

HARBOR

Love & Disaster Book 2

Tara L. Roí

BEE BOOKS

NEW HAVEN

Harbor: Love & Disaster trilogy book 2
Copyright © 2021 Tara L. Roí
All rights reserved.

Book design: Rebekah Fraser
Cover art: MacKenzie Coffman
Cover design: MacKenzie Coffman & Rebekah Fraser

First Edition: 2022
ISBN: 978-1-7353484-6-9 (hardcover)
ISBN: 978-1-7353484-5-2 (paperback)
ISBN: 978-1-7353484-4-5 (ebook)

2023 Edition features a new cover & minor content changes

Of course, for my daughter

1
Flight

THIS IS THE STATE OF OVERWHELM—POUNDING HEART, agitated mind, empty stomach. Running around the crowded airport and going through security does it to me every time. At least the TSA didn't harass me today. Now the problem is trying to dodge the clump of people gathered by this gate so I have time to pee before my flight boards. Maybe get a snack. The smell of beignets and café au lait makes the emptiness in my stomach more intense.

My phone buzzes, and Lila's youthful soprano sings "Hey, Mama," à la Kanye West. I slip the phone out of my back pocket. Seeing my daughter's sweet face on my screen softens the tension in my chest. "Missing me already?"

She sighs. "Daddy's bridezilla is driving me crazy."

"Oh, honey. I'm sorry. I wish you were coming with me to Connecticut, but—"

"Why're you out of breath?"

"Am I? Just hurtling toward the gate is all." C5, C7. Two more gates. "Hey, don't worry about Rini. Once she's got that ring on her finger, she'll chill out. And then you'll go back to having fun together."

"I hope so," she grumbles.

"It's your first flower girl gig too. How special it's for your daddy's wedding! Phew. Here's the gate."

They haven't started boarding, but all the seats in the area are full. There isn't even any wall space to lean against.

"Aren't flower girls supposed to be, like, five?"

"Jeez, I don't know, hon. Why?"

"Phoebe says since I'm twelve, I should be a junior bridesmaid."

"Tell you what, if I ever get married again, you can be my maid of honor, whether you're twelve or twenty-five."

"You might wanna go out on a date if you think you're fixin' to get married, Mama."

"Fresh!" I laugh. "Listen, Mama has to pee. I'll text you from the plane, okay?"

Of course, there's another long line to the restroom and only fifteen minutes until boarding. Sigh. The phone rings again, and I see a patient's name pop up on the screen. Can I get through this call before I make it into the restroom? Doubtful. Why does she always call two days after the appointment she doesn't show up for? It'll have to go to voice mail. Now a text from someone else:

Amira, when's my next
appointment?

I tap into the screen:

            Wednesday afternoon?
            Please check your email for the
            calendar invite.

Another patient texts.

Algebra test = F. Might fail class.

Oh, this poor kid.

            Sorry! What happened?

Can I call?

No, I'm at the airport.

I hate to share too much personal information with a patient, especially a teen.

Did you sleep the night before the test?

Nightmares all week. Trapped.
Rising waters.

Scary, I know. Remember, bad dreams help you process and heal the trauma. Did you write down your dream or do a sketch of it in your journal?

I'll try that.

Good. Then try that Yoga breathing exercise I showed you. Okay?

Got it.

Can you make up the test? Or do something for extra credit?

He sends a thinking face emoji.

Self-advocate!

Thumbs-up emoji.

Another crisis averted while standing in line for the toilet. I slip the phone back into my pocket, only to feel it vibrate again with the ringtone reserved for my most delicate patients. Oh God! I'll have to let them leave a message. I cannot take a call from a restroom stall.

How many times must I ask my patients not to contact me after hours unless they're in desperate need? And if it's really dire, to call 911 or the psychiatrist I referred them to for meds? I know I told each of them I'd be out of town this weekend. Granted, it *is* a long weekend, but I didn't schedule a single appointment for these four days because I need the break. Hearing about children's traumas on repeat takes a toll, and I'm burned out.

Once my hands are clean and I'm back on the concourse, standing in line at Café Du Monde, I text the patient: I'm not able to be present for you right now. If you're in urgent need, call Dr. Glaude. Otherwise, I'll see you at your appt. next week.

I guess I need to create clearer boundaries with my patients to protect my own mental health. The question is: How?

My phone buzzes again. Now it's the airline app letting me know they're starting to board. This line's too long. So much for my beignet and café au lait. At least I have a banana and some pralines in my purse. I head back toward the gate, reach into my bag for the fruit. Wait a minute. Where's my license? I look at my phone wallet—not there. Dig around in my purse. I don't see it. Shoot! I feel around the pockets of my jacket until I find something flat, pull it out, look at it. *Yes, Amira, it's in your hand. Relax. Ouch!*

"Whoa," a deep voice says. The voice comes from the solid mass of muscle I just ran into headlong. Elegant shirt. Mother-of-pearl buttons. Smooth chestnut skin above the collar.

Heat rushes up my neck as I brave a glance at his chin (strong), mouth (supple), and eyes (compassionate). "Oh my goodness. I'm so sorry!" I pant.

"Don't think twice," he says, holding my gaze. "Just going into the Premiere Club for a drink. Care to join me?"

His voice settles into my skin, soothes the nerves. But who asks a complete stranger for a drink at an airport?

"Thank you, no." I hurry away, resisting the urge to look back.

On the plus side, he wasn't mad about my crashing into him. His voice resounds in my mind: *Don't think twice.* Unusual speech pattern.

Something vibrates in my jeans.

Derek

Concourse C is a mob scene. Noisy, so I appreciate that the automated voice in this airport has a soothing tone like a muted trombone. Still, everyone's scurrying. No surprise someone would plow right into me. I look down at her. Cherubic face. Olive skin. Full, beautiful mouth.

"Oh my goodness. I'm so sorry," she says, her voice breathy, chest heaving.

"Don't think twice," I say, finally catching her eyes... and holy shit! The adrenaline rush is wicked fierce. "Just going into the Premiere Club for a drink. Care to join me?"

"Thank you, no," she says and continues on her way. Purposeful stride. High-heeled black leather boots. Black leather jacket. Long brown dreads dyed yellow at the tips. The way she moves... Wow!

Those eyes. Like I've been seen by some ancient soul. God, what the hell does *that* mean? I don't think things like that. It's a thing my grandmother would have said.

I take a deep breath and let it out forcefully. As I stroll into the Premiere Club and flash my ID at the guard, those fierce hazel eyes pop into my mind. Then an image of her hovering above me, her dreads cascading around my face as she lowers her mouth to mine. Maybe I should run after her. No. *No.* Three months, no romance. If I'm gonna get my act together, I need to stick with the female fast for another month. No flirting. No dating. No sex. Tough, but God knows I've been through worse. Besides, there's no ban on self-pleasure.

The voice of my men's group leader rings in my head. Observe your reactions. Write down your thoughts. Write about the feelings. The way to a more fulfilling relationship is to know yourself, to understand your motivations and reactions.

I go to the bar, order a bourbon on the rocks, and find a spot on one of the soft leather armchairs by the window. Pull my journal out of my garment bag and start writing.

Almost at the end of the detox, tempted by a woman with penetrating eyes. Didn't feel like my normal flirtation. Barely noticed her physical appearance until she was walking away. Then only saw her from behind. Spectacular view. But not... Shit. I asked her to join me for a drink. Only because she seemed so flustered. Nope, that's a lie. Lying to myself.

I sigh and circle the last three words, hearing the group leader's voice in my head. "The biggest impediment to your growth is the tendency to lie to yourself, and we all do it." Damn it. Take a long pull of bourbon. Back to the journal.

Invited her to join me for a drink because I looked at her and I felt seen even though the only words exchanged were "Oh, I'm sorry." She couldn't possibly have seen into my soul in those five seconds, though that's what it felt like. As I near the end of this, am I so desperate for female attention that I'm reading into basic exchanges? Didn't with the bartender or the security guard or the ladies at the restaurant last night or that gorgeous woman in front of me in the line to get through security today. Barely noticed her. LIE—I noticed enough to be writing about it. FACT—she didn't excite me. I did not initiate a conversation even though she turned around, checked me out, and winked. I didn't wink back. I smiled politely and looked down.

If I run out of here now, could I find the woman with the penetrating hazel eyes and the long dreads? Normally I'm not into dreads, but on her... She's gotta be long gone by now. It's ludicrous to think about trying to find her.

The airline app buzzes again, alerting me for the second time that boarding's in progress. Ten minutes before they close the door to the plane. Finish the last of my bourbon. Gather my things. Head out.

2

Hypersaturated

Derek

A GUST OF FRIGID AIR SENDS WHIRLWINDS OF AUTUMN leaves across the slate sidewalk and chills me. My heart pounds as I stand in this cold, wanting a cigarette so bad I can taste it but glad I quit. Thinking, for the God-knows-how-many-eth time, about the woman at the airport. Soulful eyes.

Focus on the present, Derek. Look at where you are.

Charming street in downtown New Haven, Connecticut. Old-fashioned lampposts lighting the way. One of the Yale dorms across the street. And a long-ass line to get into this gallery to see the artwork of my best buddy's bride-to-be.

That my best bro is about to get married chills me even more than this autumn evening in New Haven. His fiancée is good at her job, good enough to get that prestigious $2.5 million Brilliance grant from the MacKenzie Foundation. But does that mean she'll be a good wife to Wesley? Jesus, I hope so. I don't want to watch him crumble again like he did when Eve left him at the altar.

For me, one marriage was enough. I hear my accountability buddy's voice in my head: What's the benefit of telling yourself that story about staying single and safe, Derek? Protection. Is that why I'm so concerned about Wesley? Burned once, but diving in again? The dude seems crazy, but his heart is made up. He's not protecting himself. I'm gonna have to write about this in my journal.

Stepping into K-Gallery brings relief—warmth, light, and the smell of herbal tea and wine. I scan the crowd for Wesley and see him across the room, make a beeline to him, grip him in a tight hug for a moment.

"Where's the bride-to-be?" I ask.

Wesley points to the other side of the room, and I recognize the woman from the photos and news clips: Sage DesChamps. Fuck. She's even hotter in person. Several months pregnant, no less. Sage stands in a corner by the plate-glass window, illuminated by the lights of a news crew.

"She's being interviewed at the moment," Wesley says, "but when you see Sage's art, you'll begin to know her. Let me show you."

He leads me to a piece called Join Us: After the Storm. Apparently, Sage sold the piece in April, but it was damaged during one of the tornadoes that spun off from the supercell T-storm that hit New Haven in May. Wes raves about how Sage couldn't repair it, so she re-envisioned it, then added more layers and elements. "Essentially, she turned the piece into an exploration of how climate disruption affects everyone, even artists."

He's got my attention with that story. I step back a few feet until I hit a velvet rope set up as a barrier. Scanning the work, I notice the canvas printed with an aerial photo of the Mississippi River spilling into the Gulf of Mexico.

"Love the hypersaturated colors," I say.

Wes points to the patchwork of farmland. "See how she added layers of oil paint to tone down or highlight different parts of the image? Here she used rich golds and emeralds. She toned down the river and the algal bloom in the gulf almost to gray to represent the death occurring there. She could have used Photoshop instead of paint, but Sage says paint adds layers of intensity and meaning."

"She stitched the canvas with gold thread? What's the symbolism?"

"Bringing the nation together."

I move in to get a closer look, whistle. "Like she's conducting surgery on her work... What's this flaky stuff?"

"Algae collected from the spot where the Mississippi flows into the Gulf of Mexico," he says. "And get this: shards of the plate-glass window ripped through this painting but didn't touch the thread or the algae and phytoplankton."

"No shit!"

Wes's chest puffs up. "This was my favorite piece in the last show, but you've got to see the self-portrait she made when she found her studio was trashed."

The exhibition's title, Sage DesChamps: Art 4 Climate Justice, doesn't do the show justice. Looking at her work, I see what the fuss was about. Not only does Sage have vision but her aesthetic is fresh, bold, and clear. Each piece speaks on multiple levels. You don't wanna think too hard to figure the meaning. The work's simplicity makes it easy to grasp. But if you do wanna dig deeper into the layers of image and materials and meaning—and I do—then you're rewarded with an onion's worth of complexity. I see why my buddy fell in love with that work, started collecting it even before he met the artist. This piece is everything I'd want. In fact, I think I might buy it unless I see something I like more.

"Wes, how long's the show up?"

"A month," he says, leading me to another part of the gallery. "You know she set up a satellite show in your new hometown, right?"

"In New Orleans? No kidding. Where?"

"Royal Gallery in the French Quarter."

"All the same pieces?"

"Some prints and some originals. She also did a cool thing where she started with the same prints but augmented each one so they're all unique."

Amira

I AM SO EXCITED TO SEE SAGE'S NEW SHOW. SO PROUD OF her. And maybe inspired, too, because right now the poetry is flowing. I hold the phone close to my mouth, speak into the dictation app. "Do you dare to be known?"

"What?" the Uber driver asks.

"Hmm? Oh, nothing. Sorry, just dictating into my phone."

New poems come through me at the strangest times—in the shower, in an Uber, standing on an escalator at the airport. Now, crossing from the tree-lined streets of Prospect Hill where Yale's Divinity School sits next to Albertus Magnus College, into my old neighborhood, I feel that familiar excitement of coming home, mixed with dread. Parts of the neighborhood were improving, but from Mom's description and Sage's statement on the news, since the supercell T-storm last spring, Newhallville hasn't recovered as quickly as some other neighborhoods. In the twilight, it's hard to get a clear vision of anything, but as we pass my old high school, the blue tarp standing in for the roof flaps in the wind.

Do you dare to truly reveal yourself?

Hmm, I thought this poem was personal, but maybe it's also about society.

Do you care for the possibility of connection that might emerge from truly daring to be known as you are, behind the facade you display in the world?

To whom do you dare to be known?

This poem needs rhythm. I'll fix that later. Looks like the city installed a new streetlamp on the corner since my last visit. "It's right here," I say to the driver. She stops and waits while I gather my bag from the trunk. "I have to leave for Chapel Street in like fifteen minutes if you wanna wait."

"Sure," the driver says. "New Haven isn't exactly bustling for Uber drivers."

As I ascend the front steps, a spot between the door and the window catches my attention. Is part of the siding missing from my mother's house? Dear God! Mom didn't tell me about that, did she? Is that from the storm last spring?

I use the same key I've used since middle school to let myself into the dark house. The familiar smell of homemade apple pie fills my nostrils, and I feel more relaxed instantly. She always leaves the pie on top of the stove. The perfect pre-evening-out snack. I cut myself a small piece and take a bite. Heaven. After dropping my bags upstairs, I peer into Mom's room, the guest room, and finally duck into my old room for a quick change—slipping into my skinny black jeans and the flowy top with my lacy cardigan. Heeled boots. I pull my cosmetics from my backpack and dash into the bathroom, splash toner over my face, pat on moisturizer, then glide eye shadow over my lids. Quick hit of liner and mascara, a little lip gloss. Wish I could do something about my hair. The dreads are getting old. But now, out the door.

Back in the Uber not five seconds and my daughter's ringtone sings to me again. I fumble through my purse for the phone, see Lila's beautiful face light up the screen.

"Hi, sweetie," I sing.

"Hi, Mama," she sings back. Her voice still has the soprano of youth, but I think she'll be an alto. "How was your flight?"

"Good!"

How was your flight? Someone's maturing.

This is a teachable moment, and I'm taking advantage of it with some positive reinforcement. "That's so nice of you to ask. What are you and Daddy up to?"

"We're going shopping, and I wanted to buy some eye shadow, but Dad said to check with you first."

Thank you, Greg, for backing me up!

"Okay. Well, you're not quite thirteen yet. I think we made a deal about that, right?"

"But I've been doing great in school."

"You always do great in school."

"And I've been responsible with the eyeliner and lip gloss."

"You sure have. When will you be thirteen again?"

"Mama!" she says, exasperated. "You know when."

"So let's look at our calendars. Today is October 4. And your birthday is July 7, so... how many months is that?"

"Too long! Look at my eyes!" She points to her eyes. "They're naked! It's embarrassing."

"Mmmm. So, with that brilliant mathematical mind you inherited from your dad, tell me how many months until your birthday?"

She sighs. "Nine months and five days."

"Part of maturity, Lila, is honoring our commitments and being patient. We made a deal about eye shadow. I'll hold up my end to pay for it, and I expect you to hold up yours even though it's annoying. That's where patience comes in."

She grumbles. "Phoebe's mom lets her."

"Different people have different values, Lila. Hey, how was your Coastal Restoration meeting this afternoon?"

Her whole face lights up, and her eyes widen as they do when she's focusing. Suddenly she looks forty-five, not twelve. "Harry said the cypress trees we planted last spring are gonna be ready to transplant in March."

"Look at you, bringing the habitat back to health!"

"Oh. Daddy says it's time to go."

We make kissy faces and end the video call.

The driver turns from College Street onto Chapel, and my jaw drops; a line extends out K-Gallery about half a block. News crews line the sidewalk across the street from the gallery. Wow.

Never in my life did I imagine going to an event like this. Thank goodness I brought my warm coat. It's gonna be cold, standing outside in that line.

AT EIGHT-FIFTEEN, I SQUEEZE THROUGH THE CROWD INTO the gallery and search for my friend. She's group-hugging a couple and their son, looking radiant as ever. More so, actually. Pregnancy suits her. And hitting a career high probably doesn't hurt either.

"Sage," I call.

Sage looks from the family she's embracing as soon as she hears me and fixes her green eyes on me. "Amira," she sings back, her voice coming out more like a mélange of squeaks than a series of notes as she moves through the crowd.

We squeeze each other, and I inhale her familiar scent. Sage always smells so good, like cinnamon and citrus. Note to self: get the name of that perfume or lotion or whatever it is.

"You made it! How was your flight?" Sage looks over my shoulder. "Where's Lila? And your mom?"

"Lila is with her dad and Rini, who are getting married tomorrow afternoon! Then she's off to a sleepover—the event of the season apparently, and you know, now that she's twelve…" I brush my shoulder with my hand like I'm flicking away dust, then laugh. Preteens are a trip. "And, since Greg and Rini are going on their honeymoon, she'll stay with her best friend until I get back Tuesday night. My mom is stuck at work, but she promises she will be here before this thing ends."

Sage squeezes me again. "I love your hair in dreads. And this look definitely works for you!"

"Think Kath will approve?"

"Kath will be happy to see you, and Wesley's heard all about you. I can't wait for you to meet him."

"Me neither! Hey, if you don't mind, I might wanna take a moment to look at the art. I hear the artist is kind of a big deal."

"Well, la dee da. Come on." Sage takes my hand and leads me across the room toward Wesley (who I recognize from the news and from photos Sage sent) and a very well-dressed, well-built Black man who looks familiar. They stand by the refreshment table, watching a video that seems to be about dirt and water. Hmmm.

"Come meet my fiancé," Sage says.

I catch my breath, whisper, "Your what? When?"

Sage speaks softly into my ear. "Last weekend. Very quiet. Very private. Very unstressful. We were taking a bath actually. He brought me a champagne glass with cool mint tea, and this was at the bottom." She surreptitiously lifts her hand for me to see, like she's trying not to make a big show for the whole room.

I kiss my friend's cheek. "I'm so happy for you, Sage."

She is beaming. As we come up behind her fiancé and the hot Black dude, she asks, "How's the video?"

They turn, and Sage makes introductions.

"Honey, this is Amira Albright," she says, dropping my ex-husband's last name from the string of identifiers.

Wesley takes my hand in both of his—they're warm, like the kindness in his eyes. He introduces his sexy friend as Derek Foret.

"You look familiar, Amira," Derek says, his Boston accent strong. He smiles a bit too warmly, like he's turning on the charm.

"Funny. I was just thinking the same thing."

He scans both Sage and me and nods like he approves. "Homeboy told me you were beautiful, but his photos don't begin to do you justice," he tells Sage, then looks down like he made a mistake.

She laughs. "We've agreed that I'll be the photographer in the family. Right, love?"

"Absolutely." Wesley slides his arm around her waist and kisses the top of her head. My heart melts a bit.

Wesley hums into Sage's hair, and she seems to drift into another world. There's a real romance. She's been giving me the play-by-play all these months, but seeing it up close infuses me with hope.

Derek clears his throat, and I realize I'm staring at Sage and Wesley's private moment. How embarrassing. I shift my gaze to Derek, then to the snacks on the table. Grapes. Wine. Cheese. Crackers. Is it really cheese? Both Kath, who owns the gallery, and Sage are vegan. I wouldn't put it past them to sneak some plant-based concoction onto this refreshment table. I decide to taste it anyway. My stomach is rumbling. What can I do?

"How do you know Sage?" Derek asks as I spread some cheese-like substance onto a cracker, take a bite, and frown. Definitely vegan.

"She used to babysit me when she was at Yale."

"So you're from New Haven?"

"Originally, but I've been in New Orleans for the past twelve years."

"No kidding." Derek looks from me to the food in my hand. "Why are you frowning?"

I sigh. "I just prefer cheese that comes from an animal."

"Don't tell me it's that vegan crap."

I shrug and finish the unpleasant snack. "How do you know Wesley?"

"Grew up next door to him outside Boston. Spent most of my life in the area. But I just moved."

"Oh?"

"To New Orleans."

"Come on!" I tease him.

"For real." He holds up his hands.

His voice is deep, resonant, clear. I bet he's got a great baritone. "Why the move?"

He glances at our friends, who still seem oblivious to the room and its inhabitants, offers his elbow, and says, "Let's browse the art, and I'll tell you."

I ignore the elbow, gentlemanly though it is. I just met the guy, and he seems far too charming for my taste.

Derek speaks to Wesley. "Dude, we're exploring the gallery."

"What's that?" Wesley asks.

Sage shifts her gaze to us, as if emerging from a dream.

"We're going to check out your work, darling," I say.

She nods and smiles. Wow. She is in l-o-v-e. I wonder what that feels like to be so in love.

"Shall we?" Derek asks, motioning toward an opening in the crowd with his hand.

I nod and follow his gesture. Will I ever feel that strongly about any man?

"Check this out," Derek says, interrupting my thoughts.

We're standing in front of a person-sized canvas—maybe three feet wide and six feet tall—taller than Derek. I'm staring into a tornado. Lightning bolts span the height of the canvas; Sage augmented them with some sort of debris.

The card next to the piece describes how she captured the shot, found herself literally facing down a tornado and, rather than running, did what she knows best, shot it. *Goddamn, Sage! What a risk!*

"Why are you shaking your head?" Derek asks.

"She can't keep taking risks like this. She's having a child."

"True."

"And she could have died."

"You're trembling," he says. "Are you cold?"

I rub my arms vigorously. I'm not cold. I'm upset. I'm impressed. I'm scared.

"She's been like a big sister to me since I was about nine years old. I know when she was a photojournalist, she sometimes found herself in dangerous situations, but this has to be the worst. I'm so proud of her, and pissed too."

I glare at the painting.

Derek speaks softly in my ear. "Hey, she's safe now. You didn't lose her."

My whole body relaxes. Weird. I look at him: Mister Charming. And now I know where I recognize him from: the airport. He's got that voice that settles into my skin and puts me at ease.

"Thanks. Should we keep moving?"

"Let me show you this piece. Wes already explained it to me, so I can sound impressive when I talk about it."

I laugh, despite myself, and let him place his hand under my elbow to guide me toward the next piece, *Self-Portrait with Climate Change*. "Wow! This is gorgeous."

"Right? I think I might buy it."

"Really?" I look at the mid-five-figure price tag and wonder what the hell he does for a living. And does he always flaunt his wealth like that, announcing big purchases to complete strangers? Or is he one of those guys who's in debt up to his eyeballs but can't stop spending to impress people?

"What do you do for a living, Derek?"

"I'm a surgeon."

"Oh," I say, lost for words. Hot, charming, cultured, and apparently brilliant. Damn.

"It would have looked great in the place I just sold in Brookline, but I'd really like to find a place for it in my new home."

"Which is where?"

"Uptown, between Children's Hospital and Tulane."

"Nice area," I say, trying to keep the attitude out of my voice. "My daughter goes to school near there."

"You live in the neighborhood too?" he asks, his voice brightening.

I shake my head. "New Orleans is all charter schools. She takes the bus from our neighborhood."

"Which is?"

"Mid-City. You made a smart choice. Out of the flood zones."

He shrugs. "That's what my realtor said. Plus, it's near work. Hate to invest in real estate, only to have it ruined by a storm."

I nod, as if I've ever had the luxury of thinking about buying a home, never mind making sure it was out of the flood zone or even a good investment. With my part-time counselor's income, I'm lucky I have enough to invest in an IRA, but working part-time means I'm home for Lila most days after school. My mom didn't have that option.

3

Angel on the Dance Floor

Derek

USUALLY, CROWDS INVIGORATE ME—ALL THE ENERGY, the body heat, the quiet roar of so many voices. Sometimes, though, like now, a twinge of loneliness pings my heart. When we hundred-plus folks who got invited to the after-party moved en masse from the art gallery to the rooftop bar around the corner, I lost sight of Wesley and his fiancée. For the tenth time, I scan the rooftop for their faces but see only festive strings of lights and paper lanterns.

It might seem insane to feel lonely when I'm sitting with the most beautiful woman in the world and her mother. But I'm trying to avoid looking at Amira. Does she realize she's staring at me? She doesn't seem to recognize me from the airport. Why would she? She only looked up for a second. And in that second... Boom. Do I say something? Would that be weird? *You bumped into me at the airport, and I was captivated by your eyes.* Definitely weird. Anyway, what would my motivation be for telling her I recognize her? To stop the loneliness seeping from my chest into my arms because I want her and can't have her? I've never wanted to write in a journal so badly, but that'll have to wait.

"Amira." A tall blond dude with messy hair puts his hand on her shoulder. She looks up, and the look on her face when she sees him... damn.

"Elijah," she sings in a beautiful, clear voice. She practically leaps from her seat right into his arms. A pang strikes my chest. I barely know the girl. Why should I care if she's madly in love with some other man? Doesn't matter to me.

There's a certain tilt of her chin now. Is it adoration? Like she looks up to him, not just because he's got about ten inches on her petite frame, but... because why? Admiration. Has any woman ever looked at me with admiration? Well, sure, but not like that. Not like love. Elijah leads her away.

Amira's mother, Tania, draws my attention with her sing-song voice. I meet her focused gaze, and the playful wisdom in her bright green eyes lets me know I can't get away with anything around her. Expressive eyes, just like Amira's.

"Very impressive," Tania says, her voice rising a few notches to continue our conversation. The club is loud but not enough to drown out her voice. "Did you always know you'd be a children's heart surgeon?"

"My parents named me Michael Derek Foret. Some sort of autosuggestion they tried to plant in my mind from birth: M.D. Foret. Dr. Foret. Well, they got their wish, and I got mine. I want to save lives, and I really, really love kids, so..."

"Do you?" Tania asks. "You know, Amira has a beautiful twelve-year-old."

"I did not know that."

"You should meet her sometime since you're in New Orleans."

I nod.

"She's a firecracker. Very wise for her years. An old soul."

"I get the feeling that runs in the family," I say.

Tania giggles. By the way her cheeks rise and her eyes dance, I think I've pleased her. So my work here is done. Not that I need to please Amira's mother.

Amira seems kind of standoffish, stern. Not my type. I mean, I offered her my elbow, and she refused. She's probably one of those women who won't let a man open a door for her. Although she let me open the door for her when we walked into this club. Not that it matters. Why did I feel compelled to open the door for her? Was it flirtation? Nah. It's how my mama raised me. *Open the door for a lady, Derek. That's it. Good boy.*

I catch a glimpse of Amira sitting on a sofa on the other side of the rooftop, tapping Elijah's arm playfully. Nauseating. He's smiling down at her, but he's not interested; I can tell. Not that I am. But I know for sure that he isn't; he's got that too cool look on his face. It's almost paternal. And look, there's a little girl with his dirty-blond hair running up to him, and he's giving her the same look that he's giving Amira. He's definitely not interested in Amira. She can have her little crush; that's cute. It's really cute actually. Not that it matters to me. But it is cute; it's cute to watch. Not that I'm watching.

What's her mother saying now? Yale. Her job.

"So you've worked at Yale for thirty years. Wow."

"I retire in two years. Now, are you an only child?"

"Kind of. They'd had a couple of miscarriages, and my older brother died in infancy, so..."

"Oh dear."

"I'm named after him actually. If he'd lived, he'd be the doctor, and I'd be... a musician maybe."

"Really?" Tania's voice rises a notch.

"Played trombone since I was a kid. I do love medicine though."

"But they named you after him," she says, as if pondering the idea.

"It's a tradition from the 1800s or something. That's what they tell me anyway. But it's why I go by Derek. Even though they named me after my brother Michael Derek, they wanted to keep our identities separate."

"Do you want children, Derek?"

"Uh." I stumble over a few fits and starts. She has me stammering. Why? Of course I want kids. I've always wanted kids. I'm never having kids. "Some things just aren't meant to be," I tell her, hoping the old Catholic wisdom will stop the conversation on that subject. "What did you think of the artwork?" I ask.

Tania waxes poetic about Sage and what a lovely, hardworking person she is, so creative, etcetera. What she doesn't actually talk about is the art. From that, I gather she is not really an art person but showing up for Sage out of love.

Where did I get my love of art? Ma was always drawing something. Still is, and she's taking those classes I bought for her at the Museum of Fine Arts, sending pictures of her work from her iPhone. Adorable.

The music shifts from jazz to funk. Tania starts to twitch a little.

"Would you like to dance, Tania?" It's okay to ask, right? I'm not flirting. I'm being respectful of an elder.

"Sure," she says, giggling, batting her lashes, and taking my hand. I help her rise from her seat, and we make our way to the dance floor. She's got some moves for a little old white lady.

"Mom!" Amira exclaims, coming up to us. "Oh, Derek. I'm sorry."

"Why are you apologizing? I'm dancing with one of the most beautiful women on the roof."

"Honestly, Amira! I think you're just jealous," Tania says, teasing.

Amira shakes her head, laughing. "She truly is one of the most beautiful women on the roof, Derek."

Amira walks away before I get a chance to say something about her being *the* most beautiful woman here. Thank God. With those full curves and high cheekbones. Almond-shaped eyes. Those crazy yellow-tipped dreads. Sexy as hell actually. Probably better that she walked away. *Avert your eyes, Derek. Jesus.*

When funk turns into Tupac's "Dear Mama," I can't help myself; I sink to my knees and rap for Tania. She soaks it up, rolling her shoulders and getting into it. To my surprise, Amira makes her way onto the floor and belts out the background vocals. What a set of pipes—smooth and sexy, right on pitch. Damn.

Do not to look at her, Derek. Keep your composure.

"Aaaah ahhh ahhh ahh," she sings.

Shit. That voice. How can I look anywhere else? A Goddamn angel has descended onto the dance floor. I extend my arms, hoping, praying Amira will move toward me. And, holy God, she does. The woman moves to my side, puts her face next to mine, and sings. Her voice reverberates through my eardrums, right to my crotch. I'm keeping pace with Tupac but groaning inside.

When we finish the song, I look into Amira's eyes again and feel like my whole body is crumbling. Fuck. As I stand, the partygoers erupt into applause. We laugh and bow, and I try to act casual like this doesn't matter, but inside I feel like Jell-O. Amira holds her hand up for a high-five. I meet her hand with mine, clasp it for just a second. The warmth of her skin makes me weak. I am a total fucking mess. I should leave this party right now and write in my journal, but that would be shitty. I'm here for Wesley and Sage, not for myself. I don't need to flirt with Amira or even talk to her. I sure as hell don't need to look at her anymore, never mind touch her.

"Well." Tania laughs. "I certainly do feel appreciated, just like Tupac said. Do you sing that to your mama too, Derek?"

"Every damn day!"

"Truly?"

"Maybe every month. Maybe I should call and sing that to her every day. I think she likes Kanye's 'Hey Mama' better though." I allow a yawn to escape. "Excuse me. I think the travel's catching up with me. Best I head to my hotel."

Tania smiles and puts her hand on my chest to stop me. "Don't go yet, Dr. Foret. You two need to dance." With surprising strength for her size, she prods me backward toward Amira.

Amira

Where are my mother's boundaries?

I close my eyes, hoping to erase the scene from my mind. Now I feel her hand between my shoulder blades. She's old and only five feet tall, but *damn*, she's strong. "Mother!" My eyes widen in horror. I shake my head.

"Derek, Amira loves to dance," she says and presses our bodies together.

As our bodies meet, I feel pulsing in my veins.

"It's not a party if you're not dancing," Mom says, then winks at us and walks away.

I brave a glance at Derek, who's pursing his lips as if stifling a laugh. Despite the amusement in his eyes, something about the way he looks at me makes me feel sexy.

"She must have had too much to drink. I'm sorry."

"She's not always so commanding?"

"No, she is, but this is one of the more embarrassing occasions."

He laughs out loud, a full belly laugh that dispels the tension I was feeling a moment ago. I can't help laughing too.

"This will be a story passed down for generations," he says, then flinches, as if he made a mistake. "I should go."

"Really?" I ask, unable to stop myself from bouncing to the EDM pounding through the speakers. "This is the first dance I've had all night. I mean, we're already on the dance floor, so..."

"You got me there." He swivels his hips like an erotic dancer, the look on his face so ironic I double over in laughter.

"What? I'm not impressing you?"

I shake my head. "You've got some smooth moves."

"Don't you dare call me Ex-Lax."

"Wasn't planning to."

Before long, the EDM changes to old-school hip-hop. Then to a slow song. I didn't realize we were on the dance floor that long, but now his hand is around my waist and his other hand is holding mine near our shoulders. His touch is warm, tender, commanding. I'm feeling charmed and irritated at the same time. Who is this man who's just commandeered my body without warning?

"You're a great dancer." He speaks softly in my ear, and I feel that same strange sense of relaxation that filled me at the gallery.

"Thank you." I'm not out of breath. Why am I sounding all breathy and weird?

"I really enjoyed talking to your mom tonight," he says.

"That was so nice of you. She insisted I visit with everyone, but I'm sure she feels a little out of place, which probably helps explain her extra embarrassing behavior."

"Don't think twice about it. If not for you two, I wouldn't have had anyone to talk to tonight. Wesley and Sage are busy, and I don't know another soul in New Haven."

"Glad to be a friendly face," I say. "And maybe we'll see each other in New Orleans too."

"What do you do there?"

"Right now, I'm a child and family therapist with the community center in Terrebonne Parish."

"Terrebonne. I've heard of it but can't place it."

"The first climate refugees in the United States are from there, from Isle de Jean Charles. Families that have been there for generations are losing their ancestral land to subsidence and sea level rise."

"Subsidence is...?" he asks.

"The land is sinking."

"Okay. Did I hear something about sea level rise? Isn't that the same thing?"

"Subsidence and sea level rise are not the same actually. And you heard right; sea level is also rising."

"So their land is disappearing?"

"Literally. Driving to Isle de Jean Charles is like driving to the end of the world."

He whistles. "How much time do they have to leave safely?"

"Most folks have already been driven from the island by climate change, but many stayed in the region. Their community is the first undergoing a federal resettlement to a town far from the coast."

Derek steps back, a look of horror on his face. "Like a forced migration?"

"No. People have a choice about moving there. Some are refusing. It's a lot to get into on the dance floor. So why'd you leave Boston? And why New Orleans?"

"Got sick of working with people who seem to be in the job more for the status and money than for the benefit of helping others day to day. And it's a lot of pressure to have a child's life in your hands. I'm sure you get that as a parent, but—"

"Please. I can't imagine what it would be like to have a child's body and life in my hands, wielding a knife."

He nods. "So it was time for a change, and this opportunity came up with Children's Hospital recognizing the need for a children's heart surgeon who's Black."

"Specifically Black?"

"Too many communication breakdowns between parents of color and the mostly white staff. They're hoping my presence can increase the number of children who actually get surgery when they need it so they can thrive instead of being held back by poor health."

"Just your presence?"

"Well, by interacting with the parents and the children. And by speaking at schools and parent groups. It builds trust between the community and the hospital, which means parents are more likely to bring their kids in for help. Plus, you know, even showing up as a male Black surgeon sends the message that it's possible for Black kids to become doctors. Hell, I didn't grow up with a silver spoon. That's one reason I'm applying to join a social aid and pleasure club."

"You're kidding! Which one? Will you be marching in the parades?"

"Not sure which club yet, but I brought my trombone and I need to do something with my spare time."

"Oh, the pleasure club parades are so fun and such an important part of New Orleans culture!"

"So I hear. Anyway, I can only spend so many hours traveling the world or in the gym or the pool."

"You swim?" That explains the incredibly sexy muscles, I think, hopefully silently. I shouldn't have had so much to drink.

"The fly was my event back in college. I still keep up."

"The butterfly?" I say, hoping he's oblivious to me, sliding my hand along his bicep. "You have to be really strong for that stroke."

He smiles down at me. "I also do the breaststroke."

I giggle, but he grimaces and curses under his breath. Weird. I thought he was flirting with me. Maybe he's had too much to drink too.

The song changes to another slow song, and he pulls me just a tiny bit closer, forcing my face to press against his chest. Through the soft cotton of his dress shirt, I feel his pectorals, firm and warm. My nipples respond.

"Be nice to run into you when we get back to New Orleans," I say.

"I think you already did."

"Huh?"

"At the airport. You ran into me. I offered to buy you a drink."

I gasp. "That *was* you!" He remembered me? *Okay, don't make a big deal about this, Amira. It's not a big deal. Act casual.* "My God, man, you freaked me out back there."

"What?" he asks, pulling away just enough so I can see his eyes open wide.

"Who just asks a random woman out for a drink in an airport, and what kind of woman would say yes?"

His mouth drops open, and he curses under his breath, then stammers, "Well, uh. Most women say yes."

"Most women?" I ask. "What do you have, like a string of them?"

His face falls. "No—I mean—Oh God." He shakes his head and mutters something.

"What?"

He keeps shaking his head, not meeting my eyes. He says something about a journal.

"Journal?" I snort a laugh. "You mean like a *little black book*?"

My first impression was totally right. Too charming. Dr. Derek Foret is, apparently, the kind of man who keeps women on a string. Well, he may be gorgeous and brilliant and have a voice that makes me tingle everywhere good, but that does *not* mean he's the kind of guy who would ever interest me. I won't be another pearl on his string. What is it about men and commitment? No wonder I haven't fallen in love. Real men are few and far between. Just because Sage seems to have found one doesn't mean I will.

The music stops, and Derek stifles a yawn. "Hey, I've been up since four thirty this morning. I think I'd better get some shut-eye. Thank you."

"For what?"

"The dance."

"It was something. Maybe I'll see you back in NOLA," I say, sure I'd rather see just about anyone else.

4
Dare to Be Known

Amira

MOM HUDDLES IN HER QUEEN BED, THE FADED bedspread pulled up to her neck, and listens as I read.

> *"Do you dare to be known?*
> *To truly reveal yourself?*
> *Do you care for that ideal of connection*
> *The possibility that might emerge from*
> *Truly daring to be known*
> *As you are*
> *Behind the facade*
> *You display in polite society, at work, or even for*
> *your family of origin?*
> *To whom do you dare to be known?"*

I scan my mother's face for a response.

"Lovely, dear. Thought provoking. Tell me, are you coming at me with a facade?"

"Mom, of course not!"

She smiles. "Who's this for? That young man we met tonight?"

"I started writing it before I even got to New Haven."

"Someone new in your life then?"

"I never know where the poems come from; they just come."

The old heater clangs and hisses steam from the valve in the radiator.

"I hear pain in that poem. As if you're still working things out with Greg deep inside."

"Please. His constant lying and cheating is a reflection of him, not me. We've been divorced for eleven years, Mom. I think I'm over it."

"Okay," she says, but I hear disbelief in her voice.

"Honestly. I'm just glad he found a good stepmom for Lila."

She pats my leg. "You're stronger than me, sweetheart. I remember how upset I was when your father married the last of his affair partners. We'd been divorced for several years as well."

"I never knew that," I say, hugging her and squeezing tight.

"There's a lot you don't know. But dating helped."

"Okay, I know where this is headed."

"That Michael Derek Foret! He's a catch."

I snort.

"Accomplished. Sweet. Great dancer. Snazzy dresser."

"Snazzy, huh? Actually, instead of looking for a man to move into my life, I was thinking about moving you into my life."

Mom looks at me questioningly.

"Come live with us. You've been with Yale for thirty years; don't you wanna retire and chill out with us in the greatest city in the world?"

She makes that humming sound she makes when she's trying to be careful with her words. "I've always loved New Haven."

"I know." I sigh. "Me too, but New Orleans! And we have that beautiful spare room, and you could be part of Lila's everyday life. Wouldn't that be great?"

Mom looks beatific. "That would be wonderful, dear. But my life is here."

"But you're all alone."

"Sometimes, but I'm never lonely. I have my friends, my church, my knitting circle. This home has thirty years of memories, most of them involving you."

"But you could live with the actual me in real time! And speaking of this home... did you lose siding?"

"I didn't tell you about that?"

I sigh. "Mom, you don't need to handle things like that alone!"

"I enjoy my independence. I'm still young and fit. Did you see me on the dance floor tonight?"

I laugh. "I was wondering if I'd ever be able to unsee it."

She taps my hand. "Don't be fresh."

I grin. "You were amazing. You are amazing. And I miss you. And Lila misses you."

"Why don't I plan to come for an extended visit in the spring? I think I can manage an extra two weeks after spring break. What do you think?"

I lie next to my mom and hug her over the covers. "Sounds good."

"And we can plan your wedding."

"What?" I sit up and stare at her. "Did you hit your head tonight?"

She giggles. "Oh, it's so easy to get a rise out of you. But at least it will be easier for you to date while I'm there. Don't roll your eyes at me, young lady. I know you feel guilty about leaving Lila alone even though she can take care of herself."

As I kiss her good night, I think about weddings and marriage and what Mom said about my poem. God. Greg? No. That's been worked out for a while. If we hadn't gotten pregnant, I wouldn't have married him; and he wouldn't have married me. The sad truth is, Greg MacKenzie was never all that interested in me. We were young and gorgeous and had fun dating for a few months. If Lila hadn't directed the course of our lives, we probably would have grown bored quickly and moved on. But Lila, or the universe or whatever, decided to break the condom. And my mama raised me with old-fashioned values. Thank God. Where would I be without that child?

I used to think that marriage was the ideal place to be truly known. But even if Greg and I had been right for each other, would he have been up for showing himself to me? To knowing the depths of my soul? Do he and Rini even go there? Maybe in their own quiet way. They seem pretty bonded. Hell, she's the first woman he's actually wanted to marry.

Tomorrow, I get to bask in the glow of two people who are more in love than anyone I've ever seen. According to what Sage says, they keep diving deeper into each other. Daring to be known more and more.

5

Special People

Derek

THE ROCKY, NARROW TRAIL RISES BEFORE US, CARPETED with dry leaves that make it hard to tell exactly where the ground is. I step carefully to avoid slipping.

"Can't believe this place is walking distance from your house," I say to Wesley's back.

"I know. It's one thing I love about New Haven. Sage and I come here all the time."

"Even with her pregnant?"

"Not all the trails are this rugged," he says, breathing hard. "That paved trail we crossed goes all the way to the top."

We hike awhile in silence. Birds sing around us. A woodpecker hammers at a tree in the distance. I look in the direction of the sound but don't see it.

Suddenly Wesley stops and turns.

"What's up?" I ask.

He just stares at me like he's examining my face. "Something's different about you."

I laugh. "Quit stalling for time, man."

40

"I'm serious."

"You're outta breath is what you are. Losing your edge."

"That's what's missing: your edge!"

I raise my eyebrows. "I'm not the one struggling up the trail. Someone needs to hit the gym, and it's not me," I say, pointing up.

"Not that edge. The emotional one."

"Emotional edge."

"You haven't given me shit about Sage once, nothing about the changes she's made around the house, about her earning as much as me, about the baby."

"You want me to give you shit about the baby? Who does that?"

"And," he says, pointing at my chest, "you haven't mentioned one conquest this morning. There were a lot of gorgeous women at that after-party last night."

I grab my chest, feigning wounding. "Cut to the quick!"

"I guess it's my turn to ask you what you asked me last spring in Barcelona. Are you having"—he drops his gaze to my crotch—"problems?"

"Keep moving, son. No problems in that area."

"The man doth protest too much."

"Look, I'm busy. New job, new city; that's tough, man."

"So it's stress keeping you *down*?" he asks, staying in place.

"Didn't Sage say she'd have food for us at noon? We gonna make it to the top and get back in time?"

"Shit. That's right." Wesley turns and continues up the hill. "When do you start the new job?"

"Started two weeks ago."

"Did you find a new place yet?"

"Nice little property near the hospital."

"Sweet. What style?"

"They call it a double gallery. Two stories. Columns. Wide front porch. Floor-to-ceiling windows. In one of the few areas that didn't flood during Katrina."

He whistles. "Even your voice sounds different."

I sigh. Wesley is too damn tenacious. "Last summer, after that humiliating meme went out about you and Sage all over social media..."

"Thanks for reminding me," he says.

"Well, I thought about you two and how *you* really seemed different—happier, more at peace. Even that day I called you. I was telling you to forget her name. But you couldn't shake her. And then when you called to tell me you guys are having a kid... Awww. I don't know, man."

"I am happier than I've ever been in my life."

"I hear it. And by the way, I'm sorry I was such a dick about Sage before. I was just trying to protect you."

"I know. But look, everything I ever wanted is coming together. My career's in place. I'm marrying the woman of my dreams in January, and I'm gonna be a dad. What else could I want in life?"

"Right. And I looked at you, and I thought about my life. I was already considering moving to New Orleans, starting over, but... You know, when I married Riley, I wanted all that too. Wife, family, home, career."

"I remember."

"And it hit me: just because she's a toxic mess doesn't mean I have to give up on my dreams, does it?"

Wesley takes a sharp breath. "So what? Are you dating one woman now?"

"You're not even gonna believe it."

"Who is she?" he asks, his voice speedy with excitement.

"I'm celibate."

He laughs.

The base of my core tightens. I take a deep breath, savor the scent of crisp autumn air, and let it out slowly. "No joke."

"Come off it! You? Celibate? You? Mister three-date maximum? You? Mister *A Woman in Every City*? I mean, come on. How many women have you slept with in the three weeks since you've been in New Orleans?"

"None."

You'd think it was the funniest thing the man had ever heard the way he's doubled over. When I tell him about the fast though, he gets serious.

"Why are you doing this to yourself?" Wesley asks.

"To gain clarity. I looked at your life. I looked at my life. Remember that conversation we had at the airport on the way to Barcelona? You could tell I was down."

"I was worried about you."

"Was starting to worry about myself. There I was, top of my career, shitloads of cash, great shape, traveling the world with my best buddy, fucking gorgeous women, and miserable. I didn't trust anyone. Didn't wanna get close to anyone."

"Yeah, I know."

"Part of this group is we keep journals. Anytime we meet a woman, whether it's a new woman or someone we've known, we witness our reactions."

"Witness your reactions? That sounds Yogic. You taking yoga, D?"

"I'm not into that whole pretzel thing like you, but this idea of getting still in my mind, doing a little bit of quiet, a little bit of meditation to pay attention to my thought patterns... That's been really helpful."

In more ways than one. Before the program, I might not have noticed the warmth of the sun on my face, competing with the cool fall air, or the call of those birds in a nearby tree.

"So you're meditating."

"And journaling about what comes up when I'm in the presence of a woman and what comes up during my meditations. Paying attention to what's happening both inside me and outside. And there're like twenty other men around the country doing this. We went on a weekend retreat at the beginning and will go again at the end. We meet once a week online, talk about our experiences. We each have an accountability buddy, so if I meet a woman and I really want to be romantic with her, I call him."

"You mean like AA? Like a twelve-step program?"

"Kind of, but this isn't about addiction. It's about paying attention."

"Gotta tell you, D, I'm really shocked."

"I caught that."

We reach the end of the trail and look out over the tree-filled city. The view spans miles. Red rocks rise from the landscape to the west. To the north, the city's few multistory buildings and some gothic-looking towers Wes once told me are part of the Yale campus. To the east, the Long Island Sound. A few sailboats dot the harbor.

"It's about seeing the patterns," I continue.

"What have you noticed?" Wesley asks.

"Well, for one thing, fucking everything that moves hasn't worked out so great."

"Yeah, it didn't for me either."

"And just because a woman turns me on doesn't mean I need to act on it. Don't need to try to get their approval either."

"Approval?"

"Like Miss Brickson."

"Our first-grade teacher?"

"Remember that crush I had on her?"

"Did you?"

"She was awful to me, wicked racist. But now I find I'm trying to prove myself to every woman, same way I was trying to get Miss Brickson's approval."

"Geez."

"Except for one."

"What do you mean, except for one?"

"I met this woman recently. Can't describe it, Wes. She has something I've never seen in any woman, not Riley, not anyone."

"And?"

"Can't do anything about it. I can't approach her, flirt with her. I have to keep all my conversations businesslike. That's the program."

"So you're gonna let this woman get away?"

"Don't see the program through, I won't benefit from all this work I've been doing. Three weeks left. The program ends on Halloween."

"Tell me about her."

Do I dare admit to Wesley that in the space of two seconds, I've developed some sort of something for his fiancée's best friend?

"How did you meet?" Wesley asks.

I smile, thinking about her eyes. "At the airport on the way here."

"Is she hot?"

"Beyond hot. She's got this intensity like you wouldn't believe, and when she looks at me, man. I don't know..."

"So you *did* have a conversation with her. Man, you're already easing your way out of this fast."

"It's not like that. I couldn't help but talk to her."

"What were you just saying about urges?"

"I mean, she's here! You and Sage threw us together last night."

His eyes widen. "Wait. Are you talking about Amira?"

I groan.

"You are! Ha!" Wes slaps me on the back. "D, from what Sage says, Amira pulls no punches."

"What does that mean?"

"I mean, she's one hundred percent real. Gives no bullshit; takes no bullshit. And that kind of woman is perfect for you, my friend. By the way, what do you think of Sage?"

"Very impressive, dude. From the little bit I've seen, she seems true to you."

"Exactly."

AN HOUR LATER, WE WALK INTO WESLEY'S BEAUTIFUL ARTS and Crafts-style home, sweaty, thirsty, hungry.

"Baby?" Wes calls.

Sage emerges from the kitchen. "How was the hike, honey?" she asks, wrapping her arms around him, clearly unfazed by the sweat and dirt from the trail.

Yeah. That's what I want.

"Hey, when's Amira getting here?" Wes asks her.

Shit. Amira's coming? I do not want that woman seeing or smelling me like this right now. Once we get to know each other, sure. But not now. "You mind if I take a shower before we eat?" I ask. "It was hotter out there than I anticipated."

Wesley points up the stairs. "You know where it is. All yours."

"Towels are in the cabinet outside the bathroom," Sage says.

Amira's coming for brunch. How in hell am I gonna handle this?

Amira

SAGE AND I HAVE NEVER KNOCKED ON EACH OTHER'S DOORS. We've always had each other's house keys. But now, as I stand on the front porch, realizing *this* door isn't just her door, I take the heavy brass knocker in hand and rap a cheerful rhythm. My phone rings: the boy who flunked his exam the other day. I sigh. It's Saturday. Is this an issue with his impulse control? Or is it urgent? If it were urgent, he'd call Dr. Glaude. I'll let him leave a message.

The door swings open, and Sage stands on the other side, beaming. "Mimi." She takes my hand and pulls me into the house. "What's wrong? You look unhappy."

I attempt a smile. "I'm happy to see you! It's a patient issue. They know I'm off this weekend. They know they can call the doctor who's covering for me and can actually prescribe meds, which I can't. Still, they call me, text me. Sorry to walk in with drama."

"Hey, drama is the spice of life. And speaking of spice, wait till you taste Wesley's vegan cornbread! And I made chili and mole enchiladas, and there's salad."

"Geez. How many people are you feeding?" I ask as I take in a stunning home.

This is where she lives now? The hardwood floors gleam. The leaded windows look like smaller versions of the ones in the Yale library where Sage used to take me to do my homework when she babysat me. She takes my coat and hangs it in a closet in the front hall. I follow her into the living room and stare at the huge fireplace. It's surrounded by brick laid out in a zigzag pattern and a gigantic wooden mantelpiece. I envision Sage and Wesley sipping hot cider in front of a roaring fire, toasting each other's success like that scene at the end of *The Flame of Their Love*.

Sage is talking about making sure there's something everyone will love and freezing leftovers. I thought it would just be the three of us.

"Hey," a familiar voice says.

I look toward the sound and see Derek striding down the steps, skin glistening. My heart starts racing. "Hey. I didn't expect to see you here."

"Hope you're not disappointed."

"Wesley and I wanted to get to know each other's important people," Sage says, a sparkle in her eye.

Does she have other ideas as well? I should tell her about this guy's black book.

"Who else is coming?" I ask.

"No one. Just you two special people."

"We're your special people?" Derek asks, joining us in the living room. He winks at me, then looks down, as if he's disappointed with himself. Probably realizing I won't fall for his flirtations.

Sage wraps her arm around me, and I get a whiff of her cinnamon-citrus scent, which reminds me: I want it. "What's that perfume? I wanna smell like you."

She laughs.

"You smell great already," Derek says, then widens his eyes and shakes his head. "I mean, uh..."

I laugh. "Thanks. Not sure when you could have noticed."

"Dancing last night," he says, then looks even more upset.

I don't know what his game is, but I'm not playing. "Listen," I tell him. "No hard feelings. You keep your black book. I just don't wanna be in it."

He groans and leaves the room, muttering something about helping Wesley. What a strange reaction.

Sage looks amused. "I think he's into you."

I give her my best stare down, the one that says I am *not* going there today. Or any day. Then I change the subject. "I love this music. What are we listening to?"

"It's from Ceschi's latest album," she says, taking my hand.

"*Sad, Fat Luck?* No kidding! I've been listening to the first three songs on repeat. Guess I need to progress." I laugh.

"Yeah, 'Downtown' is my favorite track. But the whole album is incredible." She sighs.

"You still have a crush on him?"

"Always."

"Does Wesley know?"

"He thinks it's cute. Of course, if I wasn't all-in and one hundred percent faithful, he might not feel that way. Did you say hi to him last night?"

"To Ceschi? He was at the after-party?"

"Yeah! He even took the mic at the end of the night."

My heart sinks a little. "Oh my God. Mom got tired, and I wanted to spend time with her. I can't believe I missed our favorite Connecticut rapper!"

"Well, I promise I will give him a hug from you next time I see him." She grins.

I laugh. "You're shameless."

"Mimi, would you like a tour of the house, or do you want to see what's up in the kitchen?"

"A tour of course!"

"Let's start upstairs," Sage says as she takes my hand. "You can tell me what else I need for the nursery."

I'm blown away by the tour, the home, the way they've displayed Sage's artwork, and the studio/office Wesley set up for her. It almost makes me wish I could fall for someone like people do in movies, like Sage and Wesley did. Their entire house feels like it's filled with love.

After about twenty minutes, we join Wesley and Derek in the backyard. The guys have lit a fire in a firepit and laid out everything we need to enjoy lunch outside. I'm almost looking forward to it except that it's vegan and bound to be horrible. Thankfully, I ate well at Mom's house before coming over, and Sage has always made a great Sangria.

I reluctantly taste the food. "The enchiladas are actually good."

"Actually?" Sage asks, a warning tone in her voice. Uh-oh. I guess I telegraphed my surprise.

I laugh nervously. "I mean, they're delicious!"

Derek catches my eye and winks, then looks down and curses under his breath.

"And this salad," I say. "What is the dressing?"

"Simple lemon-EVO emulsion blended with fresh cilantro, sea salt, and a teensy dash of cayenne."

"Mind-blowing. All vegan. Lila's been begging me to go veg, but giving up oysters? In New Orleans?"

"This meal almost makes me wanna go vegan," Derek says. "You two eat like this all the time?"

"Pretty much," Wesley says. "Amira, Sage tells me you're a child and family therapist. Any advice for us parents-to-be?"

I laugh. "Yeah. Keep this woman away from tornadoes."

Wes holds up his hands in a helpless gesture. "If only I could."

"Seriously though, my specialty is disaster resilience. Kids become traumatized by these major weather events."

Derek says, "In Louisiana, seems like you oughta have enough work for a full-time job with that specialty. But didn't you tell me last night you work part-time?"

"I'm trying really hard to be available to Lila in the afternoons."

"How long is the drive from New Orleans?" he asks.

"About an hour."

"Single parenting while managing a career is tough," Wesley says. "After my mom passed, my dad switched from private practice to school counseling so he could be there for my sister and me."

"How old were you?" I ask.

"Seven. Julia was four."

Sage takes Wesley's hand, and the look that passes between them is pure intimacy. My palm tingles, as if someone is stroking it.

"Luckily, Derek and his parents and grandma were right next door, too. We went from being best buddies to brothers that year, right, D?"

"Mm-hmm." Derek lays a gentle hand on his friend's shoulder. The bond between them touches my heart.

A soft breeze passes through the crackling fire, giving the charred logs a fresh glow. A poem begins to form in my mind, something about children experiencing loss, the feelings of instability... It's not enough to write yet, just a few words starting to germinate.

"Anyway," Wesley says. "I mentioned my dad because I'm wondering if you've considered school counseling as a way to be near your daughter."

"Thank you. That's so thoughtful. I have definitely considered it, but school counseling is very limited in its scope. We now know that birth to five are the crucial years."

"Sure are," Derek says, leaning in. "And that age group is underserved across all areas of medicine, especially in the non-White community. What age do you work with, Amira?"

"Zero to eighteen. Of course, with infants, I'm really working with the parents, trying to offer preventive care and proactive strategies to manage the stress caused by the environment and the situation."

"You only work with people from Isle de Jean Charles?"

"Not at all. The center serves everyone in the region."

Derek leans toward Wesley and Sage. "Amira's working with the first group of climate refugees in the United States."

"That must be quite a challenge," Wesley says as his eyes dart to Sage. They both look as if they're trying not to smile.

What's happening right now? Was Derek just bragging about me? Or just trying to prove he was listening last night? Suddenly I feel overheated, though the fire is dying.

"I think I heard a story about climate refugees on the news," Wesley says.

"Yeah, you know, folks in Louisiana hate that term. But the fact is, the land is literally disappearing before our eyes. That's why the government's paying to create a new town for people who've had to leave Isle de Jean Charles and nearby areas. Of course, it's taking forever to build, and the fact it's far from the water means an entire way of life disappears."

"When I was shooting the Gulf from the air," Sage says, "I could see the little inlets. I was thinking about the environmental degradation. It didn't dawn on me that communities were disappearing along with the land."

"Until you're in the middle of it, it's hard to see the emotional devastation or to even get how the whole idea of being resettled triggers deep wounds and mistrust."

"So why bother with this resettlement plan?" Sage asks.

"Because if folks don't move as a community, they may lose their culture. And when you're dealing with trauma, things like routines and culture and community help stabilize folks."

"Mm-hmm," Derek affirms. "I tell parents all the time to try to keep their family routines before and after surgery. The child recovering from surgery needs extra care, but that doesn't take away the emotional and physical needs of the parents or the older siblings."

"Exactly," I say, allowing my eyes to meet his. "These people have had firsthand traumas with every major storm, plus generational trauma because at this point, the kids who lived through Katrina and the Deep Horizon oil spill are now parents. But that's a problem all over southern Louisiana, even in our own backyard."

"You're doing God's work, both of you," Wesley says.

"All three of you," Sage says, beaming at each of us.

"For now," I sigh.

Sage raises her eyebrows. "For now? Everything okay?"

"Just burned out. It's a lot, hearing people struggle every day, especially kids."

"Wait. Are you thinking of leaving the community center or leaving counseling altogether?" she asks.

"Therapy is exhausting. I spend hours of every day with other people's traumatized kids, and I don't feel like I have enough to give my kid when I'm home."

She pats my knee. "Aw, Mimi."

"We watch a lot of rom-coms, just 'cause I'm so brain dead. That's not good parenting. So yeah, I'm thinking a career change might be helpful."

"What else are you considering?" Wes asks.

"If only I knew."

"How about admin?" Derek asks.

I shake my head.

"Or working with the state," Derek says. "More stability with the state agencies."

All this attention on my stressful career is making me antsy. "I'll figure it out eventually. Sorry. I didn't mean to hijack this lovely brunch with my problems."

Sage throws her arm around me. "Oh, Mimi! You're not hijacking anything. We want to help. Right, Wes?"

Wesley nods, his affect telegraphing caring and concern.

"Derek?" She looks at him expectantly.

"Yes, ma'am." Derek's countenance reveals his compassion. I don't see a play for attention in his body language at all.

He continues, "A therapist's job is stressful enough for those who want to do it. When you'd rather be doing something else, I know that's worse. Maybe you oughta go into business for yourself."

"Doing what?" I ask.

He spreads out his palms, an open, welcoming gesture. "Happy to help you figure that out."

Right. Here we go. Mister Black Book. "Mmm."

"People say I'm pretty good to bounce ideas off," he adds.

What is that look Wesley's exchanging with Sage? And why is he looking at Derek like that?

Derek winks, then mutters under his breath. How many times is that now, that he's had some weird physical response and muttered under his breath? Does he have a neurological disorder?

6

Offending Fruit

Amira

THE SMELL OF JET FUEL ASSAULTS ME AS I SLIDE OUT OF the Uber at terminal A. Awful. Like how our coastline smelled after the Deep Horizon oil spill in 2010.

Inside the terminal, the security line is longer than I would have expected for a Tuesday morning. Then again, I don't fly that much, so what do I know? I follow a group of rambunctious, white twenty-somethings along the roped path to the guard. The guard checks my ID and scans the QR code on my phone, directs me to a conveyor belt. I heave my roller bag onto the belt, unzip my boots, and slip them into a bin with my coat and purse.

"Ma'am, you need a separate bin for your purse," the second security guard says.

I obey, make sure I have my ID in my back pocket, and walk into the full body scanner, spreading my legs so each of my feet is in a foot-shaped marking on the floor, lifting my arms above my head as the image depicts on the glass wall in front of me. The mechanical arm makes a smooth whirring noise as it swoops around me. I hate this part, but I hate what's coming next even more. The third security guard summons me from the scanning pod. I step out and spread my arms and legs wide so she can wave her "magic wand" over every inch of me. That's usually where it ends, but today, for some reason—maybe the underwire in my bra—she decides she needs to pat me down. I try not to sigh. I hate being touched by strangers.

Guard number three exchanges a look with the security agents standing by the monitor above the conveyor belt. I don't see my things on the other side of the monitor. Where are they?

"Ma'am, I need you to come with me," the guard says, her voice strident.

I follow her to an area a few feet away where I have a clear view of the monitor. The X-ray image of my purse is on the screen.

"What's in your purse, ma'am?" she asks.

"Gum, some snacks. My wallet. Is there a problem?"

"This here," says the security agent by the monitor, pointing to an image on the screen. "This looks like a firearm."

I laugh. "Goodness. I have never even touched a firearm in my life."

"You think this is funny?" the guard with the grating voice asks.

I close my mouth. "No, it's just... Have you looked inside my purse? You'll see there's nothing there."

"Well, that looks like a firearm, ma'am."

"It's probably the banana I packed for when I get hungry on the flight. Please look inside my purse."

"That looks to us like a firearm."

"I can see that it looks that way," I say. "But I don't have one, and I'm giving you permission to open my purse and put your concerns at ease."

"You don't need to raise your voice, ma'am."

I take a deep breath and adopt my most soothing therapist voice. "I'm sorry. I don't mean to raise my voice. It's just that it seems you're accusing me of doing something I'm not doing, and that makes me nervous. I carry a banana because I get hungry and I like bananas."

"We're gonna have to pull you aside."

I look at the clock on the wall and start to tremble. "My flight boards in fifteen minutes."

"Then you should have gotten here earlier, without the firearm."

"There is no firearm! It's a banana!" I say, exasperated. I look around. One white person after another passes through security without incident.

"I don't appreciate the hostility, ma'am."

"Excuse me. Is there someone else I can talk to?"

"We need to see your ID and your boarding pass again."

I slide my driver's license from my back pocket and hand it to them. "My boarding pass is on my phone, which is in that bin," I say, pointing.

My personal TSA agent grabs the bin and holds it out to me so I can retrieve my phone. It feels insanely comforting to hold it right now.

"Unlock your phone please."

"Yes, ma'am." I call up the boarding pass, noting the time—twelve minutes to boarding. *Shit.* I hold the phone up for her to see.

"Yeah, that checks out."

I try not to roll my eyes for fear it will set off this irrational person who currently has the power to strip me of my basic human rights.

"What were you doing in the state of Connecticut?"

"I was visiting my mother," I say.

"Where does she live?"

"In New Haven. She works at Yale University. I grew up there. I went home for a visit and saw some friends."

"Where were you born?"

"New Haven."

"You need to calm down, ma'am."

I can tell them all day long that I was raised in New Haven by my white mother, that my Black father was born in Rhode Island and has done biology research in Los Angeles for almost thirty years, but that won't matter. "You're going to make me miss my flight, and this could be solved so easily."

"You have a suspect item in your purse."

Right. A piece of fruit that is suspect because I am suspect because I am just ethnically ambiguous enough to look like I could be Middle Eastern. And in their minds, all people from the Middle East are Muslim and all Muslims are suspect.

I look at the clock. Nine minutes. Fuck. "Are you going to open my purse and put this issue to rest?"

"What do you do for a living, ma'am?"

"I'm a therapist. I work with children who suffer trauma."

I've tried to be rational. I tried to be calm. That's not working. I'm tempted to raise my voice to show these power-trippers how loud I can project.

Because, you assholes, I am a trained singer, and I can get really fucking loud.

But I don't. Instead, I take my volume up just enough to call attention to what's happening, but not so loud that I sound hysterical. "It seems you are engaging in racial profiling. Again, I ask you to get your supervisor or look through my purse or give it back. That is my personal property, and you may not hold it indefinitely because there's a banana inside!"

As if I'm invisible and inaudible, they ignore me and keep their focus on the X-ray image on the screen.

Seven minutes.

Inside, I'm laughing at the absurdity of it all. Outside, I'm shaking. "Please just open the purse and put your concerns at ease so I don't miss my flight."

I look up and see a familiar face looking back at me from beyond the security guard. Derek.

He looks at me questioningly. I widen my eyes in what I hope is a clear *help me* signal. Some emotion flickers across his face, and I realize that if he does come help me, he could be putting himself at risk. These idiots apparently see anyone without a peachy complexion as a threat to national security.

Derek does not move a muscle in his face. But the look in his eyes brings me an instant sense of calm. I take a deep breath and let it out slowly. He nods almost imperceptibly, turns, and walks toward the gate.

Idiot number four tells me to sit on a bench and wait to be interrogated. At this point, I realize I have no choice but to comply, so I follow their instructions. Six minutes.

My feet are cold. I want the comforting weight of my purse in my lap, but it is sitting on a conveyor belt, being scanned repeatedly by an X-ray machine so that everyone can examine the shape of my wallet, the shape of my lip gloss tube, the shape of my granola bar, the shape of my tampons, the shape of my notebook, and the shape of the deadly banana.

I think of the stories I'll tell when I get through this, how Sage will both laugh and completely sympathize. She's told me about similar experiences. It is a crime to be ethnically ambiguous in the United States of America, and I am tired of the system that perpetrates these aggressions on me and my loved ones.

Breathe, Amira. Do the same thing you tell the parents you work with. Take a deep breath. This. Too. Shall. Pass. Count backward from ten. Breathe.

A gospel song pops into my head, something we once sang in my high school choir about being abused and scorned. And the chorus: *Glory Hallelujah.*

Looking at the ground, staring at my feet, cold in their cute little socks. Other feet pass hurriedly by. Work shoes, dress shoes, impractical heels, more stocking-clad feet. Now a very expensive-looking pair of men's driving moccasins stops in front of me. My father used to have shoes like that.

An argument pops into my head: Dad wearing those shoes, telling my mother he was so sorry he couldn't pay child support that month. *Too many mouths to feed, Tania.* The hard expression on her face. *What did you pay for those shoes, Jason?*

"Amira."

I know that voice. Just like before, it sends a wave of peace throughout my body. This is not my father. I look up. His soft dark eyes soothe me. "Amira, this is Rosalin Donoghue, head of security at this airport."

A redhead even shorter than me extends her hand and shakes mine briskly. Her weight makes up for what she lacks in height, giving her an imposing stature. "Dr. Foret informs me that you are being harassed by my agents. Is that true, Ms. MacKenzie?"

"They're holding my belongings because they claim that the banana in my purse looks like a threat. My flight boards in two minutes. And I need to pick up my daughter when I get home, but I don't know when I'll be able to get home if I miss my flight. They've asked one ridiculous question after another."

"Are you two traveling together?" Ms. Donoghue asks.

"No," we say in unison.

"How do you two know each other?"

"Socially," Derek says. "Her best friend is marrying my best friend. We were with them this weekend."

"Small world," she says.

"Indeed," he says. "Perhaps you've heard of them. Wesley Williams and Sage DesChamps."

I glance at his face, notice a small twitch at the corner of his mouth like he wants to smile but is restraining himself. Clever man, dropping their names like that. Derek just sent a subtle message to this woman that anything that happens to me at this airport could become news.

"Williams... DesChamps." She looks at the ceiling, as if in thought. "The fainting proposal. Right? They were on TV after they both won that big Brilliance Award."

"That's them," I say, looking directly into the woman's eyes.

Ms. Donoghue takes a deep breath and blows it out forcefully. "Where is this offending fruit?" she asks her TSA agents.

Idiot number four points to the image on the screen.

"Have you bothered to open the woman's purse, or are you just staring at the screen, waiting for something to happen?" Ms. Donoghue asks.

The TSA agent stammers something unintelligible.

"Because if you were staring at the screen, waiting for something to happen… For the fifteen minutes that you stood over Ms. MacKenzie, threatening her, you have actually been racially profiling and harassing her. Do you understand what that means?"

Ms. Donoghue turns to me. "I am very sorry that you had to experience this. I don't take situations like this lightly. Smith, get the woman her shoes, give her the purse. Ms. MacKenzie, may I open your purse and show my employees the *fruit* that they have been staring at in terror for the past fifteen minutes?"

"Of course," I say, sliding into my boots. "I've been asking them to open it so we can just move on."

"I'm sure you have," she says, her voice trembling with irritation.

The TSA agent with the grating voice hands Ms. Donoghue my purse. She removes the banana and hands it to me without a word. I can't help smirking in triumph.

Ms. Donoghue takes a deep breath, apologizes to me again, and hands me her business card in case I have any issues at this airport in the future. She also assures me she will call the gate and have them hold the flight.

I smile my appreciation at her, then look at Derek. "I didn't realize you were flying today. We could have shared an Uber."

"Can I help with your suitcase?" he asks.

I gesture to the roller bag at the end of the conveyor belt. "What flight are you on?"

"United 9432," he says, striding away.
I catch up with him. "Me too!"
We rush through the small terminal.

7
First Class Team

Amira

GRAY WALLS AND CARPETING FLASH PAST ME IN A BLUR as we hurry to the gate. Actually, he's not hurrying. I'm just struggling to keep up. His legs are a lot longer than mine, and heels aren't made for running.

"Derek, I can't thank you enough," I pant.

"Don't think twice."

When we arrive at the gate, the customer service rep waves us toward the door. I place my phone face down on the scanner, and she admits me to the jetway. No need to run now, thank God. I take a moment to catch my breath before continuing onto the plane.

Odd that Derek hasn't caught up yet.

I look back, don't see him. Should I go make sure everything's okay? What could have gone wrong between the gate and the jetway? Maybe he forgot something. Just as I turn around to find out, he strides down the jet bridge, a huge smile on his face.

"Getting on the plane, Amira?"

Embarrassed. Do I admit that I was worried about him? Which looks worse: I was worried about you, or I was catching my breath, or...? *Do you dare to be known?* Excellent. Now my poetry is chiding me.

"Umm... I was just going back to make sure you were okay," I say, looking at my feet. These really are amazing boots. The leather is supple and beautiful, and I love the stacked wooden heel. The faux buttons and loops complete the steampunk look. Even Lila likes them.

"...of you," he says.

"What?" I ask, realizing I've tuned out.

"That's very sweet of you. Let's get outta here."

He puts his hand on my upper back, as if to guide me. I submit and stroll down the jet bridge beside him.

When we get inside the plane, though, Derek winks at me, then slips through a curtain on the left. Lucky him, sitting in first class.

I turn right and make my way down the narrow aisle, the hard shell of my roller bag hitting me in the calves as I look for my seat: 31B. Got it. Now, is there any room in one of these overhead bins? No, no, no, okay, maybe this one. I start to lift the bag above my head when a strident voice behind me says, "Ms. MacKenzie, can you please come with me?"

My heart stops.

Not again. Didn't we already go through this?

I lower the bag, take a deep breath, and turn to see the flight attendant smiling, perfectly coiffed blond hair in a hair-sprayed shell.

"What's the problem?" I ask.

"No problem," she says. "You've been upgraded."

"Excuse me?"

"You've been upgraded to first class."

"What? How?" I ask, thinking about the balance on my Visa card. I hope they didn't charge me for this.

"Another passenger thought you deserved a treat."

I don't know what to say about that. How to respond? It must have been Derek. I feel excited and kind of uncomfortable. This would never be in my budget, and here he is...

"Ms. MacKenzie, we need to take off soon, so if you could just follow me."

"Of course," I say, following her down the aisle, through the gray curtain, and into a very spacious cabin. Big leather seats. Only two seats in each section, not three like in economy class.

The flight attendant leads me to the second row on the right, where there's an empty seat next to Derek.

"Did you do this?" I ask.

He smiles. "After what went down back there, I thought... Anyway, do you prefer the window or the aisle?"

"The aisle is great," I say, thinking of how often I will need to pee and how embarrassing it would be to climb over him or ask him to move every time. "Thank you." I settle into the comfortable seat. "Wow, this is so much nicer than economy!"

He smiles. "Right?"

"Ms. MacKenzie, what can I get you to drink before we take off?"

"What's available?"

The flight attendant runs down the list from the well-stocked bar.

"How about a mimosa? Do you like champagne and orange juice?" Derek asks.

"That would be perfect! I don't normally drink before noon, but..."

"With the morning you've had," he says.

The flight attendant smiles and walks away.

"You are just so sweet," I say, pulling out my wallet. He waves it away. I look at him confused.

"It's covered," he says.

"Don't tell me you paid for that too!"

"It's included with the fare. It's free. Just like your snacks."

"You mean I don't have to eat this bruised, mishandled fruit weapon in my purse?"

"There are reasons people pay extra for first class."

"I'd pay extra just for the comfort. This seat is amazing!"

"Did you see how it reclines?" Derek shows me how to raise the footrest and lower the seat back like a Barcalounger.

"Oh. My. God. Boy, Derek, you sure know how to treat a woman."

"I like to think so." He smiles and winks, then swears under his breath.

He either has a really strange habit or a nervous tic. Now's not the time to ask. Anyway, once I settle down with my mimosa, I'm going to start revising that poem.

The flight attendant brings a mini wineglass with my beverage. I take a sip. Heaven.

"I'll be back for that glass just before takeoff," she says.

"Thank you," I say, then turn to Derek. "Do you always fly in first class?"

"With the job stress I've had in the past fifteen years, I really felt it was worth it to treat myself whenever possible."

"I sure can see why."

"I sleep better on overnight flights in first. Eat better. Who wants to eat junk out of a box if you don't have to?"

"Yeah, I always bring food."

He laughs. "I bet you'll be rethinking that strategy after today, huh?"

I laugh too. "I sure won't be bringing bananas."

I recline and sip my mimosa until the flight attendant comes for the glass. Following Derek's lead, I put the seat back upright and the footrest down for takeoff, then fish my notebook and pen from my purse.

The vibrations of the wheels on the tarmac reverberate up through my feet as the plane pushes back from the gate until it gains speed and lifts off the runway. Even from the aisle seat, I have a pretty good view out the window.

"Bye-bye, Connecticut," I say to the orange and yellow trees that get smaller as we rise.

Derek smiles but keeps his gaze outside, giving me a chance to notice his strong profile. Strong and secure. He's far too much of a player for a woman like me, but he is kind and *very* nice to look at. Heat fills my inner thighs.

It's a one-and-a-half-hour flight to DC with a layover that's really only long enough to use the restroom, then hightail it to the gate for our connecting flight. To my amazement, Derek has floated my first-class ticket on the second flight too. Once we get in the air, he shows me how to control the TV screen embedded in the seat in front of me. Since this flight is over two and a half hours, I choose a classic chick flick from the selection. He chooses the same movie.

"Are you a fan of Meg Ryan?" I ask.

"I've never watched one of these movies."

"Come on."

"Really. Never thought it was my thing."

"Then why watch now?"

He hesitates. "Trying to do things different, do new things. So my new friend Amira's watching this; it'll give us something to talk about."

Is he trying to come on to me, or is he genuinely curious about my interests? If he hadn't come to my rescue at the airport, I'd think he was hitting on me. But he did come to my aid in a really big way. I'm gonna give him the benefit of the doubt and assume he thinks this is a way to get to know me better.

My favorite scene comes up. I can't help but watch his face. Is he getting the joke? Is he enjoying it? Why do I need to worry about what this guy thinks of what I'm watching on a plane? It does happen to be one of my favorite romantic comedies. But really, who cares what he thinks?

About halfway into the movie, the screen goes black.

A deep voice comes through the intercom. "Ladies and gentlemen, this is the captain. We are diverting to Charlotte due to weather in New Orleans. Flight attendants will be coming to take your trays and beverages momentarily."

Weather in New Orleans. My heart starts pounding. "What weather could be serious enough to divert a plane?"

"I don't know, but I'll find out," Derek responds, his voice calm as he whips out his phone.

I don't feel calm. What weather? When New Orleans has "weather," things fall apart.

"CNN says a torrential downpour dumped over four inches of rain between seven and eight a.m."

"Which means?" I pull out my phone and scroll my social media feeds. WWL-TV always posts updates on Twitter. "Shit. Runways are flooded."

"What about the rest of the city?" Derek asks.

I text Lila:

You okay, Li? I hear there's flooding.

She doesn't respond.

Where is Lila? We spoke this morning. Everything was fine. She was getting ready for school with Phoebe. Did they make it to school? Or are they home? Stranded on the road somewhere? Shit.

I exhale.

Gather information before you react, Amira.

Derek scans his phone. "Looks like a freak lightning bolt hit a transformer and knocked out power throughout southern Louisiana. Took out most internet and a couple of cell towers. Still pouring. Apparently, something called a turbine is also down."

"If a turbine is down, the city is flooded." I groan.

"Yeah," he says. "Guess there's flash flooding throughout New Orleans."

I envision cars trapped on the highway, unable to move as floodwaters rise. Is Lila in one of those cars? "People die in flash floods. They get caught in their cars. They..."

Okay, Amira, breathe.

I try to take a deep breath in but can't quite seem to inhale.

I take my phone out of Airplane Mode and dial my daughter. Her cheerful voice invites me to leave a message.

"Just checking in, honey," I say, forcing calm into my voice. "My flight was diverted, so I'll be home late. Please stay with Phoebe, and I'll see you as soon as I get home."

I look at Derek. "What if she doesn't get my voice mail? I have to call Phoebe's parents." I scroll through my contacts until Elara's and Zaki's smiling faces pop up. Dial. This time a recorded message plays. "All lines are busy. Please try your call again later."

Panic rips through me. I try to text them, but my hands are shaking so badly I can barely even tap the numbers.

"Want me to do it?" he asks.

I nod, tears springing to my eyes.

"What would you like to say?"

"You all safe?" I say, my voice cracking. "My plane got diverted to North Carolina because of the floods."

Derek taps in the message and hits Send. "Any others?"

"To my ex-husband, Greg," I say, tapping on the image of his face.

"What would you like to say?"

"On the plane. Diverted to Charlotte. Can't reach Lila or Phoebe's parents. Assuming you guys made it out for your honeymoon. Hope so."

Derek types that in and hits Send, then hands the phone back to me. I stare at it, willing a response to pop up. None comes. It feels like an eternity I'm staring at the phone, waiting for a familiar text tone.

"What if they're trying to call me?" I ask Derek.

"Chances are they'd text first," he says, his voice taking on that soothing tone. "Besides, if the cell towers are out…"

"Send another one to Lila please," I say.

"Okay. What would you like to say?"

"We've never been separated during a storm. I think you're safe with Phoebe and her parents, but if you're not, don't be afraid. Just get to safety. I'm coming for you."

Derek

MY HEART JUST ABOUT BREAKS OPEN HEARING THE MESSAGE Amira asks me to send her daughter. By the time the girl receives the message, we'll probably have found her. But Amira's understandably distraught and having trouble doing basic things like texting. I need to help her get to Lila.

"Anyone else you want me to message?" I ask, just as my pager starts beeping. A message from the hospital.

"Yeah, can you text my mom and Sage and tell them I need help finding Lila?" she asks, her voice rising in pitch. "I need them to try to call."

"One second, lemme check this," I say, pulling the pager from my pocket and reading the message:

All staff report current availability for duty to supervisor, regardless of schedule, STAT.

I tap a message to the chief of surgery:

D. Foret PedsCardiac U/A—out of state. Patient update?

"Is that a pager?" Amira asks.

"Yeah." I stare at the screen on my pager, willing a response. None. They must be scrambling to make sure the patients are covered and the staff are safe.

"I didn't even know they still made those."

I take a deep breath and let it out slowly. "Hospitals use pagers because the old-school tech works ninety-nine percent of the time, even when the power and internet are down."

"And what do they say? Everything okay there?"

"No news yet. They're bringing staff in. I'll hear something soon, I hope."

For now, I return to her phone and get her message out. Both Sage and Tania respond immediately that they will call until they have some answer. Amira's mom expresses concerns. Nobody tells Amira it will be okay. I want to even though there's no way for me to know whether it will be. She looks into my eyes. Hers are clouded over with fear.

"Want your phone back?" I ask.

She takes it, opens Instagram, scans until she finds what must be her daughter's page. All the images reveal a younger, paler version of Amira.

"Nothing," she cries. "Damn it."

"Hey," I say, trying to be gentle. "She'll be okay."

"How do you know that?" she asks, breathing heavily.

"I don't, but I believe it. What I know is, it's totally natural for you to be afraid right now. And holding on to that feeling won't help Lila. Do you meditate?"

"Ha. I'm always telling my patients to."

"Then let's do it together. I just learned this a couple of months ago myself."

She smiles. The plane starts descending. I look into her eyes.

She does something weird with her lips and takes a long, slow, deep inhale, holds it, then exhales through her nose.

"Aren't you supposed to inhale through your nose?" I ask. *What? Come on, man! Cut the woman some slack.* "I mean, that's how I learned."

She nods and speaks more slowly than I've heard her speak before. "There are different types of meditation and pranayama."

"Prana what?"

"Yogic breathing exercises. This one cools excess heat in the body. Great for anger, stress."

"Wanna teach me?" Sometimes teaching is the best way to forget a problem.

"Sure. Make a tube with your tongue and inhale slowly. Now close your mouth and exhale through your nose. Feel that? Feel the difference with that exhalation?" she asks, holding my gaze.

I nod *yes*.

"Let's do that again. Inhale through the curled tongue for ten, and close your mouth and exhale. Repeat." She repeats the counting, and I feel my eyelids getting heavy. "If you feel like you want to close your eyes, that's okay. Let them close. Keep breathing."

She leads me through another few rounds of this anger-reducing breath. I learned through my program that when you control the breath, it helps relax the parasympathetic nervous system. Meditation experts call it the lizard brain, the part of the brain that makes people go crazy and panicky when they feel threatened. It's connected to the amygdala.

By teaching me now, Amira's not only soothing her nervous system, she's also having an experience of being in control in the middle of a situation where, sadly, she has literally no agency. Having control over the breath is helpful. Now I'm getting a new firsthand experience with that too.

"Got it?" she asks.

"Mm-hmm."

"Good. If you wanna keep meditating, you can count in your head, or if you're ready to stop, take one long, deep breath, open your eyes, and let it go. I'm gonna stop instructing you and keep going," she says, and I can hear her inhale slowly, deeply through her curled tongue, then exhale slowly.

Amira

My meditation is interrupted by a stream of ideas about how to get to Lila as quickly as possible. Now, as I feel the plane descending, I recognize I need to actually make a plan. That's why I'm plagued with those thoughts. This is important. I turn to Derek. "What are you going to do when we land?"

He opens his eyes wide. "You mean what are *we* going to do when we land?"

"We?"

"Why would I let you deal with this alone?"

"Well," I begin.

"There's no *I* in team," Derek says. "So the only question is: What are we as a team going to do to get back to New Orleans and get to your daughter as soon as possible?"

Wow. A team. I'm used to handling everything solo. A little breeze of relief passes through me. "I guess we have a couple of options. We can try to get on a plane to Atlanta. The problem with that is we don't know what the weather is going to be like there. Even if it's fine now, the storm could change direction. If we get diverted again, who knows where we'll end up?"

"Good point. We rent a car; we'll have the freedom and control to move quickly. Storm crops up in front of us, we can find another highway."

"Besides, when you think about the time we'll have to wait for a flight to Atlanta, if there are even any seats available, and then the time it takes to fly there and then the time it takes to get off the plane and get our luggage and get to the rental car agency..."

"Could take longer to fly into Atlanta or Birmingham and drive than to just drive from Charlotte," he says.

"Also, it should be less expensive than flying. I hate to say it, but I don't have that much room on my Visa card."

"Let me take care of this."

"I can't let you do that."

"Why not?"

"It's too much!"

"We're talking about getting to your daughter, right? If you had the money, you'd spend it, right?"

A knot tightens in the base of my stomach. How can I not have the money to handle this emergency? I think about the no-shows last month, the time I allotted for patients and didn't get paid for. I feel sick.

Derek squeezes my hand. "Besides, it's not like it costs more to have you ride in the car."

"But you wouldn't be rushing back to New Orleans if not for me. You could stay in North Carolina or go back to New Haven or—"

"You kidding? I have children counting on me, children I operated on."

"Of course. I'm sorry. I didn't think of that."

"So it's settled, right? I'm renting us a car, no matter the cost because I would be renting one anyway." He opens the Hertz app on his phone and books a vehicle. "Plus you don't weigh enough to add to the gas expense significantly." He grins.

I scowl at him. "Not that my weight is your business."

He opens his mouth as if to speak, then closes it and shakes his head. Now a series of emotions seem to travel across his face. It's actually quite entertaining. If I wasn't so stressed, I might start laughing. As it is, even though I feel sick, I really wish I had something to snack on right now. Eating always takes my mind off my problems.

8
Plane to Nowhere

Derek

OVER THE INTERCOM, THE CAPTAIN SAYS, "LADIES AND Gentlemen, welcome to Charlotte, North Carolina. We're going to sit on the tarmac until they have an open gate. For your safety, please stay in your seats until the plane comes to a complete stop."

I wonder how long we'll be sitting on this tarmac. Do I need to rebook the rental car?

Amira looks at me again, fear in her eyes.

"We've got this," I say.

She takes my hand, and my whole body feels alive.

"Thank you, thank you, thank you," she says.

"Anytime. We're gonna get through this. We will get back to New Orleans, and we'll get to your daughter."

I wish my pager would vibrate or beep or something. Has anyone messaged Amira back? I'd ask, but I don't want to encourage her to keep checking her phone. That will raise her anxiety and undo all the good of the meditation.

Amira is the first woman I've held hands with in two months. The women I spend time with, we don't typically hold hands. This almost makes me dizzy.

The seat belt sign goes off, and she slips out of her seat and heads toward the restroom. Thank God. A moment of privacy. I grab my journal from my bag and write:

> Held hands with Amira. Find myself wanting to take care of her. Why? Barely know her yet feel as comfortable with her as if I've known her all my life.

She returns, and I stick the journal under my leg. From the back of the plane, I think I hear someone crying.

The captain speaks through the intercom again. "This is Captain Domenico. We know many of you are concerned about loved ones in New Orleans. Rest assured we are seeking whatever information we can find. What we know now is the storm was unexpected and three of the city's five turbines are down at two of the pumping stations. Emergency teams are doing their best to rescue people who are stranded in or on top of their vehicles. The crew here in Charlotte says they'll have a gate and jet bridge for us in about one hour. If they had stairs to fit this aircraft, we'd be able to let you out right here, but they don't. In the meantime, we'll put on some free entertainment for you and flight attendants will be coming down the aisles with carts of snacks and beverages on us."

As if on cue, the flight attendant comes over with menus. Amira orders salmon. I choose the steak with au gratin potatoes. When the flight attendant arrives with Amira's food a few minutes later, I help her take the tray table from its stowaway spot in the armrest. Then the flight attendant brings my meal. We dive into our lunches as the movie resumes.

Amira's still holding my hand, using her left hand to eat. I don't wanna take my hand away. I'm definitely gonna have to journal about this.

Amira

Thank God for this salmon and salad. Stress always makes me hungry, and this meal is surprisingly tasty. Flaky salmon. Fresh mesclun mix and avocado. Cherry tomatoes. The white wine is a nice touch, though I'm careful to sip it slowly so I can keep my wits about me when we get off this plane.

We landed in Charlotte at half past noon. The pilot said it would be one hour. Now he's telling us there's still no gate and he doesn't know when there will be one. He says he hopes it'll only be another hour. My flesh is crawling from the desire to get off this damn plane. Still, since I'm stuck here, I'm very grateful to be in a first-class cabin. I would be positively claustrophobic squeezed into one of those tight seats in economy.

I try to send telepathic messages to Lila. How am I going to function if I don't hear from her soon? The only things keeping me tethered to reality right now are the food and the warmth of Derek's hand in mine. Isn't that strange? I barely know the man, and two days ago I thought he was a total jerk, but I find his presence so soothing.

The Meg Ryan film ends and another begins. The flight attendant brings dessert and more drinks. I switch from wine to tea. The new romantic comedy plays on the screen in front of me. I hear it. I see it. I've watched this one at least a dozen times, but right now I have no idea what's happening.

I'm always telling my clients to sit with their discomfort. My own discomfort seems unbearable. I think about the parents I've worked with who were separated from their children during any number of the storms and floods we've had. How did they prevent themselves from screaming at anyone who tried to have a normal conversation with them? God, are my patients okay now? I didn't see any reports on Isle de Jean Charles or Pointe-aux-Chênes or anywhere in Terrebonne Parish. The last thing these families need is more trauma. I think about Ruby and her grandparents, the boisterous Courteaux family, and poor Christian and his failing math grade. It looks like his dream was prophetic, not that he hasn't been through floods before.

Somehow, I've been spared all that. These past twelve years, every storm we've had, Lila has been with me. And we've been easily able to connect with Greg and make sure we were all safe. Now my mind feels like it's leaving my body. Still no word. Mom hasn't reached them. Sage hasn't reached them. They're still trying, thank God. But what can I do? Nothing. That's the thing I just can't seem to accept; this is literally out of my control. I cannot get in touch with my child right now. *Breathe.* Hold Derek's hand. Breathe some more. At least I can be fairly certain she's with Phoebe, Elara, and Zaki.

Two and a half hours.

Derek's looking antsy as well.

"You've been so attentive and helpful to me these last hours. How are you doing?" I ask.

He rubs his face. "Worried about my patients. Last operation I did before leaving was a five-year-old with a previously undiagnosed condition that would have killed him by age twenty or younger if we hadn't caught it. I hope to hell the auxiliary electric system is functioning. Makes me sick to think about it."

"Oh my God. And he can't be the only person or even the only little kid recovering in the hospital."

"For some reason, I can't sign on to the staff portal. There's no way of knowing how any of my patients are doing until I get a message on my pager. That five-year-old is from the Lower Ninth. You know how easily the roads wash out in that ward. What if his parents got trapped? Is he lying in his hospital bed with no family nearby?"

"Oh God, Derek," I say, knowing that type of situation is all too realistic. It's what brings families to me.

"They both had to work, were visiting him in shifts. Two older kids at home." His eyes fill with tears. "I'm the only Black pediatric surgeon, the only face that looks somewhat like his among the doctors. And he might be lying there alone."

Now it's my turn to offer comfort. "You'll be there as soon as you can. Tomorrow at the latest, right? Maybe the flooding will subside quickly."

I don't actually believe that, though it would be nice.

"Do you think the folks in the Lower Ninth have food?" he asks.

"Good question. Unless it's flooded, Cotlon's store must still be operating. But it's probably flooded, and even on a good day, the selection is pretty limited."

"Yeah, you can only fit so much in a small space. If Burnell got washed out, will the Ninth go back to being a food desert?"

"You've been in New Orleans three weeks? And you already know Burnell Cotlon by his first name?"

Derek shrugs like it's no big deal, but I'm impressed. True, folks in New Orleans are friendly, but Derek's connected with him in such a short time.

"You have so much weighing on you, Derek. Yet you're a picture of calm." I squeeze his hand.

He looks at me, says nothing, just holds my gaze. I think there's a message in those eyes, but I don't know what it is. What I sense from his gaze, though, is warmth, compassion, and seeking. What is he seeking?

Derek

At this point, Amira's hand in mine feels natural, like it's supposed to be there, like it's always been there. Thankfully, I'm right-handed, so I've still been able to journal about this. I don't know what the program would say about holding a woman's hand for two hours, and I don't really care. This woman is in a horrible situation. Frankly, so am I. What's happening here isn't sexual. There's no attempt at romance. She reached out to me, and I was there for her. Period.

Too much time sitting on a goddamned plane going nowhere. Thank God they're finally wheeling us to the gate.

Amira's eyes are fixed on her phone. Looking at her, I get a flash of a much older woman. Suddenly, I feel as if I'm also thirty years older and we'll be sitting here like this, going somewhere together after a lifetime. After a lifetime.

There's a poem by Rumi my grandmother used to read to me when I didn't feel like doing my homework.

> *Tend to your vital heart*
> *And all you worry about will be solved.*
> *Your donkey is afraid of work.*
> *Tie it up and make it carry many loads*
> *Of patience and gratitude for a hundred years*
> *Or thirty, or twenty.*

"Ladies and gentlemen, welcome, again, to Charlotte, North Carolina. Local time is three-fifteen p.m. Flight attendants will be disarming the doors in a moment. If you need to book a flight back to Hartford or another city, gate agents are standing just outside the Jetway to assist you. If you stay in Charlotte until we have clearance to operate in New Orleans, we'll help you rebook at that time."

One thing I love about flying in first class is we're the first people off the plane. No standing in line for half an hour just to leave the flying tin can. Now, in the terminal, I have room to stretch and move. I've been on some long flights, but I have never sat on a plane that was not moving for so long, and I never want to again.

"Bathroom," I say to Amira, who's stretching next to me. She nods, and we separate for the first time since we stepped onto the jet bridge in Hartford. That seems like so long ago.

It feels like something is missing from my arm. Her hand. We've been holding hands for the past few hours. Now we're separate people again. Not that we were ever united.

Soon as I step into the stall, I dial Ned.

"Derek, my man!" His raspy voice brings relief.

"Dude, you know that woman I texted you about the other day?"

"Amira, right?"

"She was on my flight. Whole drama that I won't get into, couldn't be avoided, but now we're about to drive from North Carolina to New Orleans together—it's like ten hours in the car or something."

"Temptation!"

"Exactly. What do I do? I feel this attraction. I don't know if I even can assess my motivations in her presence and in this crazy situation."

"Not possible. So just keep the principles in mind. Remember, no matter how solid she seems, she's carrying generational trauma from toxic masculinity."

"Right."

"But it's not just what she's gone through; it's what her mother and her grandmother and her sisters and friends have experienced."

"She doesn't have sisters."

"You know what I mean. Epigenetics, man. The male species has oppressed and violated women in every possible way, perpetrated unspeakable crimes against women, and unfortunately for better or worse, we're now paying for it because our forefathers didn't know how to be real men. If your dad taught you to be a real man, you're lucky."

"My daddy has always treated my mama like a goddess. It's how I treated Riley until I found her in bed with that scumbag. After that..." I sigh.

"Hang in there, buddy! You've got this. In fact, it's a great opportunity to connect with a woman without letting sexuality enter the dynamic. It's good practice for you."

"Thanks."

MOMENTS LATER, I HAND THE TIRED-LOOKING YOUNG MAN behind the car-rental desk my credit card, tell him I booked an SUV with four-wheel drive. Amira puts her card on the counter. I take it.

"Derek," she says, and I don't like the tone in her voice.

"What?"

"At least let me contribute."

"Really?" I say, raising my eyebrows and pressing her credit card back into her palm. "We made an agreement on the plane."

She flares her nostrils at me, which makes me laugh.

"Look, Amira, this is no big deal to me, so just drop it okay?"

"But—"

"Do you always have a problem with people taking care of you?"

"No! Yes! I don't know. What does that even mean?"

I look into her eyes and inhale slowly and deeply, hoping that modeling the relaxation technique will help her calm down and gain some perspective.

She follows my lead. After a few breaths, the fierce look in her eyes softens. "This is really nice of you actually. I feel bad that I can't pay for the fancy SUV. It's just not in my—"

"Hey," I say, taking her hand—*not* a romantic gesture, thank you very much. "We're in this together. All right? It makes me feel good to do nice things for people. Okay? Just nod."

She nods. I squeeze her hand and let go.

THIRTY MINUTES LATER, WE THROW OUR BAGS INTO THE back of the SUV. The vehicle is high and she's petite, so I assume she'll need help getting into the passenger seat. As I offer my hand, Amira wraps her arms around me. "Have I said thank you for this?"

"Don't think twice."

She squeezes me tighter. Shit. What do I do about this now? I don't want her to feel rejected. It's not romantic. Just appreciation. I wrap my arms around her lightly, careful not to pull her too close or press our bodies together. I can't help but catch a whiff of her hair though. A soft, sweet scent. I might go crazy if we stand like this much longer.

"Seriously, Derek. Without you here today, I'd probably be sitting in a cell in Hartford, and if by some miracle I did make it onto the plane, I'd be squeezed between two smelly, drooling old men for hours, feeling hopeless and hyperventilating about my daughter."

"Two smelly old men, huh?" I laugh.

"Yes." She laughs and looks up at me.

Damn, those eyes! Bewitching. My hands start moving against my will. Stroking her hair, running down her back.

Stop, Derek. Stop right there. Do not do any more "soothing." Damn, you have some journaling to do.

9

Drive

Amira

DEREK'S CALMING CARESS LINGERS ON MY BACK EVEN as I settle into the passenger seat of the SUV. More relaxed, I'm able to focus on our next move. How long will it take us to get home from here? I map the directions on my phone. Looks like a ten-plus-hour drive. That's not so bad. It's not so good either.

"It's basically a straight shot from here to New Orleans," I say. "Once you get on 85 South, you go all the way through North Carolina, through Georgia, and into Alabama before we get on 20 West, then 459 South, then 59 South. That brings us into Louisiana, then we'll take 10 West into town."

"I'm never gonna remember all that. Ooh, I love this song." He turns up the volume on the radio and sings along. His rich baritone fills the rental car and sends tingles throughout my body.

I lean back in my seat and let the vibrations soothe me as he maneuvers out of the airport roads and onto the highway.

"Where'd you learn to sing like that?" I ask.

"Everyone in my family sings."

"That's so sweet. Were you in choir or something?"

"Too busy playing trombone."

"Oh?" That old joke about men who play wind instruments being good with their tongues springs to mind.

"Did you just coo?"

"Uh..." Oh my God. Did I just make an audible cooing sound? How embarrassing. "I think you mentioned your instrument when we were dancing," I say. "Do you play with it often?"

Derek bursts out laughing, and I gasp as I realize what I just said.

"I mean, play it. Do you play it often? The trombone."

Heat rushes to my cheeks. I avoid looking at Derek by staring out the window at the lush forest on either side of the highway.

"Huh. I never realized the leaves change color in the fall here too. I thought that was only a northern thing," I say, hoping to take attention away from my embarrassing comment.

"So what do you like to play with, Amira?" he asks, then laughs like a mischievous teenager.

"Ha. Ha." I take a deep breath. "Sometimes I take dance lessons."

"What kind of dance?"

"Belly dance."

"Really? Do they let men into those classes too?" he asks, then curses under his breath. There he goes again. What's up with that?

"I've never seen a man in a class. Would you like to join us? They say it helps someone prepare for childbirth."

"I definitely need that," he says, and we both start laughing. It feels good to laugh, except the release also uncorks a torrent of tears. An image of newborn Lila flashes through my mind, and the floodgates really open.

"Oh no! What did I say?" he asks.

I shake my head. "It's just the situation. And my baby."

"Hey," he says, taking my hand again. "What can I do to help?"

"You're doing it. Keep distracting me."

"Okay. What else do you do for fun?"

"I watch a lot of chick flicks, read, write poetry, sing."

"What part?"

"Mezzo, but I have a pretty big range. I can go down to a high tenor and up to high soprano."

"Impressive. You have any poems with you? Care to read something now?"

"There's one I started working on during the flight to New Haven. It definitely needs work though."

"Let's hear it," he says, turning off the radio.

"Okay, um…" I pull out my notebook and start reading "Do you dare to be known?"

I try not to edit the poem as I read it aloud to him.

When I finish, he sits in silence for a while. A long while. My throat tightens. "Uh, you know, it's still a work in progress. It's…"

"I'm just taking it in. It hits home."

"Oh?"

"It's along the lines of something I've been pondering for the past couple of months."

"Which part?"

"How much I'm willing to open myself to people, or not. And what I gain and lose from keeping walls up."

"Wow," I say.

"Would you send me a copy of that poem when it's finished?"

"I'd be honored to."

"I've got some friends I'd like to share it with, if you don't mind. They're doing this kind of work with me. We have an accountability group, and…"

"An accountability group? What do you mean?"

"A group of individuals who are working toward a similar goal and meet up at regular intervals to talk about what actions they've taken, the challenges they faced, their successes... like that."

"And then what happens?"

"I've only been in this group for a couple of months, but so far, I think it's really helped me. Reflecting with people on what they're doing, what I'm doing. To feel like I'm not alone in some of the goals and challenges I have. To be able to support other people in what they're striving for—it's powerful."

"My friend Celeste runs one of those. It's like group coaching?"

"Kind of, yeah."

A beeping sound comes from his side of the car.

"Shit," he says, pulling the pager out of his pocket and handing it to me. "Can you read this please?"

I look at the black-and-white screen and read: "Dr. Foret, your patients are covered."

His shoulders visibly drop as he heaves a sigh of relief. "Oh, thank God. Thank God! Can you respond: Trying to get home. Will check in ASAP."

"Of course," I say, pressing the keys with my thumbs. "Gosh, I forgot how hard these little keys are to use. Like on the old cell phones."

"Right?" He laughs. "Hey, do you have any other poems you wanna read?"

"Maybe," I say, flipping the pages of my notebook. "Oh, there's one on my phone you might like. Here it is. It's about ethnic ambiguity. Wanna hear it?"

"Definitely."

> *"I recently learned I am white*
> *From the Black, Latino, First Nations children*
> *In my refugee support group.*
> *They don't like to be called refugees*

And I don't like to be called white.
But the government assigns these labels
And labels once affixed
Stick
And are hard to shake
No matter how hard you try to break
The mold of societal conditioning
And patterning
There's always something
Rattling
In your brain and your cells
That says your Self
Is not quite right
Because you are not white
or
Black
or
Latino
or
Of a First Nation
You are a conglomeration
And nobody knows
What to do with that."

Derek exhales. "Amira. Shit. That was powerful."

"Really?"

"I learned so much about you in that one poem."

My cells feel alive with the compliment. I smile at his profile.
"And you like it?"

"Everything about it."

10
Making Groceries

Derek

FOUR HOURS ON THE ROAD, NOT INCLUDING STOPS FOR food and restroom breaks. She's been trying to reach her daughter. No luck. She's doing a great job of keeping herself together, and she hasn't been holding my hand too much in the car, thank God. Though I do miss her touch.

I like sharing this small space with her; warm and cozy.

The scenery is lackluster, cinderblock wall on one side and defoliated trees on the other. Still, better than being on the plane, in part because we're moving and in part because there's no one else around.

"So we're approaching Atlanta. What do you want to do, woman?"

"Eat. Make groceries. Keep driving."

"Make groceries?"

"If you're gonna live in New Orleans, friend, you best learn the lingo."

"Educate me then. What is *make groceries?*"

"Shop for food. No telling what we'll find at home. What did the radio announcer say? How long has power been out?"

"Almost twenty-four hours."

"Stores with generators might be running out of gas to keep the electric on. People mighta bought them out. Nobody's barbecuing if the streets are still flooded."

"Barbecuing?"

"You'll see. Anyway, best make groceries while we can. If they don't feed us, they'll feed someone. And we'd better get several gallons of water for drinking and bathing, and wet wipes. By the way, don't even think about pulling out your wallet in that store. I'm buying since you paid for the car."

"Yes, ma'am."

WE'RE SELECTING FRESH FRUIT IN THE SUPERMARKET WHEN Amira asks, "You know that accountability group you were talking about?"

I glance at her but return my attention to the apples quickly. Granny Smith or Fuji? Why not both? I fill a bag.

Her voice softens. "Forgive me, Derek. I can see I just made you uncomfortable. I'm sorry for violating your privacy."

I take a long, slow breath and clear my throat. "Nah. It's okay. The music got wicked loud in here all of a sudden though, huh?"

"I don't think so," she says, placing her hand gently on my arm. "You know, we don't have to talk about this. That's a lot of apples."

Her touch on my arm… If only she knew what she was doing to me. Maybe if I tell her, it'll make being in her presence easier. "We're each doing a fast of sorts."

"But you've been eating."

"Not that kind of fast." Do I dare share this with her? In the supermarket? I look around for eavesdroppers.

"You're making a little growling sound," she says.

"Mmm," I say, moving my mouth closer to her ear. "It's supposed to be a fast from females."

"Excuse me?" Amira turns her face toward mine so quickly that our lips almost graze. I'm tempted to close the distance, but I take a half step back.

"I think you heard me," I say.

"You said a fast from women?" Her formerly gentle voice takes on a hard edge, and her nostrils flare.

"You got it."

"What does that even mean?"

"How about we finish this conversation in the privacy of the car?"

She purses her lips and nods.

THIRTY MINUTES LATER, WE LOAD THE BACK OF THE SUV with coolers full of cold drinks, ten one-gallon jugs of water for washing up, fresh fruits and veggies we can eat without much preparation, and bags of nonperishable items, pouches of soup and curries, a couple of loaves of bread. It's way more food than we need or could possibly eat. But we don't know who we'll meet in the flooded streets. Amira also thought ahead and grabbed candles, lighters, and flashlights.

Now she opens an ice cream bar from a package of three and climbs into the driver's seat. "Continue," she commands.

"Huh?"

"Fast from women," she says, her voice curt like a displeased school teacher. Miss Brickson.

"Have you ever got so caught up in an unhealthy pattern of dating that you felt like you needed to clear your head?" I ask.

"I haven't dated much actually."

"Gorgeous woman like you?"

She raises an eyebrow, as if she either doesn't hear or doesn't believe the compliment. "Having a kid kind of kills the buzz for most guys. Why? Were you in a bunch of toxic relationships?"

"No."

"Then why fast from women? And how do you do that anyway?"

"You don't touch them, don't date them, don't have conversations with them of a personal nature. You don't flirt."

"But I hugged you. And we were holding hands on the plane."

"I know. I had to call my accountability buddy for help from the bathroom at the car-rental place this afternoon."

"Help from me?" she asks, her voice rising a notch.

"Not help from you. Help cleaning my head of the experience of…"

"Touching me."

"Mmm…"

I hear she's taking this the wrong way.

"Did I violate your female fast?" she asks, that unpleasant tone returning to her voice.

"I don't know you that well, Amira, but I feel a connection with you. When you bumped into me at the airport in New Orleans—"

"What?"

"Remember? You bumped into me at the airport. I looked into your eyes. I felt something. That's why I asked you for the drink."

"Oh that," she growls.

Damn it. I'm really screwing this up.

"Maybe your eyes set me off because I've gone two months without the company of a woman. But I don't think that's it. I think you might be special to me."

I glance at her. She's staring at me, her mouth agape. She takes the last bite of her ice cream bar, opens another one, and puts the car in gear.

"When you were in need at the airport this morning, I had to help you. I thought buying you that first-class ticket was okay. I thought it was a nice thing to do for a nice person who had a rough morning. Maybe somewhere deep inside there was a little romantic idea there."

"And that's a problem."

"It is while I'm on this fast, yeah. I'm supposed to be clearing my head, assessing my motivations and my actions."

"What did you do in your dating life that was so bad?"

"Nothing, but it wasn't fulfilling."

"Tell me more."

"I went through a difficult divorce, decided love wasn't for me, but I'm a red-blooded, virile man." I try to keep my voice even, to practice sharing my story without either judging myself or dismissing my behavior. "I've got needs. Women have needs. I dated casually. Very casually."

"What does that mean?"

"No strings attached. Ever. No more than three dates. Ever. I didn't wanna get close."

"Oh," she says. "What was so rough about your divorce?"

Do I tell her about Riley's continual infidelity? How she blamed me for her affairs and for some reason I still carry shame, as if her cheating was the result of some deep flaw in me? "You know, I don't wanna get into that now if that's all right. Suffice it to say, after ten years of casual dating, watching Wesley fall in love and shift his whole attitude and life for Sage, seeing how happy they are together... You know after that fainting proposal, I told him to forget her."

"You did?"

"She said no."

"Well, she didn't mean to say no. She was just stunned."

"He's explained all this to me, but at the time, he thought she said no."

"Oh no, she didn't. She called me when everything fell apart. She was so devastated she couldn't get out of bed for days."

"I understand that now, but when I first heard about it, when I saw the meme and spoke to him on the phone and heard how much pain he was in, I said, 'Forget her. It's not worth it.' But he couldn't. Have you ever felt that way about somebody, that no matter what misunderstandings you had or how badly they hurt you, you were still willing to try?"

She sighs. "Actually, I haven't."

"Me neither. But watching them, I realized I'll never give myself the chance if I keep living this lifestyle. So I decided to take this new job, move to a new place, and do this female fast. The way it works is if I have contact with a woman of any kind, I write about it in a journal. I document my feelings, my reactions. When I read back to the early days of this program, my notes are a lot different than they have been recently. Even meeting you and spending this time together, starting to maybe feel something that seems crazy since I've only known you for a few days."

"We've spent a lot of time together in the past two days."

"True dat. So, question is: What am I feeling? What's it about? Is it an antidote to loneliness? Do we have a connection? Or is it trauma bonding? We're both in a very stressful situation—you more than me—and I'm able to help you. That can create a false sense of connection. I don't know yet. I've started to explore this and journal and talk to my accountability buddy."

"Sounds like you're doing a lot of inner work."

"Wesley thinks I'm crazy to be doing this."

"It does sound a little... intense."

"But I think it's helping."

"Huh... Hey, I really appreciate you opening up to me like that."

"Thank you."

Amira doesn't say anything about her feelings. Did I give her an opening? I did say I was starting to maybe feel something. I took a risk, shared my emotions with her. She didn't respond.

What is this feeling in my shoulders and upper back? I think it's fear. I breathe in. Fear, but what's underneath it? Vulnerability. There we go. She makes me feel like I'm at her mercy.

Come on, Derek. Grow up. You've both got more important things to worry about. You've got patients who may be in distress, and she can't reach her child. How can you think about romance? How can she? Would you even be interested in her if she could think about romance at a time like this?

11
Washed Out

Amira

I THOUGHT THIS MIGHT HAPPEN. AS SOON AS WE GET TO Bayou Sauvage, Route 10 is underwater. It is passable, but I have to slow the car to about five miles per hour, so we don't go hydroplaning across the highway and careening into the bayou.

Derek wakes, grumbles. "What's happening?"

"We're close to home. The highway's washed out."

"Shit."

"I know. How'd you sleep?" I ask, not daring to take my eyes off the road to look at him.

"Good. Just enough. We still have any of those fries, or did you finish them?"

"I think I left you some. I tried to leave you some."

He roots around in the paper bag and starts munching. "I'm starting to rethink our plan."

"What plan?"

"The one where we drive into New Orleans right now. If this highway is washed out, won't roads in the city be a mess? Returning in the dead of night seems pretty foolish."

I sigh. There's a logic to what he's saying, I know. It's hard enough to see through floodwaters in daylight, never mind pitch-dark. But everything in me says to keep going until I find Lila, no matter what it takes. "I hope you can understand why stopping just isn't an option for me right now, Derek."

He takes a deep breath and lets it out slowly, puts his hand on my shoulder. "I do."

"At this point, I'm all adrenaline. I know I'm not thinking rationally, but... anyway, it's too late to turn back. We're practically in New Orleans."

Derek

AMIRA SAYS SHE'S HIGH ON ADRENALINE, BUT LOOKS TO ME like she's on the verge of falling asleep.

"Hey," I say. "Why don't you let me take over for a while?"

She shakes her head and continues singing along with Bob Marley.

"Amira, come on. I can tell you're exhausted."

"You don't know the roads," she says, eyes fixed straight ahead. "It's so easy to get stuck in New Orleans during a flood, to get trapped in a vehicle or swept away in floodwaters. I know the neighborhoods. I know which roads tend to flood and which ones usually stay dryer. I know which streets have the neutral ground."

"The neutral ground?"

"Man, if you're gonna live in New Orleans, you need to understand the neutral ground and the way water flows in the streets. The streets are higher in the middle and lower on the sides, so water runs toward the houses and pools at the curbs. On all the major thoroughfares, a strip of grass runs down the middle of the street between the two sides of traffic. That land is elevated. So if ever there's a risk of flooding, you park on the neutral ground so your car is less likely to get destroyed in the flood. I plan to drive around the cars on the neutral ground as much as possible. It takes knowledge and practice to navigate New Orleans in a flood, and to be honest, it's really dangerous. What I'm about to do is foolish. But I don't care. And I hope you're with me in this because if we don't take this risk, I don't see how else I will get to my child and you will get to that little boy lying alone in his hospital bed."

"I'm with you. Of course, I'm trapped in a moving vehicle, so I don't have much choice." I laugh. But what she said hits me hard too. She's not just thinking about her child. She's thinking about little Tyrell even though she doesn't know his name. She's on my team. We're in this together.

Again, I see a flash of Amira and me decades from now: her hair is white, and her dimples have turned to deep grooves that frame her mouth. She must be in her sixties, which would put me in my early seventies. Driving in the dark, holding hands, still singing along with Bob Marley.

12
Too Quiet

Amira

MOONLIGHT PROVIDES THE ONLY ILLUMINATION ON this street. Granted, it's past midnight, but New Orleans is a city that's up all night usually. The streetlights should be glowing even if the houses are dark. Something else noticeably lacking in the neighborhood we're driving through right now is noise. There's no music, no yelling, only the sound of our tires moving through water.

"Maybe the car is muffling outside noises," Derek says and lowers his window. An awful smell fills the vehicle, and he quickly presses the button to raise the window.

I choke. "I should have warned you not to do that. The sewer lines tend to back up during floods."

AN HOUR LATER, AFTER EXHAUSTING EVERY POSSIBLE ROUTE and finding roads barricaded or with visibly high water levels, I stop in the middle of the street and try to think of my next move.

"You okay? What's happening?" he asks.

I sigh. "I don't think I can get home."

"Home? I thought we were trying to get Lila now."

"I tried. It's not possible. Mid-City, where we live, is like the lowest point in the basin. Always fucking flooding. But there are weird low points even in the generally safe neighborhoods. Phoebe's family lives in one of those. Their house has never flooded 'cause it's on piers that elevate it about four feet from the ground, but their street is impossible to get to, or out of, once the waters rise."

"What neighborhood are they in?"

"Uptown."

"Shit," Derek says, a note of panic in his voice. "That's where I live. The Realtor said it wouldn't flood."

"They're probably right. Most of Uptown is well above sea level. And most of those homes are set several feet back from the road and elevated from the ground."

"Mine is, thank God. I might even have electricity."

"I think the whole grid got knocked out, Derek."

He grumbles. "Why'd we come to Mid-City if no one's here?"

"It's where I live. Where else would I go?"

"Do me a favor and stay with me."

I clear my throat. "Uh… female fast?"

Derek waves away the suggestion. "If the female fast is about abandoning women in their time of need in order to navel gaze, I'm not down with that. I've got a four-bedroom home that might not have flooded. And if it's dry, there's plenty of room for you and your daughter once we get her."

I smile, genuinely touched. After what he shared about his struggles with women, I know my instincts were right; he's not the man for me. But he is a kind soul, and I think we could develop a lovely friendship.

"You two can take my bed. I'll sleep on the couch in the other room."

"Why not just put us in one of the other bedrooms?" I ask.

"They don't actually have beds yet. But we'll get beds as soon as possible."

"But...," I protest.

"What are your other options at the moment?"

"Umm..."

"I guess you could sleep in the car tonight, but what will you do once you get Lila back? We'll get beds."

"We." He's thinking about all three of us, not just himself.

"Don't know how I can say it more clearly. I don't feel good leaving you alone in this situation. At least until your home is safe again, you're on Team DF."

"Team DF," I say and raise my eyebrows.

"Team Derek Foret." He grins.

I laugh, feeling a tiny bit of tension slip away for just a moment. "Thank you."

"Don't think twice. Let's go home. Uhh, I mean my home. Okey doke?"

"Okey doke. Where do you live?"

13
A Natural Crush

Derek

By the time Amira pulls onto Nashville Street, it's nearly three a.m. and my eyes are starting to cross. Good news is my street is dry. Halle-fucking-lujah. I knew this was the best neighborhood to buy a home. That place I looked at in the Marigny neighborhood was walking distance to all the great music spots, but the Realtor warned me the Marigny, the Bywater, Mid-City... all those neighborhoods are hit-or-miss and getting worse as the city subsides and the sea level rises.

I lower my window and sniff the air. No sign of sewage. Thank God. All this bodes well for my patients, too, except that Amira was right about the electricity. Pitch-dark except for the moonlight. Is the hospital's generator functioning? I'm tempted to drive by and see if the lights are on, but if they are, then I'll be compelled to go in and check on my patients. I haven't had more than a catnap in almost twenty-four hours, haven't showered since yesterday. Without my white coat, nobody recognizes me. Clearly it's best that I wait, go home, take care of myself, and let Amira take care of herself before anything.

"It's this one on the right," I tell her. She pulls into the driveway and parks under the carport. My heart stops. "Shit. Where's my car?"

"You left it here?"

"Hmm? Oh wait, no. I drove to the airport. Okay," I say, exhaling in relief. "Thanks for driving."

"Of course," she says, her voice soft and kind.

"I know the landscape of the heart, the music that travels its byways, the pulsing of its denser spaces. New Orleans is another matter."

"Poetry at three a.m.," she purrs.

Can't help but smile at the compliment.

"Did you just make that up?"

"Nah. I wrote it when I moved here, and it crosses my mind every time I get lost in this city, which is a lot."

She giggles.

"There's more. Ready?"

"Hit me."

"Though I listen for the beat of the drum circle at Congo Square, I get lost following the sound. Every note echoes off the walls built by my ancestors."

"Your ancestors?" she asks.

"My father grew up here, moved to Boston after his parents died, met my mom, never looked back. Or at least I thought he never did until I told him I was moving here."

She yawns. "Oh, excuse me I really want to hear more, but I think the adrenaline is wearing off. It's lucky I kept my eyes open driving here."

"Don't think twice." I step out of the vehicle and go around to help her out of the driver's seat. She takes my hand, and I can feel her trembling. The woman's exhausted all right.

"Let's get our bags and the food," she says.

As we gather our things, I hear my father in my head, caution tightening his voice. *You sure you want to move there?*

"Mm-hmm."

"A city with a proud past and a sordid history can trap a man. You know about Buddy Bolden."

"Yeah, Daddy, you told me."

"He was and is a New Orleans legend."

"I know."

"The man created jazz, inspired none other than Louis Armstrong."

"Sure did."

"Died in an asylum."

"Daddy, I know," I say. "I'm going down there to save lives and uplift people. The music is secondary."

"But you will play."

"I'm bringing the horn. Might even join a Social Aid & Pleasure club."

"Your great-grandfather was part of the Zulu. Not for Hurricane Audrey, we might still be there, playing in the front line."

"You might. I wouldn't exist if you hadn't met a certain young lady named Althea."

"Ain't it so."

"Ain't? Who are you? You never let me say ain't."

"Talking about New Orleans brings out the native son in me, I guess. Shhh. Don't tell your mama."

The sound of my daddy's laughter carries me to the front door, where I wait for Amira.

She carries two gallon jugs of water. "These are for tonight."

"How much water do you drink?" I laugh.

"For cleaning up."

"Oh man, after this long day of travel, I can't wait to take a shower."

"We can't," she says.

"Huh? Why not?"

"City water is generally not safe for several days after a flood, even in neighborhoods that didn't flood. You know, 'cause we're all on the same system."

I groan.

"So, we'll take these jugs of water into the showers and clean off with soap and bottled water. It's our best option for the moment."

"Well, that fucking sucks."

"Yup. But we're lucky we have so much bottled water. Most people probably don't."

Perspective is a beautiful thing. Amira just helped me shift my mindset from annoyed to grateful.

Amira

AS WE STEP OUT OF THE SUV, I TAKE IN DEREK'S MOONLIT house. Double-gallery-style homes, with their dual-level porches that span the full width of the structure, columns, and slip head windows that go from floor to ceiling have always been my favorite of the New Orleans architectural styles. Some people spend hours on shoe porn or on sex porn. I swoon at house porn.

"Amira?"

"Huh?" I lift my gaze to his face, feeling heat in my cheeks. I scan the wide porch. "Those are gorgeous. Are they hand-painted?"

"What?"

"The tiles on this porch."

"Nice, huh? The previous owners did a beautiful renovation," he says.

Derek unlocks the door, and we step inside. He flips the light switch to no avail. "Guess it's good we didn't buy too many perishables," he grumbles. "Let's get this food in the kitchen though."

Even in the moonlight, the home looks amazing. Gleaming wood floors in the hallway, plush-looking sofas in the living room, more hand-painted tile in the kitchen, granite countertops, or maybe marble. Hard to tell in this light.

"How much money do you have?" I blurt, then immediately regret it. "I'm sorry. Don't answer that. My God, I'm rude."

He chuckles. He's probably rethinking his whole *Save Amira* idea. "Pediatric heart surgeons get paid pretty well," he says, unloading the food into the cabinets and fridge. "It's still on the cool side, probably good for the fruit, right?"

"For another twelve hours anyway."

I'm drawn to the wall of windows framed in beautiful carved wood at the back of the kitchen. In the backyard, a pool reflects moonlight and something we rarely get to see in the city due to light pollution—stars. The sight of the night sky shimmering in the pool is incredibly relaxing.

Derek takes my roller bag and carries it through the living room and upstairs to the master bedroom. I follow. He lifts my bag onto the upholstered bench at the foot of the king bed. Everything looks plush. I run my hand along the duvet cover and nearly melt. So soft.

"This is very nice."

"Glad you approve," he says with a wink, then shakes his head, curses, and makes that strange grunting sound he makes after every interaction that borders on flirtatious.

"You know..." I laugh. "The first few times I saw you do that—"

"Do what?"

"Every time you wink at me, you, like, chastise yourself."

"You can tell?"

"Of course I can tell! You make a funny sound and you shake your head, and—"

"Oh hell."

"I thought you either had a nervous tic or a neurological disorder."

He groans. "Nope. I just lack self-awareness and social grace."

Seeing him break into a wide smile warms me in the exact wrong places for this moment. The insides of my thighs tingle.

Oh God, Amira. Get yourself together!

"Anyway," he says. "It's good to see your beautiful smile... Damn it!"

"You know, you don't have to give yourself such a hard time," I say, giggling.

"Thanks for understanding. Let's get out of the bedroom, and I'll give you the lay of the land."

"Good idea." Was he having fantasies too? I have a nice smile.

"Why are you sighing?" he asks.

"What? Oh. Was I? Oh dear. I just love this house."

And the effect you are having on me.

We walk into the master bath, and I want to cry with relief. A double-wide soaking tub with a bay window overlooking the backyard, a glass-enclosed shower big enough to practice yoga in—or other activities. "Look at this oasis. I hope the water's safe soon so I can take advantage of this tub," I say.

"Me too," he says. "I'd love to see you relax in it. I mean... Damn!"

I can't stop myself from giggling.

"Not that I'll be watching. I just, uh... Shit. I'm tired."

I'm too tired to speak, and now that I've started laughing, I can't stop. I'm doubled over, putting my hand on his shoulder to steady myself. Now he's laughing too.

"You're gonna make this hard," he laughs, then sputters, "Aw, Christ almighty! Come on, man!"

I'm gasping, crossing my legs. "You're gonna make me pee."

"Oh no!" He laughs. "That's my cue to leave this room. I'll be in the hallway when you're finished."

A moment later, he walks me past the two guest bathrooms—smaller but equally beautiful versions of the master bath. I peek into the extra bedrooms, and I see why no one is sleeping there. Not only aren't there beds, but the rooms are filled with boxes. "Still unpacking, as you can see," he says. "After I clean up, I'll be downstairs if you need anything."

"I feel bad taking your bed."

"Don't think twice," he says.

"At least let *me* sleep on the sofa."

"Not a chance. Your daughter will be with us tomorrow, and I'm not having you two sleep on a couch."

"But tonight."

"For God's sake, woman, I can sleep on the couch."

"Are you this kind to everybody?"

"I guess it depends who you ask."

"Thank you."

He reaches his hands toward my shoulders, then quickly slides them behind his back. "Sleep well, my friend."

"You too, Derek."

"Tomorrow, we get Lila."

"I can't wait."

As I reach the bedroom door, I turn and see him standing by the bathroom door. It's hard to tell in the dim light, but it feels like our eyes meet. "Good night, Derek," I whisper.

"Good night, Amira."

"Thank you for everything."

"You said that."

"Is it getting old? I don't feel like I can say it enough."

He must have just winked because I hear him growl and curse under his breath.

I giggle.

"Sleep well, dear," he says, then slips into the bathroom.

I RETURN TO THE MASTER BATH, STRIP, PULL A WASHCLOTH from the towel bar, step into the glorious shower, cover myself with liquid soap, soak the washcloth with bottled water, and scrub everything. Then I pour the remaining water from the jug over my head, face, neck, torso, arms, backside, legs and feet. At last, I feel and smell clean. Hallelujah!

Stepping out of the shower onto the bathmat makes my feet tingle, as if they're getting a little massage. The sensation of the bath towel against my skin—pure delight. It's the perfect texture. Where did he get these amazing towels?

The bed is even more luxurious than the towels. When have I ever experienced a bed like this? So perfectly plush and firm at the same time. So perfectly... Derek. Sumptuous. Plush. Firm. I giggle, envisioning something else that's plush and very, very firm, entering me.

Lying in bed, I can't help imagining what he looks like in the shower. Rock-hard pectoral muscles. A solid six-pack. Velvety-smooth dark skin. A line of hair guiding me toward a magical tool designed to bring pleasure. He pours the water over his legs. Rivulets glow in the moonlight, traveling down the well-defined muscles. As I imagine the water dripping off his skin, I can almost feel the strong leg muscles under my fingertips, the tight glutes under those boxer shorts. Are those silk boxers? I help him slide them off.

What is wrong with me? How could I possibly even have that kind of a fantasy at a moment like this? My city is a mess. My home and car are most likely flooded. I haven't been able to reach my child in almost twenty-four hours. And I'm thinking about sex?

Amira, get yourself together!

It's disaster arousal. That's what it is. I've discussed this very phenomenon with several patients over the years.

A soft knock sounds on the door.

"Yes?"

Derek pops his head in. "Do you have everything you need? Are you comfortable?"

"More than everything I need except for Lila."

"Understood. Good night."

The door closes.

He's beside me, caressing my cheek with soft fingers. "Everything will be all right, Amira," he says, looking into my eyes. "Close your eyes. I'm here."

I let my eyes close, relax into his gentle touch. His fingertips graze my forehead, stroke my eyebrows, the length of each cheekbone. He gently caresses the outside of my ears, squeezing the earlobes. Outrageously relaxing.

"Amira?" That deep, quiet, soothing voice. "May I kiss you?"

"Mm-hmm."

His full, firm lips meet mine. Heat first, then pressure. Safety and warmth. He parts my lips with his tongue, probes into my mouth. Our tongues entwine, dance together. I lick the roof of his mouth with the tip of my tongue to stimulate him. He groans. Then he does the same to me. His hand slides down my neck, my shoulder, my arm, onto my waist, slides back up my rib cage, my waist until he's cupping my breast, gently kneading the nipple, rolling it between his thumb and forefinger.

His other hand slides down the center of my chest onto my belly. The heat of his palm on my stomach lights my internal fire. He moves his fingers down farther, touches my pearl ever so lightly, glides around the lips. One hand on the inside of my thigh, the other hand on my breast.

I groan.

"Amira?" Footsteps sound in the hall.

Suddenly I'm awake.

He knocks on the door. "You okay in there?"

Oh. My. God. Did I just have a sex dream and moan aloud in his bed?

"Uh, I'm fine. I must have been dreaming."

"Okay. Just checking. Hey, if you wake before me, don't leave, all right? Let's stick together. Make a solid plan so we all stay safe."

"Sure." There's that word again: *we*.

It's just a crush. It's a natural crush. I'm in a stressful situation. I need something else to focus on. There's nothing wrong with me. I haven't slept in twenty-four hours. My mind is mush right now. I can't help what I dream anyway. It's just a crush. It's okay. It's just a crush.

My heart slows.

14

Temptations

Amira

THE TUB LOOKS EVEN MORE TEMPTING IN THE GLOW of morning light than it did in moonlight. But I doubt the water is safe to bathe in yet. It's definitely not potable. The pool in the backyard catches my eye. That water looks clean. Of course, I don't have a swimsuit with me. Would he notice me skinny-dipping? I laugh out loud. Would he notice? Uh-huh. Thinking about how he reacted to me last night. Wait. Why am I worried about whether Derek would notice?

I speak to my reflection in the mirror: "My life is not about a man I just met. This is a pleasant distraction, a very kind person helping me. It's natural that I would develop disaster arousal, even a crush, especially on someone so fine."

I like the look I see in my eyes reflected back at me: compassionate, kind, soft. I envision Lila's eyes in front of me. "Look at them, Mama; they're naked!"

Okay, God. I will buy her that damn eye shadow she wants and go vegan. A yawn escapes. My eyelids are drooping. I realize I'm leaning heavily against the bathroom counter. If I don't get some coffee right now, I may fall asleep on the bathroom floor. I drag myself into the hallway and slowly descend the stairs. Coffee.

As I tiptoe past the living room, I resist the temptation to peek at Derek in repose. His soft snores remind me of a cat purring. Cute.

Focus, Amira. Coffee. Then meditation, then strategy.

I need to plan a safe route to Phoebe's house, but my mind is blank. A little yoga and a swim will activate my brain. Plus the swim will replace bathing.

Thankful for the twenty gallons of water we bought in Atlanta, I pour eight cups into the coffee maker, then hunt for the beans. Once I find them, I realize I don't have a clue how to run this fancy thing. Is this an espresso machine? What does this lever do? I press it and nothing happens. I try the red button at the top, but that doesn't work either.

Because, Amira, the electricity's out. Remember?

Irritating. Plan B. Cold brew. That takes hours to make. Instant? A quick search through the cabinets yields nothing. Why didn't I think to buy instant at the supermarket? Plan C… What kind of stove is this? Not gas. Darn it. Don't all the fancy people with their gourmet kitchens prefer gas stoves to electric? Does the man have a gas grill outside? I can boil the water in the teakettle, then brew the coffee like Greg does—filter above the mug, pour the water over it, and drink.

Greg… where are you?

I check my cell phone for a signal. Nothing. Wi-Fi remains down too. Nothing loads on the browser. Frustration wells up inside me, and I want to yell. My God, I hope my patients haven't been trying to reach me. Of course they have. I hope they're safe. We have zero communications channels available. It's eight a.m. I'm operating on about four hours of sleep and no caffeine. Is it too soon to go get Lila? Probably. No one's going to school or work today, so they'll sleep in, at least the kids will. Zaki and

Elara may be awake. If I had a signal, I could call. Patience. Also, Derek made me promise not to leave the house without him, an attempt to ensure my safety.

Better go outside and look for that grill.

I open the french doors and step onto a brick patio laid out in a herringbone pattern. Beautiful! And hot under my bare feet. It must be eighty degrees in the sunshine. Inside, with shade and windows open, I felt so comfortable I didn't even notice the temperature. Outside, it's hot and humid even for October in New Orleans. That should do wonders for mold growth in all these flooded homes like mine. Fantastic.

Home. Lila. I cannot wait to see her.

A headache forms behind my eyes. Coffee. There is no grill in sight. Shit. I'm gonna try the cold brew method. I'll let it sit on the hot patio to brew while I swim, do yoga, and meditate to clear the cobwebs from my brain.

In the kitchen, I discover the situation is worse than I realized. There are no coffee grounds at all, only whole beans and an electric grinder. Great. Plan Z: I pop a bean into my mouth and start sucking on it. Not horrible. But I'm not giving up on the beverage. I put about a half cup of beans onto the wooden cutting board by the sink, put the jar over them and put all my weight on the jar to crush them. It kind of works, but not really. I smash the partially broken beans with the heels of my hands. Ouch. Bad idea. Does he have a meat mallet? I search the drawers until I find one, then start smashing beans. This turns out to be a great frustration reliever as well as somewhat effective. I put the pulverized beans in a jar, cover it with water, close it, and step back onto the sunny patio.

With the coffee brewing—I hope—on the hot brick patio, I tiptoe to the edge of the pool, strip down to my panties and bra, and slip into the water. An audible moan escapes my throat. Heaven. The water temperature is just right relative to the heat in the air. And the faint scent of chlorine, not something I normally enjoy, reassures me this water is safe.

I'm really only good at two strokes: the sidestroke and the breaststroke. I start the breaststroke, and suddenly what Derek said at the after-party flashes through my mind. "*The fly was my event in college. I also do the breaststroke.*" Then he got that horrified look on his face. Now I'm giggling, which makes it hard to swim. I pause, take a deep centering breath and release it slowly, then begin again. Counting the strokes from one to ten and starting over becomes like a meditation mantra. Soon the numbers fade to the back of my mind and I focus on the movements of my muscles, the caress of the water over my skin. At some point, even the laps blur. It's just sensation, breath, movement.

"Good morning."

"Morning," I say, trying to maintain the rhythm I've established, though it's difficult when I can feel his eyes on my body. I flip onto my back and do a gentle backstroke so I can see him while I swim. What a view.

Derek

THERE'S A BEAUTIFUL SIGHT TO WAKE UP TO: AMIRA IN MY swimming pool, wearing nothing but lingerie. I'm fasting. She's tempting. My eyes travel the length of her body. Beautiful curves. She says good morning and flips over, revealing a taut stomach and full breasts that make me want to... I let out a slow breath, glance down. Jesus! I should have put on gym shorts, swim shorts, something over my boxers. The tent pole is sticking out of the tent. Nothing to do but turn around and walk back into the house. I'd call my accountability buddy if we had a goddamn cell signal.

Properly attired in my swimsuit, I step back onto the patio with a towel for each of us. "How's the water?" I ask as I set the towels down on the bench by the pool.

"Beautiful. Coming in?" she asks, not breaking stride.

I answer by diving into the deep end and racing underwater toward her. I emerge at her side and adopt her rhythm, facing her in the sidestroke. "Feels great. You've got a nice stroke."

"So do you." She grins, eyes dancing. "Though I'm no pro or anything, not like you."

I laugh. "Having been on the college team twenty years ago doesn't quite make me a pro."

We reach the end of the pool and flip onto our other sides, facing each other as we do the next lap. I could get used to this—swimming with my lady every morning, finding a rhythm together, breathing in sync, occasionally speaking, but mostly just feeling the water support us. Then of course we'd end the swim kissing, and then I'd take her to the outdoor shower and run my hands along her soft skin, and… "Whoo, wake up, Derek."

She giggles. I remember what she said about thinking I have a neurological disorder or something. Oh man. What do I do? Maybe I should just own it. *Amira, I know it's crazy because we just met, but I see myself growing old with you.* Nah. I told her I was feeling something for her yesterday in the car. Somewhere between North Carolina and Georgia. She might not know just how strong the feelings are, but she knows they exist.

You need to chill the fuck out, man. That's what you need to do. Take a cold shower, once the water's safe to bathe in. Let her laugh at you; she needs a little comic relief right now. Course I'd rather give her sexual healing. "Oh, for the love of God!"

"What's wrong?" she asks, breaking stride at the shallow end.

I shake my head. "Ignore me. We've got a job to do. And I just had an idea that may make things easier for both of us."

She looks at me, waiting.

"Children's Hospital is an easy walk from here. They'll have electricity, possibly internet. Plus, I can check on my patients."

"If you need to go to work today, I don't wanna hold you up. I only waited for you because you made me promise. Also, the coffee situation is bleak. I'm hoping that jar contains something resembling a caffeinated beverage by now."

"They'll also have coffee at the hospital. And I don't need to stay at work. I'm not scheduled until tomorrow and no surgeries until Friday. But, for my own mental health, I need to know my patients are okay. You know?"

"Mm-hmm."

"I keep thinking of that sweet little five-year-old. Major surgery. What if his family couldn't get to him after the flood? They were visiting in shifts because they have older kids and jobs. Imagine being alone in a hospital bed for days at age five."

Her hand flutters to her heart. "Poor baby. I was just thinking about my patients too. I doubt I'll be able to reach them, but it would be nice to see what the news says about how the storm hit there."

"So we'll get dressed, head to the hospital—"

"I need to hold my child first. I mean, I'm sure she's safe at Phoebe's, but—"

"Of course! Thoughtless of me. We'll get Lila, then go to the hospital. Or… I'll go to the hospital alone after dropping you two here, if you want. Okay, woman? Or we go to the hospital, get you a coffee in a go-cup, then I stay there while you get that girl."

Amira presses herself out of the pool gracefully, stretches toward the sun, then bends forward, placing her fingertips on the ground. She takes a deep breath as she rises up, shakes out her whole body, and reaches for the jar with beans and water in it. She shakes it, opens it, takes a sip, pulls a face. "Eww. It's like tinny water."

I join her, handing her a towel and running one over my face. "No one's ever raved about hospital coffee, but in this instance…"

"Oh, that hospital coffee will taste gourmet compared to this. Is there an option four? What if you go to the hospital while I get Lila, then we meet back here and you bring some of that delightful hospital coffee for me? With almond milk instead of regular?"

"You got it!"

"I've decided to go vegan with Lila. Solidarity, you know?"

"That's wicked sweet."

Amira

I SLIP INTO A PAIR OF FLORAL SKINNY JEANS AND A FLOWY rayon top. Maybe not the normal poststorm attire, but whatever. I'm not normal. For good luck, I slip the gold chain with the charm Lila gave me for my thirty-third birthday around my neck and fasten the clasp. I finger the amethyst triangle in its solid gold casing. How a twelve-year-old saved the money to buy such a thing astounds me. I know her father helped her pay for it. I think my mom did too. Still, she chose it months earlier, figured out how she would pay for it, saved money, and then asked for the help she needed. What an amazing little person. Little. An inch taller than me.

Even if she were not with Phoebe's family right now, I believe Lila could have found a way to be safe during this flash flood. She can advocate for herself. She's bold. She would ask for help, even from strangers. She's intuitive. She would know who was safe to trust and who wasn't smart to trust. She's just an amazing child. How I got so blessed to birth and raise that person is truly beyond my comprehension. But there it is. And here is a beautiful reminder of that. Nestled between my collarbones. I place my fingers over the amethyst, say a silent prayer of gratitude. *Thank you, God, for Lila.*

I look in the mirror, consider the mascara in my cosmetic bag. Not a good idea. Tears will only wash eye makeup away as soon as I see that beautiful girl in front of me.

15

Home

Derek

THE ELEVATOR DOORS OPEN TO REVEAL THE now-familiar hallway with fuchsia walls and white floors. I pass the sign identifying the space as the Cardiac Intensive Care Unit, nod to a colleague in blue scrubs, stroll past the Family Respite Lounge and down the hall into room thirteen, where Tyrell lies alone, his back to the door. Alone. Goddamn it.

"Heyyy, champ," I say, softening my voice so I don't startle him. "Tyrell, how you doing?"

The little boy rolls onto his back and turns his head to me. The tubes coming out of his arm make it almost impossible to roll onto his left side and face me. "Dr. D, you're back."

"It took a long time. I had to drive a long way. You know my airplane couldn't fly home because of all the rain? Did you see all that rain?"

He nods.

"So I had to drive. Took me a whole day to drive here to see you. How's your body feeling?"

"Okay."

"Breathing all right?"

He nods. "My mommy and daddy didn't come since before it rained."

I sit at his bedside and take his hand, feeling the pulse in his wrist. Nice rhythm, thank God. "I'm sorry. The roads weren't safe for them, but they'll be here as soon as they can. Because they love you and miss you so much. And that's why I'm here right now. Checking on my special friend Tyrell. How's our Nurse Loreen? She treating you right?"

"I got a blue slushie for dessert."

"Right on. You feel like doing anything? Coloring? Playing with those Legos your mama and daddy brought? Reading a book?"

"Can you sing me that song?"

"*Guardian*?"

"'Keeper of life.'"

Alanis Morissette doesn't normally do it for me, but these lyrics really resonate. I put a jazz spin on the tune and turned it into my personal theme song. Now Tyrell watches my face as I sing, and when I get to his favorite lyrics, about being his keeper of life, he smiles, then closes his eyes like he's soaking it in. I stroke his baby 'fro while I sing, keeping my voice low but pouring my heart into the song. When I finish, I scan the monitors again. His eyes are still closed. I check his chart again, make a note for someone to keep trying to reach his parents. If their car flooded and they can't get here, can I go get them? Use the hospital boat? Nah, that's for search and rescues. Shit.

"I'll be back in a while, Tyrell," I whisper. He's asleep again.

My only other patient, little baby Maureen Laughlin, is in room 28. Thank God she rests in her mother's arms right now. Maureen's father lies snoring on the pullout couch by the window.

"Glad to see you nursing that child. That'll help her recover as quick as anything else," I say. "How're you folks doing?"

"We were here during the storm, Dr. Foret," Maureen's mom whispers. "My parents were going to try to come yesterday afternoon. Obviously, too late. I think she's thriving though, don't you?"

The note of panic in Mrs. Laughlin's voice gets my attention. I lay hands on the infant's back, conduct a cursory examination while she's at her mother's breast, then review her chart. "Looks like everything is progressing well, Angela. How are you and Eamon holding up?" I sit next to her, waiting for a chance to hold the baby.

"Fair. I'm just thrilled she took to nursing. My milk came in last week, and this seems like the only place she wants to be." There's that note of panic again. What she really wants to know is: Is this normal for my baby to be latched onto my body twenty-four seven, or is it because she's not thriving?

"That's perfect," I say to reassure her. "Mother's milk is the best medicine, so make sure you take care of yourself too. Rest every chance you get to replenish your milk. The oxytocin should be kicking in. Are you feeling extra relaxed when you nurse her?"

She nods.

"Good. Remember to eat healthy, keep up your strength, and let Eamon take her for a few minutes each day so you can stroll the grounds and get some fresh air. Understand?"

"I can't leave her."

"She keeps progressing like this, you'll get to take her home before you know it and take her on walks with you. But for now, it's important you take care of yourself so you can give her what she needs."

At last, little Maureen lets her mother's breast fall from her mouth. Angela covers herself, and I reach for the baby. "May I?"

"Of course, Dr."

I hold the infant, coo at her, listen to her heart, feel the pulses in her neck and on her tiny wrist. She came in at six pounds four ounces and has gained over a pound. Rumblings in her lower half let me know her digestive system is active. Good sign. I look at the little scar on her chest. "Healing nicely, Mom. Good job," I whisper, handing the child back to Angela. She smiles.

"I'll be in and out today and tomorrow, working a full shift this weekend. Rest assured, even though cell phones are still out of service, the hospital can reach me on my pager if need be. Okay?"

"Thank you so much, Dr. Foret."

"It's an honor."

Amira

THE ONIRYMBAS' STREET IS STILL COVERED WITH ABOUT two inches of water, not enough to pose much of a threat, definitely not enough to keep me from my daughter. My body vibrates with excitement as I park on the neutral ground across from the Onirymbas' quaint rose cottage. Normally I take a moment to savor the bright colors and gingerbread trim on their porch.

Now another force seems to overtake me, because the next thing I know I'm standing in their living room, holding my child and never wanting to let go.

We stand in each other's arms silently for a while, cheeks pressed together until Phoebe's mom invites me to sit with them for a bit. I accept, feeling layers of stress practically fall off me.

"Wow. This is the first moment I've felt I could relax in over twenty-four hours."

"Why?" Lila asks.

I laugh. "Oh my goodness, kid. We've never been separated during a storm before. That was enough to freak me out. Then my flight diverted to North Carolina and we had to drive all day and night to get to you."

"We?" Lila asks.

"Derek. Ah... Sage's fiancé's best friend. Turns out he lives here too. Long story. Anyway..." I lift my shoulders and let them drop, letting a loud sigh fall out of my mouth. Then I shake some of the tension from my body.

"We've got some lukewarm sweet tea, or would you like something more potent?" Phoebe's dad offers, holding up a bottle of rum in one hand and a bottle of bourbon in the other.

"Tea would be great, Zaki. You know, Derek and I bought a lot of extra food and bottled water on the way down from North Carolina. Are you fully stocked? Because we're happy to share."

Phoebe's parents bob their heads in sync.

"We have everything we need." Elara laughs. "You know how Zaki likes to prepare for the end of the world."

"And aren't you glad I do?" he asks.

"Of course, sweetheart," she says, kissing his cheek. They always seem so much in love, these two.

"How long have you two been married?" I ask, apropos of nothing but what's inside my head.

"Twenty-five years," they say in unison, then smile into each other's eyes.

Zaki continues, "We've been through many storms, many floods, both real and imagined."

"Real and imagined," I repeat, tucking the idea into the back of my mind.

They smile at me, then Elara returns her gaze to her husband. "And he is always my safe harbor."

"We are each other's safe harbor," Zaki says.

It's like watching a rom-com in real time, except this isn't so much funny as it is swoon-worthy. I may have just sighed at the sweetness of it.

"So," Elara says, "you are home. And it's all clear?"

"Not by a long shot. We couldn't even get near our street. Mid-City was under at least a foot of water last night."

"Oh dear," Elara says.

"Thankfully, this person I met over the weekend is able to offer shelter."

"How wonderful." Elara gives me that look that says she knows something's up. "Who is this person?"

"Derek. The guy I mentioned. Wesley's friend. He's a heart surgeon for kids, and for the moment, he's our harbor in the storm."

Lila and Phoebe exchange a look that I'm not sure how to decipher.

I add, "In fact, his place is just a few blocks away. And, Lila, there's a swimming pool."

"That's nice," she says, not displaying even half the enthusiasm I would have expected.

"Mom, I've missed you so much," she says as we get into the SUV.

"I missed you too. I was terrified. I kept trying to reach you and your dad."

"They went to the Park View hotel Saturday after their wedding and then to their honeymoon in Costa Rica. Rini was all excited about them being off the grid."

"Thank God," I breathe. "I have good news for you."

She raises her eyebrow.

"These past twenty-four hours, as I was desperately trying to reach you and wondering where you were and if you were safe and fearing I might not see you again, I decided that when I found you, I would buy you some eye shadow."

"Really?" Lila asks, wiggling in excitement.

"If it's okay with your dad."

"It will be," she says brightly.

"Well, don't count on that, but I'll convince him. And I'll even teach you how to apply it."

"Oh, Mama, they have YouTube videos for that. There's this girl I've been watching for years. She's amazing."

"You've been watching for years?"

She nods. "I probably know how to apply eye shadow better than you. Whoa," she says as we pull into Derek's driveway. "This is really fancy."

16
Hairbrained

Derek

THE SUN BEATS HOT ON MY BACK, AND MY BODY TINGLES everywhere as I ascend the steps of my porch. Going to meet Amira's daughter in a few moments. I hope she likes hot chocolate. Twelve-year-olds don't drink coffee, do they? I juggle the go-cups (a New Orleans term I've learned in the past few weeks that actually makes sense to me) as I press down on the door handle to let myself in.

"Hello," I yell, toeing off my shoes as I enter the foyer. I'm tempted to call out, "Honey, I'm home!" But I don't think Amira would appreciate that right now. Not yet. Maybe someday. Maybe soon. "Amira?"

"We're in the back," she yells.

I follow the sound of her voice to the patio. The girls sit at the edge of the pool, facing me, dangling their feet in the water. The pictures don't do justice to the resemblance between mother and daughter. Except for height (Lila's taller) and hairstyle (Amira's dreads, Lila's soft brown ringlets), and skin tone, Amira and her child could be twins.

"Reunited at last," I say.

"We sure are," Amira responds, putting her arm around her daughter and squeezing. "How are your patients?"

"Safe, stable, healing. All I can ask for under the circumstances."

"I'm sure seeing you was comforting," she says.

My cheeks warm at the compliment. "This must be Lila. I'm Derek. Pleasure to meet you."

"Hi," the girl says, examining my face, then meeting my eyes. I see why Tania described her grandchild as an old soul.

"You like hot chocolate?" I walk to the other side of the pool and hand the go-cup of coffee to Amira. She takes a long sip and sighs in satisfaction.

"Is it vegan?" Lila asks.

"Almond milk okay?"

She smiles and reaches for the go-cup. "How'd you know?"

"Your mom," I say, sitting next to Amira, slipping off my socks and dropping my feet into the cool water. "Ooh, that feels good."

"Doesn't it?" Amira looks at me.

Amira nudges her daughter playfully. "In addition to deciding to buy you eye shadow, I also promised God I'd go vegan once I found you."

Lila sucks in a sharp breath. "Seriously?"

"It's a fact." Amira pulls from the coffee again and flashes a thumbs-up at me. "Gourmet, Derek. Truly."

"But you don't believe in God, Mama."

"You don't?" Derek asks.

"I'm not waiting for a man in the sky to save me if that's what you mean. But I do believe there's something greater than us all—a creative force beyond human comprehension. What do you believe in?"

"A lot of surgeons act like they *are* God. But when I open up a child's chest and see this miraculous organ pumping life of its own accord, how can I not believe in the creative force in this universe? I don't care what you call it: God, Goddess, creator; I don't believe we just popped up here randomly because of some astrophysical event."

"That must be amazing to see the inside of a body, still pulsing breath... or not," she says.

"Have you seen a dead body, Derek?" Lila asks.

"Ahhh... well, I had to open up cadavers in medical school and, you know..." I let my voice trail off. I will not tell this child that I lose about three patients each year.

"What?" Lila asks, looking horrified.

Nor will I reveal that, nationwide, of every one hundred kids to have heart surgery, between one and twelve die, depending on the surgeon. How did we get on this topic?

"How's the hot cocoa, Lila?" Amira asks, placing a comforting hand on my shoulder.

I put my hand over hers for a second, send a silent thank-you with my eyes.

Home.

"It's good," Lila says. "How's your vegan coffee?"

"I'll get used to it, I'm sure. Derek, you sure have been my angel, *our* angel, these past couple of days."

"Awww. I'm no angel," I say. "How we feeling? Not much to do in this house without electricity."

"I can think of one thing," Lila says, gesturing at her mother's head.

"What?" Amira asks.

"The dreads, Mama. They're cheugy."

"Lila!" Amira gasps.

No clue what the girl just said, but the meaning's clearly not good. I cringe at Amira's palpable embarrassment.

"Forget the eye shadow. I'll wait until I'm thirteen if you'll do something about your hair today."

"You are being rude, young lady."

"Sorry." Lila looks down, then sneaks me a conspiratorial grin.

Uh-oh.

"Derek, don't you think she'd look better with her normal hair?"

"Uh…" I lift my hands in a helpless gesture and look from mother to daughter. "Haven't seen her normal hair, but I imagine your mom looks pretty even without hair."

Lila snorts. Shit. Why did I say that? But a little smile crosses Amira's face, so maybe it was worth that small trip up. Was that my unconscious motivation? To make Amira smile?

"Let's shave it," Lila shouts.

"What?" Amira's eyes go wide.

"You'll look badass with a shaved head, Mama."

Amira bursts out laughing. "That's what you want? A badass mom?"

Lila shrugs. "Why not? It's better than…"

Amira narrows her eyes and flares her nostrils at the girl. She closes her mouth. They take a deep breath together and release it. Amira looks from her child to me and back again. "I have been getting tired of this look. Dreadlocks are heavy."

Amira

AN HOUR LATER, I STAND IN FRONT OF THE BATHROOM mirror, shifting my gaze between Lila's reflection and Derek's. His battery-powered clippers feel heavy in my palm.

"Are you guys ready?" I ask.

"Are you?" Derek asks.

"She's ready. Anything's better than what's happening on her head now."

I laugh. "Fresh."

Lila giggles. "Just kidding."

"Let's do this," I say and turn on the clippers. Derek reaches for them, but I hold back.

"Wait! You don't wanna shave your own head, Amira. You even know how to use these?"

"How hard can it be?"

He cocks his eyebrows and turns the corners of his mouth down. "Uhhh, how about you trust the surgeon with this?"

"Please, Mama. It looks bad enough already." Lila makes a dramatic gesture to illustrate her point.

"Enough, Lila," I warn and give her my *mom look*.

"And, you know, these aren't kiddie scissors, woman. They're sharp blades moving back and forth at high speed."

A picture of me with a head full of stitches flashes through my mind. Definitely worse than what's happening now. I sigh, turn off the clippers, and hand them to Derek. "I leave the fate of my head in your hands, Dr. Foret."

Derek's mouth quirks up into a smile and he turns on the clippers. The motor whirrs, its buzz filling my ears as he brings the instrument to my head and shaves one side. The dreadlocks fall from my scalp.

"Oh my goodness."

"Sure you wanna go through with this?" he asks. "You could just stop here, go with that half-shaved look that's trending right now."

Lila shakes her head emphatically.

I glance at my reflection and can't help grimacing. "If I was nineteen, sure. But now?"

"You can pull it off," he says.

I groan.

"No, Derek, she's right," Lila says. "She'll look like one of those old ladies who thinks she's young."

"Lila!"

"Sorry, Mama," she says, looking appropriately chagrinned for all of ten seconds, then breaking into a raucous giggle.

"Don't make me laugh. I might cut your mother's head."

Derek takes another pass with the clippers, and dreadlocks fall to the floor.

How long will it take my curls to grow in? Half an inch a month… I'll be sporting a pixie cut for at least a year.

Derek finishes the job. I stare at my reflection in the mirror. Derek's staring at my reflection too.

"Well, at least I have a normal-shaped head."

"You look hot," he says, then curses himself under his breath.

Lila laughs until I give her the *mom look* and clear my throat.

"What do you think?" I ask.

"I think it will be way less embarrassing to walk around with you in public," she says.

I wrap my arm around the child and grumble. She returns the grumble and flashes a beatific smile. We share a long hug.

As Lila kisses my newly bald head, she adds, "If you wear chunky hoops, you'll look like that pop star you love. You know, the old lady from the 1990s?"

"Whoo, girl, you gotta give your mama a break," Derek says, the playful note in his voice matching his smile.

For a split second, I worry about Lila's reaction. Will she take it personally? Worry he doesn't like her? *Does* he like her? Does it matter? Why am I worried about a virtual stranger's opinion of my child? We won't be here too much longer. They can get along for a few days.

"Is anyone else hungry?" I ask.

17

Double Take

Derek

AMIRA SEEMS DISTRACTED. SHE'S TAKING THE vegetables out of the refrigerator and washing them with bottled water, and she keeps looking toward the living room where Lila sits reading. I thought she would be ecstatic with her daughter home. Instead, she seems tense. Maybe I'm missing something.

I reach for her, then pull away. *Damn fast.* "Everything okay?"

"Fine."

"Lila okay? I tried to make her feel welcome by bringing the hot cocoa. She seemed to like it."

She places a hand on my shoulder, and I feel a zing. "That was so thoughtful. It's probably silly, but I feel a pull to be next to her all the time, and I'm worried she doesn't feel comfortable in the kitchen with us."

"Why wouldn't she be?"

She shrugs. "Maybe she thinks she has to give the adults some space or something. I probably just need to go check on her. You've got this. Right?"

"Making salad?" I laugh.

"You're probably better at chopping vegetables than I am, with you being used to wielding a knife."

"A scalpel isn't the same as a chef's knife, but yes, I got this, Amira."

She walks away, and I feel a pull on my heartstrings.

Lila screeches. "Mama! Your head!" Her giggles bounce off the bare walls.

I know the feeling. I've been trying to keep my cool around the woman, but every time she walks into a room, I do a double take, even though I'm the one who shaved the dreads off.

Now they're speaking in low tones, but the sound of their voices carries from the living room into the kitchen. Is that annoyance I hear tightening Lila's voice?

I pour the bottled water over the vegetables, then start slicing a red bell pepper into thin strips. Hope they like their peppers sliced this way. People can be very particular about food preparation. Wesley sure is, and I get the feeling Sage is too.

Amira returns, and I start at the bald head, try to keep my face placid.

She's got a sheepish expression on her face. "Apparently I'm being overprotective."

"Really?"

"I guess my daughter feels like it's no big deal for her to sit in the other room and read a book, and why am I worried? And why does she need to come in the kitchen and help us prepare salad when she doesn't even like to cook?"

I laugh. "Guess she's got a point, doesn't she?"

"Seems so. She likes to eat. But that's not the same thing as cooking. And just because she wants to be vegan doesn't mean she wants to cook vegan."

"Must feel good to have her home though."

Amira sighs and hugs herself. "It really does. I feel bad that we're not in our own home but grateful to you for sheltering us."

"Don't think twice. Hey, didn't I promise you a conversation about your work?"

"Did you?"

"When we were at Sage and Wesley's house, I told you, you could bounce ideas off me."

"Oh, you were serious."

"What did you think? Why else would I say that?"

"I... Uh, never mind. You know, it's funny. After we lost communications yesterday, even though I was stressed as hell being unable to reach Lila, I started feeling more relaxed than usual in some ways. Where are the knives?"

I pull a paring knife from the drawer under the island counter and hand it to her.

"A knife block in a drawer? Cool." She selects a bunch of carrots from the colander and proceeds to remove the tops and ends.

"Why do you think you've been more relaxed?"

"I haven't heard from any patients, and it feels great. Is that terrible?"

"Terrible? Nah. Informative though. They call a lot?"

"Twenty-four hours a day. Texts, calls, emails. Very often to confirm appointments. Sometimes because they're struggling. Sometimes because they're upset and just want to vent. One kid called me at ten p.m. because he had a zit and thought he should stop taking his antianxiety meds. I don't even prescribe."

I don't mean to laugh, but a kid calling her about a zit? "Come on! Seriously?"

"No joke. And it's not like I get paid for phone calls."

"What? It's 2019. How can you not get paid for phone sessions?"

"Insurance companies won't pay for them. If I spend two hours talking someone off a ledge, that's on me."

"Sounds like you're dealing with some boundary issues."

She sighs and nods. "That's what Greg says too. And I know it's true, but... how do I handle this? I care about my patients. I want them to thrive."

"At Wesley's, you said the demands of your patients were affecting your mothering. You often feel that way?"

"All the time."

"You want my advice here? Don't wanna overstep the boundaries of our relationship."

"I'm at a loss, so shoot."

"Start making lists, or... What do they call those things? With the circles and the lines... Mind maps. Make a mind map."

"Of what?"

"List the areas where you feel your job encroaching on your personal life. Make a mind map of all the aspects of your job—the day-to-day details as well as the irregular events. Put hearts by the things that make you feel good. Just to see on paper the effects this work has on your life."

"What a great idea! Where'd you come up with that?"

"A good buddy dropped out of med school to become a life coach. I let him practice on me."

"There's a career shift you don't hear about often."

"Right? So... mind map and list. Just start by gathering information."

"And job postings."

"I'd hold off on that for now."

"Really?"

"Get clear about what you want so you don't end up in the same situation."

She rocks on her heels. "Like that quote: No one can solve a problem from the same..."

"From the same level of consciousness that created it," I finish. "Exactly."

Again, in a subtle way, we're on the same page. How many people even know that Einstein quote? I'm feeling good with this woman. Wicked good, in fact. She feeling it too?

18
Goals

Amira

I COULD GET USED TO WORKING LIKE THIS. LYING ON A chaise by a clear pool, shaded from the hot sun, looking up every so often to see my daughter relaxing in the water. The gentle breeze riffles the pages of my journal, drawing my attention back to the mind map, list, and action plan I just made.

<u>Work Goal</u>: Solve the burnout problem by setting and keeping clear, healthy boundaries with my patients.

I can set and keep boundaries. I don't need a new career, just the willingness to stand up for myself, at least for now.

<u>Action Step</u>: Hire an answering service to help me keep the limits I have tried over and over to set with patients.

<u>Plan for Future</u>: Step away from patient care. How?

How can I continue to help traumatized kids and families without providing direct service? Derek asked if I'd consider systems change, working in policy. That's not me. I don't have the personality for politics or fundraising. The idea will come. I just need to keep an open heart and an open mind.

<u>Personal Goal</u>: Move out of flood zone.

<u>Action Step</u>: Ask Greg to pitch in more money every month to support Lila.

Paying the minimum in child support is ridiculous when he has so much. Our daughter needs to live in a home that doesn't regularly flood. And none of us thinks Lila living with him full time is a good idea. Girls need their mothers, especially girls entering the teen years. I won't take him to court over this. That would be a nightmare for everyone, and I'm sure I can show him it's fair and logical to increase his monthly payment.

<u>Plan for Future</u>: Find a new apartment.

I knew all this in my head, but somehow seeing it on paper makes everything seem clearer. I rise from the chaise and stretch. "That's it for now."

Lila looks up at me, starts, and falls off the floaty with a splash. She comes up, wet curls plastered to her head, then laughs. "I can't get used to it, Mama."

"Come on." I laugh, running my hand across my shaved head. I feel like an alien, but Derek said I look hot. "It's better than those tired old dreads. Right?"

"Definitely."

I dive into the pool and swim to Lila. As I emerge from the water and grab onto the floaty, I reflexively flip my hair back, but there is no hair. What a weird sensation. Instead, the water just runs down my forehead. I wipe it away like I've seen old bald guys do. God, I hope I don't look like an old bald guy. Again, I hear Derek's voice in my head and feel instant relief. "You look hot."

"Mama, since the floodwaters receded, will I have school tomorrow?"

"Nah, not with the electricity out. Maybe next week."

"Phew!"

As soon as the electricity is back on and the cell towers are functioning, I'll research answering services and get in touch with Greg.

🙰

Derek

A SOFT BREEZE CARRIES THE SCENT OF CHLORINE ACROSS the patio. The sounds of Amira and Lila chatting and laughing that drift through my office window fill my heart with joy. Savoring this moment of peace, I write:

> Can't reach Ned with the cell towers out, but I don't need to talk to him right now, except to boast. I made it through two nights with the most beautiful woman in the world sleeping upstairs in my bed. I've got this down. With nineteen days remaining in the program, I am solid. I am secure. I am fit for female companionship. I did not put a single move on Amira. I did not fall to the temptation, even when my body craved her touch—still does. Growing hard just thinking about her. Shit. But mindfulness is my ally. Time to meditate.

19
Patina

Derek

I FINISH MY MEDITATION, OPEN MY EYES, AND LET THEM readjust to the light. The past month—moving, starting my new job, then traveling and meeting the woman of my dreams, dealing with the aftermath of the storm... It's been a lot in a short period of time. Meditation brought serious relaxation, but the remaining tightness in my arms tells me it's time to play the horn. And this is the right place to do it. This room, with its dark wood trim and simple white walls reflecting the golden afternoon sunlight brings me back in time.

As I pull the instrument from the case, I have a flash of connection to my forebears. Whose hands hold this trombone right now? Mine, or my grandfather's? Of course they're my hands, but sometimes I get the feeling my ancestors are moving through me, sharing my experiences. Especially since coming to New Orleans.

A big afghan rug would do well in this room. Maybe Amira can help me find one later.

I lift the horn to my lips, set my embouchure, and run a few scales.

"What are you playing?" Lila asks as she bounces into the room.

"Just warming up right now," I say.

"How come your trombone looks all janky?"

I smile, run my fingers along the brass. "You mean the patina? That's about one hundred years of love on this horn."

"Where'd you get it? An antique shop?"

"My granddaddy played this, passed it down to my daddy, passed it down to me. Just like your mama passed her beautiful singing voice down to you."

Lila's eyes widen and her pale cheeks flush.

"I hear you singing around the house, just like your mom. You make beautiful music together."

I would like to form a trio with those two. The MacKenzie Foret Trio sounds right. I pick the horn back up and blow the opening bars of Big Pun's "Still Not a Player" from memory.

"That's my mom's favorite song."

"She told me." I play a few more bars, hoping Amira will hear.

"When?"

"On that very long drive from North Carolina. It was on the radio." A full sense memory arises: Amira singing along and dancing in her seat, rolling her shoulders in that way that made me wanna reach out and—

"Awww. You like my mom, huh?"

"Of course I do," I say, trying to sound casual.

"No, I mean, you *like* my mom."

Nervous laughter escapes my throat. Shit. How do I respond to this? "You know," I say, failing to keep my voice under control, "you're a lot like her. Very direct."

"Mm-hmm. And your voice is getting all squeaky like the boys in school when they say hi to Miss Nelson in the hall. Then they all watch her walk by, tongues hanging out of their mouths." She giggles.

I am being humiliated by a twelve-year-old.

"I think I'll go back to playing my horn. You wanna sing along?"

"Sure."

I lift the horn and channel my nerves into the music. The fact that this, of all songs, is Amira's favorite, floors me. It's all about the choice I'm making to turn my life around. Although some of the lyrics are pretty lewd, which I never quite noticed until right now, listening to Lila sing them. Damn. Time to play a new song. With one sustained note, I slide from Big Punisher to Sade's "The Sweetest Taboo."

"Hey," she complains.

I wink at her and keep playing.

Amira

LURED BY THE SOUNDS OF A TROMBONE AND MY DAUGHTER'S precious little soprano, I pull myself from my comfy spot on the patio and find my way into a beautiful room filled with a music stand and an old-school rolltop desk with an antique-looking desk chair.

Lila lies sprawled over the meditation cushion in the corner.

Derek stands by the window and plays a beautiful rendition of one of the most romantic songs ever.

"Did I hear Big Pun a minute ago?" I ask.

"Yeah, but now he's playing this boring music," Lila says, shifting uncomfortably. "This is the tiniest bean bag chair I've ever sat on. Is it, like, for babies?"

Derek blurts out an errant note. Our eyes meet, and I have to bite my lip to keep from laughing.

"What?" she asks, looking from me to Derek and back. "What's funny?"

"Hmmm? Nothing? That thing you're clearly not enjoying is a meditation cushion. You sit on it cross-legged, and it helps position your knees below your hips," I explain.

Lila adjusts her posture to match my description. "Ohhhhhhh! Yeah, this makes way more sense."

"So I hate to interrupt the concert. But the barbecue should start soon. Wanna go?"

Derek raises an eyebrow and lowers the trombone. "Barbecue?"

"It's a New Orleans tradition," Lila says, jumping up. "Like the second line and jazz funerals."

"I'm confused."

"Do you have any meat in your freezer?" I ask.

He nods.

"If it hasn't gone from thawed to spoiled, we'll bring it along with anything else we want to cook. Somewhere on the block we'll find people with grills set up in the neutral ground or in the middle of the street."

"It's the best part of the storms. Really the only good part. Come on," Lila shouts.

"What're you gonna eat, Lila?" he asks.

"Grilled veggies and tofu."

"You down, Derek?" I ask.

"Sounds like a good time." He puts his trombone in its case and follows us into the kitchen.

We root around the freezer and fridge and fill a shopping bag with a pound of thawed steaks and a package of chicken legs.

"Ooh, you're a dark meat man," I say, realizing immediately it sounded way more sexual than I intended. Dear God.

"We on the same page about poultry also?" he asks, emitting a low whistle. I laugh. The same page about poultry. What a goof.

"Mama, did you get *anything* I can grill?"

"We have potatoes, corn on the cob, portobellos..."

"What about tofu?"

"Sorry, I didn't think about tofu, baby."

She sighs. "Okay. Maybe someone else will have it... or veggie burgers... come on, come on, come on, you guys," she says, already at the front door.

"Manners, Lila," I say.

"Sorry, Derek," she says as she bounds outside.

"Don't think twice." He smiles at me and lowers his voice. "Think it's a good sign she's comfortable enough with me to be a little unruly."

Again, the tone and timbre of his voice soothe me. But what a strange thing to say: it's a good sign she feels comfortable being unruly around him? The last thing I want is to raise a child who's disrespectful to the people who are helping her, or anyone for that matter. Sure, we play around and tease each other but... "A good sign? For what?"

"Uhhh." The kindness in his eyes turns to confusion. "I, uh. I don't know. I just..."

"You're an incredible host, a beautifully generous man, Derek Foret."

Now he looks sad. Why? I just complimented him.

"Let's get to that barbecue," he says, gesturing for me to lead the way.

Outside, Lila's already bounding in the direction of Phoebe's house. Midway between Derek's place and the Onirymbas, we find a group of neighbors hovering around seven or eight grills. Elara, Zaki, and Phoebe seem to be presiding over the food prep until Phoebe sees Lila. She squeals, breaks away from her parents, and rushes to my child. The girls hug and disappear into the crowd. I introduce Derek to Elara and Zaki, and they introduce us to other neighbors.

"So," Zaki says, eyeing Derek, "you are the one who rescued our friend Amira."

Derek's mouth quirks up into an embarrassed smile and he meets Zaki's gaze. "Rescued is a strong word. I've been happy to help a new friend in need."

"Helping someone to weather a storm is no small thing," Zaki says, continuing his visual examination, then extending his hand. "Zaki Onirymba."

Derek grips Zaki's hand and introduces himself. The two share a bit about their careers and backgrounds, how they ended up in New Orleans. Zaki explains the rationale behind the post-storm neighborhood barbecues and introduces Derek to Elara.

She gives Derek a flirtatious bat of the eyelashes. Funny. I've seen her do that many times over the years, and it's never irked me until now. Does it bother Zaki to see his wife flirting with another man? My stomach tightens. I bend over to hide my irritation, pretending to search for something in the shopping bag.

"What're you looking for, hon?" Derek curses under his breath. "I mean... Amira."

"Didn't we pack tofu for Lila?"

He squats beside me and whispers, "You okay? You just told Lila we didn't buy any."

Now some other sensation is flooding my body. He's checking on me, as if we're... I don't know what to do with this. "I'm fine," I say, hoping he'll let it go. "I just... I guess the heat's getting to me."

"Do you feel light-headed?" He places his hand between my shoulder blades. His touch is soft, warm, comforting.

I shake my head, take a deep breath, and let it out slowly. *Come on, Amira. Get it together.*

Derek stands and holds his hand out to help me up.

Elara and Zaki stare at me, concern in their eyes.

I laugh as I take Derek's hand and rise. "My goodness. Sometimes my memory is..." I don't even know how to finish the sentence.

Elara hugs me. "You've been through a lot this week. Do what you're always telling me to do: be gentle with yourself." She kisses my cheek and whispers in my ear, "And let this wonderful man take care of you, Amira. He's someone you can weather many storms with."

I search her eyes for more.

"Not everyone has that capacity. I see it in him, and I can tell Zaki does too."

20
The Power

Derek

A HUM FILLS THE AIR. AM I AWAKE OR STILL DREAMING? What is that hum? I open my eyes to the morning light, look around. The overhead light seems to be glowing. A surge of energy fills me. Does this mean what I think it means? I throw some athletic shorts on over my boxers and stumble into the kitchen where the hum gets louder. I place my hand against the refrigerator.

"Halle-fucking-lujah," I yell. "Yeah, boy!"

This means real coffee, not that tired hospital crap. This means television and radio and connection to the real world. I throw my hands in the air and do a little victory dance in the kitchen, chanting about electricity.

Her giggle stops me. I turn, try to adopt a nonchalant stance, point my thumb at the fridge. "Power's on."

Amira nods, not even trying to hide her smirk. "So I see."

Is she appraising me? Sure looks like she's running her eyes up my legs to my thickening crotch, past my tensing stomach until she meets my gaze. Heat fills my groin. A low hum escapes my throat.

Keeping her eyes on mine, she moves to the fridge, places her hand on it, and wiggles. "Oh!"

I raise my eyebrows.

She wiggles again, shaking her body from head to toe, that smirk making her look sassy as fuck. Oh man.

"Oooh. I feel it, Derek. I feel the electricity pulsing through my body. Oh. My. God." Her voice rises as if she's climaxing. "Whoooo! I've got the pow-ah," she sings, then breaks out into a victory dance that matches my own.

Amira sings Snap's lyrics better than they did. I join in with the rap to "The Power," and we dance around the kitchen, laughing and singing.

"Oh. My God. You guys are so weird," Lila says from the doorway.

I freeze, look to Amira for the appropriate response. She stops dancing and wraps her daughter in an embrace. "Good morning, little one. Power's on. You know what that means?"

"Yes, Mama. I'm twelve, not two," Lila says with an unpleasant, snarky tone. "I already plugged in my phone so I can call Phoebe and Daddy ASAP."

Amira flinches but keeps her voice soft and upbeat. "And we can go home!"

"Really?"

"After I clean, we can."

Is that why she was celebrating with me? Because she can leave? Suddenly I wish we could go a few more days without electricity. At least I'm on duty today. Meditation and journaling help, but sometimes there's no better remedy than a good old-fashioned distraction. Gotta see how my buddy Tyrell's doing and baby Maureen.

Amira

As soon as I turn on my phone, it starts dinging. From other parts of the house, I hear Derek's and Lila's phones dinging nonstop as well. Derek usually speaks softly, but right now his voice booms from the other room. "Good to hear your voice too, Mama. ... I know. ... The house is fine. ... We weren't here for the storm, just the aftermath. ... Uhhh, a friend... Her name's Amira. I'll tell you about her later. Hey, the hospital's beeping me. ... Love you too. Bye."

I have twenty-five voice mails and 107 text messages. About half are from my family and out-of-state friends, and another half are from patients. Dear God. Being the dutiful daughter, I call my mother first. After reassuring her we're all right, I call Greg, and he informs me he's on the other line with Lila. Just as I'm about to dial my brother, he calls.

"Josh!"

"My God, sis, how're you doing?"

"As good as can be under the circumstances."

"Where are you? Did you find Lila?"

I give him the lowdown quickly.

"Sorry I wasn't able to help when you texted from the plane. Celeste and I were ending our relationship at that moment."

"What? Oh, that's terrible. Are you okay?"

"Heartbroken, but I'll survive. It was for the best."

"Hmm." I find it hard to believe their breakup actually was for the best, but I can't get into all that now. "Listen, Josh, I want to hear all about it, but right now I have about sixty messages from patients to read and a bunch of voice mails to listen to, just to make sure no one is in an imminent crisis. Plus, we've gotta get over to our place to clean it up so we can move home."

"Gotcha. Glad you guys're safe. Talk soon. Hug Lila for me."

Celeste and Josh broke up. How depressing. They were such a great couple. Did he cheat on her, too? He is our father's son in that regard. Jerk. Well, maybe that's not what happened. I'll have to call him soon.

"Who wants oatmeal?" Derek calls up the stairs.

"I'd love some," I say as I go to the landing and smile down at him. God, he's handsome.

"Me too," Lila yells from the living room.

TWENTY MINUTES LATER, FEELING GOOD ABOUT CLEARING most of my text messages, I'm sitting in the breakfast nook with my daughter and Derek, savoring the first real breakfast I've had in days.

I smile at him across the table. "Delicious!"

His eyes shine. "Good. Listen, I'm on duty today. I'll walk to work and leave the SUV for you, all right?"

"You sure?"

"Absolutely. Won't be back until late tonight, and you two should do whatever you need to do today."

I sigh. "I think I'll be on the phone with patients for a while. Honey, do you have homework?"

Lila grumbles. "That history project's due next week."

"And you have your laptop?"

"Of course."

"Maybe we'll see about making groceries. See if anything's open, huh?"

My daughter brightens. "There's a Whole Paycheck nearby. Elara and Zaki shop there all the time."

I'll bet they do with their professor salaries. "I guess we'll check it out."

"I'll leave money for you," Derek says.

"Excuse me?" I say, directing my mom look at him: flared nostrils and a glare that sends most people scurrying.

He returns my challenging look with a warm, soft gaze. "I expect I eat more than you two combined. Appreciate it if you pick up a few things for me, please."

Now I feel chagrinned. "Of course. But you don't need to leave money. I told you in Atlanta I'm covering food."

He raises an eyebrow. "I want to. It's only fair, Amira."

The way he speaks my name—low, resonant, gentle—warms my abdomen and lowers my resistance.

It's only fair.

Not really. He's trying to take care of me again, to pay my way. I hate it. I hate it so much. I'm an adult, capable of taking care of myself and my child. I don't need his help. But he keeps offering it, and when he does, the warmth in my stomach travels down into the insides of my thighs and back up into places I shouldn't be thinking about at the breakfast table.

21
(In)Dependence

Amira

H's HELPING ME AGAIN. YESTERDAY IT WAS GROCERIES. Today he's bringing me home and helping me clean. My thighs aren't the only body parts tingling right now, and this is not a sensation I want to be having with my child in the back seat.

Derek pulls up in front of the Onirymbas, and Lila leaps out of the car and bounds up the steps to their front door. Phoebe must have been waiting by the door because she swings it open before Lila has a chance to knock and before I even make it up the stairs. Phoebe sees me, squeals, "Amira," then covers her mouth.

"Phoebe," Elara scolds, then sees me. "Oh. Well, now I see what the fuss was about."

The girls rush into the house, and Elara comes out to the porch and gives me a once-over. "I love your shaved head—so bold and confident."

"Thanks!"

"Interesting outfit though." She grins.

"I borrowed the old T-shirt and shorts from Derek since I don't have any junky clothes at his house and may want to wash or toss all the clothes in my dresser rather than try to wear them. These are a little big though," I say, lifting the shirt high enough to reveal the belt cinched tight around my waist.

"Hmm," Elara says, her voice rising and falling several notches. "Is that him in the driver's seat?"

Heat rises to my face. I know what she's thinking. What Elara said at the barbecue has been running through my mind for the past twenty-four hours. "He's also insisting on helping me clean."

She beams. "What did I tell you, Amira." It's not a question.

A lump forms in my throat. "Derek seems like someone a woman could weather many storms with someday. But he's working through his own demons, and just because he's got potential doesn't mean he's ready for any kind of relationship right now."

"Men who aren't ready for a relationship don't insist on loaning you their clothes and helping you clean."

"But he's a doctor."

"So?"

"He's very focused on health. He'd do this for anyone."

Elara shakes her head and laughs. "You have a knack for refusing to see what's right in front of you. You know that?"

"And I've got a kid to raise. I can't be dating. I tried that. It's too distracting."

"You're not ready. Maybe you will be. Try not to overthink it. Now, Zaki and I are going to make groceries. The girls will probably stay here."

"Of course."

"Lila's welcome to spend the night."

"Thanks. Let's see how the cleaning goes. Maybe Phoebe will want to come to our house."

We hug goodbye, and I stride slowly to the car.

What if he was ready?

"I really like your friends," Derek says as I buckle my seat belt.

I throw a sidelong glance his way. "They like you too. Shall I set up a playdate for you?"

He belts out a laugh. "Now I know where Lila got that wise-ass sense of humor. How do I get to your house?"

As I direct Derek to Mid-City, I lay out my plan: First we'll see what furniture I can save. We'll drag the rest out to the curb, then we'll open all the windows for ventilation and clean the house. With luck, we'll be able to finish today, and Lila and I can move home in a couple of days after the place airs out.

Fifteen minutes later, we pull onto my street. Thankfully, the water's gone. In its place, though, is about an inch of sludge. Why am I always surprised? It's not like all the stuff stirred up by the water evaporates or just flows down the storm drains.

"I would've parked on the neutral ground had I known this would happen," I say, pointing to the wide strip of elevated land that runs down the center of the street. "Looks like some of the cars there might be salvageable. You can park in front of that little Honda Civic."

Derek parks the SUV in front of my car. Stepping out of the passenger seat, I note a pinstripe running the length of my Civic that indicates the water and sludge reached almost to the door handles. I sigh. "Another one down."

"What?" Derek asks.

I don't have the money to buy another car. Better make sure I file claims for car insurance and renter's insurance as soon as we get settled.

"Whenever there's a flood, I have to replace my car. When the first car flooded, I tried to find a mechanic to fix it. The good ones won't. They say, most times, it costs more to pull it apart inside and out and replace all the damaged and moldy parts than the vehicle's even worth."

"Can't imagine it'd cost more to fix my Tesla than buy a new one."

"Will it even still run if it's been flooded?" I ask.

"Never happened before."

"Floods, especially salt water, wreak havoc on electrical systems."

He takes a deep breath and scans the street. "Sweet neighborhood."

"Thanks. This purple-and-green house is ours. Well, we rent it, but..."

Our house is right on the street, and the water/sludge line crosses the door and siding at about fifteen inches above the ground.

"And this is called a shotgun house?" Derek asks, as I unlock the door.

"Because it's long and narrow and the way the rooms flow, you could fire a gun through the front door and the bullet would exit out the back door."

"Sordid bit of history."

"Right?" I laugh. "The cultural mindset was a bit different back then."

I push the door open, then recoil at the smell. This doesn't bode well.

"Glad you told me to wear rain boots," Derek says, as we step through the front door into my living room. Sludge covers the floors. "Hate to ruin a nice pair of shoes stepping in this."

"Be careful. It's probably slippery," I say. "And leave the door open for ventilation please."

"Yes, ma'am. Cute place."

"It's the third home we've rented in twelve years," I say as I lead him through the wrecked house.

Even with bandannas tied around our faces, the stench is a nauseating mix of sewage and mildew.

"This is why I keep trying to find a place on Esplanade Ridge or somewhere less flood prone. But it's way more expensive there."

"Tough to keep moving."

"Especially with a kid, but you know I've gotten very good at getting rid of things. Every time there's a flood, something gets destroyed."

"Amira," Derek says, pointing to the black mold that covers the baseboards and rises another few inches.

"Every damn time. This is why we keep moving." In some spots, the mold climbs as high as three feet above the floor. "It's also why I don't buy expensive furniture. The sofa and chairs are a loss obviously. Let's see if I can save anything."

Derek makes a grumbling sound, which I ignore as I lead him into the room Lila and I use as an office/study space.

"Smart to elevate your filing cabinets," Derek says.

"I learned the hard way." I scan the rest of the room. "The desks look cleanable. Those office chairs have gotta go, though. Next time, I'm buying wood or metal office chairs and putting cushions on them. What do you think about the books?"

"Probably mold climbing up behind them," he says as he opens the windows as wide as they'll go.

"Right. Okay, let's see about the kitchen." I lead him into our cute eat-in kitchen. "I can definitely salvage the kitchen table and chairs," I say as I envision scrubbing the wood with bleach.

Derek shakes his head. "Amira, no."

"No, what?"

"You can't salvage this stuff. Your files? Probably, if they're in plastic.

"They are."

"But nothing else."

"Why?"

"It all has to be bleached. And, uh…"

"Mold comes off."

He sighs. "I'm gonna call Wesley about this. Get the epidemiologist's perspective. Will you listen to him?"

"Derek, we go through this all the time. We'll just air it out, clean it out, get rid of the severely damaged stuff and…"

"Amira, you can't be serious about staying here."

"It's the only home we have." I sigh, wishing I had options, more money saved. But when you have to buy a new car every couple of years and you have to move every couple of years and your income is unsteady… My body fills with frustration.

"You have a home with me as long as you need it."

"Fish and company stink after three days. We've already overstayed our welcome."

Derek

OUCH. I PRESS MY LIPS TOGETHER TO KEEP FROM SAYING something I'll regret. The woman is being stubborn as hell, and this is not the time for it.

"Why are you glaring at me?" she asks.

I can't tell her she just insulted me. Can't say, "*But I already think of you guys as family.*"

I grumble. "My whole life is about saving lives, keeping people healthy and safe. This situation…" I sweep my arm across the kitchen. "…is neither healthy nor safe."

"But we'll clean."

"You have a child."

She raises her eyebrows. I know I'm in deep waters here, stepping into a danger zone, but I can't stay silent for long. Maybe she'll never speak to me again, but if I can prevent her from bringing her kid back here, it'll be worth it. First though, I'm going through the place, taking pictures, and sending them to Wesley. Seems there's no other way to get her to see reason.

I choke as I walk into the bathroom where sludge fills the bathtub. The tiny window in the bathroom doesn't actually open, and the stench is worse here than in the rest of the house. Mold extends from floor to ceiling. I can't get out of here fast enough.

"Looks like the sewer backed up into your tub, woman," I say as I hurry down the little hallway into Lila's bedroom.

Amira stands in the middle of the room, appearing to scan the space.

Out of respect for her, I open the windows. Still, I see nothing salvageable. Mold extends from the walls onto the curtains. I text a few shots to Wesley with the message:

> Amira thinks we can clean this
> place and it'll be safe for her and
> her daughter. Thoughts?

Hell no. Black mold. Toxic.
Completely unsafe.
Lung/brain damage.

"Amira, what means the most to you in here?"

She turns to me, tears in her eyes. "Lila was so excited about that bedspread. She bought it with money she earned babysitting. And those photos..." She points to mold-covered picture frames on the wall. "The one of Lila and Greg and the one of our whole family at our wedding... We don't have digital copies of those. They've survived all this time. I shouldn't have let her hang them on an exterior wall. I should have known better."

I take photos of the images and text them to Wesley:

> Can we save these pics?
> Covered in black mold.

Maybe. Wear gloves.
Remove from the frames. Leave in
the sun twenty-four hours. Then
scan them so she has digital copies.

I text him a thumbs-up and the appreciation hands, then show Amira the text exchange about the photos. Her eyes light up. "Thank you!"

"Any other important items in here?"

"Lila's clothes."

"Buy new ones."

"That's expensive."

"Ask her father. If he can't or won't; I will."

"Derek, that's too much!"

I raise my eyebrows. "We're talking about your child's health. It's not too much. What about in your bedroom? Anything you can't part with?"

I follow her into her room, where she shows me a ceramic box painted with a baby foot and baby hand. It says LILA 8-7-2007.

"She was one month old," Amira explains.

"Ceramic's easy to clean. Anything else?"

"Clothing, but..."

"Nope. I'm buying."

She sighs. "A few special dishes in the kitchen."

"Good. Let's go outside and discuss the new plan."

"New plan?" Amira asks, following me out the back door into her little fenced backyard. A palm tree provides much needed shade from the bright sun and heat.

I slip the bandanna from my face, suck in the fresh air. "I cannot let you stay here."

"Excuse me? You cannot *let* me? Like it's your decision?"

"You're right. I'm outta line."

"Damn right you are!"

"But I'm worried about you and Lila. I've been texting Wesley. He warns me that black mold is toxic and can cause permanent lung and brain damage. Amira, I'm sure you know this. Didn't you say something about your patients suffering lung diseases because they keep living in homes with mold?"

She looks down, toes the ground with her boot. "Well..."

"Well, what, woman? What's more important than your health? Than Lila's health?"

She raises her gaze to mine and bores into me with those soulful eyes. "Are you telling me how to parent?" The edge in her voice is ice.

"Do you need me to?" I keep my voice low but firm. "Seems you're unable to think straight right now."

She stares at me, nostrils flared. A tear slides down her face. "All I can smell right now is shit."

"Me too," I say, putting my hand on her shoulder. "Let's put on the gloves you were smart enough to bring, grab the photos you want and that ceramic box, your special dishes and your files, and get the fuck out of here."

"But where will we stay?"

"Aren't you comfortable at my house?"

She nods.

"Then stay with me."

"Derek, you've been too generous already."

"No such thing. But if you won't take me up on my offer, then get a hotel until you find a safe, new apartment."

Amira stares at me. "I don't have money for a long stay in a hotel. I don't have money for a new car. I don't have money to move."

"Look, I'm inviting you to stay. You're not fish, and I think you're pretty good company, except when you're being stubborn like this."

She flares her nostrils at me, but I keep going. "I'm sure this is stressful as hell and that's why you're being unreasonable, because I know if you were thinking clearly, you would not even be considering cleaning this place up and moving back in."

Amira paces the backyard, talking to herself about money and mold and health and how she could be in this situation. After a minute or so, she stops and stares at me. In her eyes, I see a terrified little girl. Who could blame her?

I open my arms.

"Female fast?" she asks, standing still, arms by her side.

This is not a come-on. There's no part of me trying to woo her right now. I walk to her and bring her close, rub her back. She cries into my shoulder, and I feel the tension start to ease just a bit.

"Hey, let's get this done so we can go home and shower. Then you can figure out your next step."

"Okay." She sniffles.

22

Taking Care

Amira

HEARING GREG'S VOICE BRINGS A WAVE OF RELIEF until we get past *hello*. Ten seconds into the call and he's already lecturing me about being more responsible and choosing a safer place to live with our daughter.

Didn't we used to be friends? Before all this wedding stuff, weren't we friends? What happened? I guess I should have spent more time chitchatting about their wedding. Instead, I got straight to the point. Not a good strategy.

I resume pacing around the pool, wishing I had taken time for a swim to burn off some of this nervous energy. His voice has always had a whiny quality to it, but for some reason, it's really standing out to me now.

"You're asking for more money," he says, sounding surprised. "I just spent $30,000 on a wedding, and you think this is the time to ask for more monthly support."

"Our apartment is filled with black mold, Greg. The car is a loss. I can't keep putting Lila through move after move. It's not fair to her."

"You should have mentioned your financial troubles before, Amira."

The muscles in my face tighten. Is he really giving me a hard time about this? "So you're refusing to help us move?"

"She can always come live with Rini and me."

"We both know that wouldn't work for a whole host of reasons. Besides, where would I live?"

"You're not my responsibility."

"Okay, you know what? I'm sorry I asked."

"Why don't you just take on more work?"

"I'm not asking for career advice. Besides, aren't you the one who's always telling me I need clearer boundaries with my patients? You think if I take on more patients and work harder, that's going to give me stronger boundaries?"

"Don't work harder. Work smarter."

I sigh. He's sounding like he did at the end of our marriage. "Thanks."

"Listen, I'll talk to Rini, but I don't see how we can help anytime soon. Our savings went into that reception."

"You know how lucky Lila is that I'm not the kind of mother to tell her that her father places more value on his new wife's wedding dress than on his child's safety?"

"Tell her."

"Are you crazy?" The pitch of my voice is rising to an unpleasant level.

Calm down, Amira. Breathe.

"That's the kind of thing that fucks a kid up, Greg, knowing their parent doesn't prioritize their well-being. Which is why I'll never tell her, and Lila will keep looking up to you. By the time she's old enough to realize how selfish you are, maybe you will have matured."

"You're not making your case, Amira."

"I shouldn't have to, Greg," I whisper. "It's not about me. It's about our child. Wake the fuck up."

I end the call, slip out of my clothes, and dive into the pool. Through one lap after another, the angry energy increases, propelling me into the next lap.

That lying, cheating... Does he cheat on Rini the way he cheated on me? Or was she his last affair? If they had a kid, would he be more responsible with them than he is with Lila?

I need to scream. I finish my lap, drop my feet to the pool floor, take a deep breath, lower my open mouth into the water and yell as loud as I can, letting the water take the sound.

What are we going to do? Derek has offered his home, but...

God, he's not even Lila's father, and right now he's showing far more concern for her well-being. I don't know if I can accept his help. I don't know if I can afford not to. What I must do, though, is find some way to show my appreciation. When else, who else, has ever gone so far out of their way to help me? My father sure hasn't. My ex sure hasn't. It feels weird to be taken care of. I don't know if I like it. But I guess I prefer it to being abandoned.

Derek

HAVEN'T SPENT MUCH TIME AT THIS ROLLTOP DESK UNTIL now. Before last week, I basically lived at the hospital, meeting colleagues and families of patients, diving into the work. Now sitting in my home office feels like I'm in another universe.

Jot a quick note in my journal:

Amira arguing with ex on the patio. Speaking in low tones but the anger in her voice carries. Glad Lila's at her friend's house. Strong desire to take Amira into my arms, comfort her, and more. More time we spend together, deeper my need to take care of her. These feelings may be an escape from the female fast, but I don't believe that. Recurring visions of us old and gray, moving through our days together.

As another one of those visions takes hold in my mind, I feel the new but now-familiar sensation of my heart expanding, as if a million fragments of light are emanating from my chest throughout my body and into the room. Wow! Other than the actual feeling of climaxing, this has got to be one of the peak experiences of my life, and it happens every time I envision a future with Amira.

I take a deep breath and let it out slowly.

It's time to get my head together, to plan my day. I pull out my Franklin Planner and write my punch list:

Check surgery rotation,

Get car from airport,

Call Ned re: Amira,

Extend SUV rental for Amira if she'll let me,

Clear out guest room for Lila,

Book flights to men's retreat,

Laundry (water safe yet?)

"Derek?" She stands in the doorway, a towel wrapped around her, droplets of water on her shoulders reflecting the light.

I stiffen to the point I need to adjust my pants, hard to do surreptitiously with her staring right at me.

"What's up?" Other than my flag pole.

"Are you working tonight?"

"Let me double-check."

I call up the new surgical schedule online. The patient I had scheduled for yesterday is now on for Monday. Monday's surgery has been moved to Tuesday. Wednesday, we're back to normal, if that's really possible.

"Not till tomorrow. Today I need to get my Tesla from the airport."

"Great. Let's do it. And... what's your favorite meal?"

"Was also thinking I could return the rental car."

Amira's face falls, but she quickly forces a smile.

"Or... I could extend the rental for you or rent a smaller vehicle. Don't think any of the car dealerships are open yet, are they?"

"Oh my goodness, Derek. Are you serious?" she asks. "That's—"

I hold up my hand. "Don't even say it."

Amira closes her mouth. "You're right. I was going to say *that's expensive* and protest."

"Please," I say. "Now that we know airport parking is open, I can get my Tesla. There's no reason that you shouldn't have a vehicle."

"Derek, I can't tell you how much I appreciate this. Yes, I will take you up on that very generous offer."

"Good!"

"And to thank you for all your kindness. I want to cook your favorite meal. Meat. Cheese. Whatever. Just 'cause I'm vegan doesn't mean you should suffer."

"That's very kind."

"Lila's spending the night at Phoebe's, so I have some freedom. Of course"—Amira smiles—"I'm not like a gourmet cook or anything, but—"

"Who is? Nothing like a box of mac 'n' cheese. Though I actually don't like mac 'n' cheese..."

"Do you cook?"

"Oatmeal."

"And you make excellent oatmeal. Tell me what you want, and I'll look up a recipe and try not to poison us," she offers.

She's adorable. I'm still feeling the tingling in my body from that strange heart-opening experience a few minutes ago, and now she's here looking all sexy and wet from her swim and offering to cook for me. I grip the arms of my desk chair hard.

"There is a dish I had in Portugal with clams and white wine that's become my new favorite. I eat it every time I go there."

"How often do you go?"

"Every couple of years. I like to alternate. Wesley and I always take a guy's trip in March when he has spring break. Last year, we went to Barcelona. This coming year, I don't know... with his baby coming, he may not to be able to go."

"So that clam dish is your favorite?"

"One of them."

"What else do you love?"

"Cioppino."

"What's that?"

"A tomato-based seafood stew. Kind of the signature dish of San Francisco. You soak up the broth with fresh sourdough bread. Mm." My stomach rumbles just thinking about it. "New England fish chowder was a favorite growing up, and my mother makes it wicked good. She also made a Creole version of oyster stew that my dad says reminds him of his childhood."

Amira taps her phone screen, pulls a face. "I hear that you really like fish and seafood stews. But I just double-checked, and it's not safe to eat fresh-caught seafood for about a month after a big storm or flood."

"Really?"

"All that sediment and other fun stuff gets stirred up and trapped in the shells of mollusks or something, so..." She frowns. "I'm sorry. What else would you like?"

"Anything with good solid Mexican chocolate."

"There's dessert. What about dinner?"

"How about you make what you would enjoy making?"

"I want to cook what you would enjoy eating. Sounds like you're kind of into stews and soups. Do you have a favorite kind of bread? Favorite drink?"

"Bourbon on the rocks, and there's plenty of that in my liquor cabinet. Bread... depends on the meal but I love any good quality... I love arugula, grilled cauliflower, red peppers."

"How do you feel about mushrooms?"

I flash two thumbs-up. "I try not to eat too much red meat or processed meat. But my mama makes a New Orleans-inspired corn chowder with andouille sausage that feels like home and happiness."

Amira's face broadens into a smile. "Do you have the recipe?"

"I'll call my mama."

Won't she be happy to hear a woman's making my favorite dinner? I'm gonna have to rein her in, keep her from getting all gushy. Wouldn't do any good to try to tell her I'm cooking it. She'd laugh her ass off, probably post something on Facebook about her son pretending to cook.

23
Recipe for Temptation

Amira

LET ME GET THIS CLEAR IN MY MIND. I'M NOT USED TO cooking two versions of a meal, but since I made this commitment to change my diet and also promised Derek his favorite chowder, here I go. I get out two soup pots and put them side by side on the stove. I review the recipe for Althea's Andouille Corn Chowder and the recipe for Best Vegan Corn Chowder I found online.

The sweet potato smells like it's almost done roasting. I open the oven and test a sweet potato cube with a fork. Perfect. I pull the baking sheet from the oven and set it on a brass trivet to cool while I start the soups.

Into the vegan pot, I add:

6 tablespoons olive oil

1/2 cup diced onion

1/2 cup minced celery

1/4 cup diced red bell pepper

1/4 cup diced green bell pepper

1 tablespoon minced garlic

4 1/2 tablespoons paprika

1 1/2 tablespoons freshly ground black pepper
1 tablespoon salt
3/4 teaspoon filé powder
3/4 teaspoon chili powder
3/4 teaspoon crushed red pepper
1/2 teaspoon ground cumin
1 tablespoon cayenne pepper
1 tablespoon dried oregano
1 tablespoon dried thyme

Into Althea's version, I add:
4 T butter,
all the same veggies and spices in the vegan version, plus
1/2 pound andouille sausage, cut into bite-sized chunks.

While everything cooks, I blend two cups of frozen corn with five cups of vegetable stock on high speed until it forms a creamy consistency. Once the onions are translucent, I add the creamy corn/broth mixture to the vegan version, stir it well, and then add another cup of frozen corn kernels plus the roasted sweet potato cubes.

To Althea's version, I add three cups of frozen corn kernels, one cup of heavy cream, and four cups of vegetable broth.

While the soups simmer on the stove, I slice a small cauliflower into steaks, coat each one with olive oil, lay the steaks in a single layer on the baking sheet, and season them with the filé, oregano, thyme, salt, garlic, and paprika mixture. Those roast at 450 degrees. Now I'm ready to make the salad. But I can't find a proper bowl.

"Derek?" I yell. "Where are the salad bowls again?"

I keep looking. Here's another hand-painted ceramic bowl. It's so beautiful it should be on display, not just lying around in his cabinet.

"Smells wicked delicious in here."

Startled, I lift my head too fast, catch it on the edge of the marble countertop, then sink to the floor in pain. Tears fill my eyes and a moan escapes my throat. "Ow," I manage.

He's at my side in a flash. "Amira, are you alright? Where does it hurt?"

His touch confuses my body. There's pain in the top of my head and neck, but the touch of his fingers lightly palpating my shoulders and neck sends sensations of pleasure everywhere.

"Nothing seems out of place. Vertebra in your neck are in line."

Another groan emerges.

"Aww, honey. Can you stand?"

Who knows? What I'd like to do is curl into a ball on the floor until the pain in my head subsides. I feel the gentle pressure of his fingertips on my scalp.

"Looks like you're getting an egg on your head. Want some ice?"

I whimper my assent. He steps away from me, and a slight panic flashes through my body. What is wrong with me, aside from this awful pain? He returns to my side and places something cold and soft on the painful spot. "Here. Lean against me."

Derek sits on the floor with his back against a cabinet, slips his hands under my arms, and lifts me into the space between his outstretched legs. I lean into him, feeling his heartbeat against my spine. He holds the ice pack on my head, whispers in my ear. "That okay?"

"Mm-hmm."

"I'm sorry, sweetheart."

He's calling me sweetheart and honey in that soothing voice. I'm leaning on him. We're in his kitchen. Something about this feels just right. An image flashes through my mind, and it's so real I swear I feel it. *I'm leaning against Derek, feeling his heartbeat, him holding me, resting his head on my shoulder, looking at the baby in my arms. The family we're building together.* That can't be right. I hit my head harder than I realized.

"Derek?" I whisper.

"Hmm?" he whispers back.

"I think I have a concussion."

"Really?" He slips one arm around my upper back and one arm under my legs, turns me around to face him. He pulls me onto his lap and looks into each eye. "What makes you say that?"

"I…"

It's hard to speak with him so close like this. Our lips are almost touching. And I suddenly realize it's not just trauma bonding. I want him. I want his lips on mine. I want his fingers lower on my body. No. I hit my head. It's not desire. It's confusion.

"I want… I mean… I hit my head."

"Open your eyes," Derek says. As he scans my face, he runs his thumb lightly along my cheekbone, over my eyebrow, along my jawline. "Do you feel confused?"

I nod. He's so close.

"I think I'm hallucinating."

"What do you see?"

The sound of his voice travels through my mouth, down my throat, right into my core. My abdomen tightens, along with other parts of my body.

"Amira, honey, what do you see?" He sounds concerned now. And what do I tell him? I saw our baby?

"Amira?" he asks again.

"Ummm… I… uh… it's nothing." My breath catches in my throat. I close my eyes again, try to clear my brain.

"Are you having trouble breathing?"

I nod. "But my head is starting to feel better."

"Hmm," he says, sounding confused.

"The ice is helping, I think."

"Are you still seeing things?"

"No, it was just for a minute."

"What did you see? Stars? Sparkles?"

"No."

"Hey, look at me. Are you seeing double? How many fingers am I holding up?" He holds up a closed fist.

"Zero."

"Good job. Now?" he asks as he raises three fingers in the air.

"Three."

"Do your eyes hurt?"

"Just the top of my head and my neck."

"Hmm. You don't seem to have a concussion, but I'll keep an eye on you. What did you hallucinate?"

"A baby in my arms."

"A memory of Lila?"

"It wasn't her," I whisper, thinking of the baby's brown skin, a few shades darker than me and lighter than Derek. Big brown eyes like his.

"A baby," Derek says. Did he just stiffen under me?

Now I'm tingling. I think wetness just spilled into my panties. I need to get off his lap. Instead, my body presses into his against my will. He clears his throat, focuses on the top of my head. Suddenly my mind is clear. My nipples are hard. His neck curves gracefully as he examines the egg on my head again. My lips almost graze his neck; I could end his female fast in a split second if I wanted to. I lean against him, rest my head on his shoulder, and press my nipples into his chest. It's wrong of me, I know. I think he's trying to pretend nothing's happening, but I know he wants me too. I see the way he looks at me, the way he stares when I'm swimming or working or... doing pretty much anything. There's something between us. I bring my lips to his ear and whisper, "Thank you."

Since I'm not willing to blow this fast for him, literally or figuratively, I may as well stand up and finish dinner prep. But when I push my hands against his shoulders to rise, my tingling legs go limp.

"Whoa," he says. "What happened?"

I haven't been turned on like this in a while, but as I recall, this is pretty much what happened the last time too.

"My knees just went weak."

In one fluid motion I don't even understand, Derek stands with me cradled in his arms. He carries me to the living room, lays me on the sofa, and kneels beside me. The scent of roasting cauliflower fills the air and something else. The faint scent of charcoal?

"Derek, the soup."

"What about it?"

"I think it's burning."

"That's okay."

"No! I worked hard on it. Just turn it off and the oven please," I whine. I hate it when I whine.

"Be right back."

He dashes into the kitchen.

"Stir the soup please so it doesn't stick," I call, hoping it's salvageable.

"Amira," he yells back, as if he thinks I'm being silly.

"I'm serious."

"God, you're bossy when you're hurt."

"Stir it please."

"Yes, ma'am. Do I need to take this stuff out of the oven?"

"Yes!"

I hear the oven door open and close. Then Derek's by my side again, looking into my eyes. This time I don't close them. I stare back, trying to convey my desire and caring.

Can you see how I want you, Derek?

"I can," he says, caressing my cheek with his thumb.

"What?"

"I can see your desire."

"Oh God. Did I say that out loud?"

He smiles, and deep dimples I somehow never noticed before frame his supple lips.

I want those lips. I hope I kept that thought inside my head.

Derek brings his face closer to mine, touches my nose with his, and whispers, "Can you see how I want you, Amira?"

"Mm."

He strokes my ear. "I want to take care of you."

"But..."

"That baby you saw..."

"It was..."

"Have you had visions like that before?"

"Never. Well, except right before Lila was conceived. I saw her swaddled and lying between her father and me in bed. I saw us kissing her cheeks."

"And this time?"

"It was different."

Please don't ask more. I can't answer more. Not yet. Not until I've figured out a few things.

Derek inhales, as if he's breathing me in, and backs away, shaking his head. "I want everything about you."

My heart lights up, but my brain fires a warning. "You don't know me."

"I know enough. But now's not the time. Sixteen days to go."

"The fast?" My voice comes out in a tired squeak.

"The last four days'll be easy though."

"How?"

"It's a four-day men's retreat in California. No temptation from you."

My heart feels like mush right now. He just suggested I'm temptation. Me. A single mom with a shaved head and an empty bank account.

"How's your head?" he asks.

I nod slowly, not just to let him know it's better but also to see if the movement brings the pain back. It doesn't. I breathe a sigh of relief. "Better."

"Shall we eat this delicious meal you prepared?"

"I never got to make the salad. It was going to have arugula, and..."

"Let's save the salad for tomorrow," he says, standing and holding his hand out to help me up.

With the exception of the smoky flavor caused by burning, the chowder is quite good. Derek raves about it, but I think he may be being extra kind because... well, because he is genuinely kind.

I smile at him as he takes a bite of a cauliflower steak. He beams and makes sounds of appreciation. Warmth floods my chest. It feels good to please him. And that scares me. I've never wanted to please a man, other than my father, and I gave up on that at a pretty early age.

But now I sit across from a man who radiates care, who has welcomed me and my child into his home and his life, who spent hours of his free time, helping me salvage what I could from a moldy, stinky home. And I'm thinking I want to please him. It scares me to imagine staying here much longer, to think about getting closer before we're ready, before Lila is ready for me to be close to anyone.

When we finish dinner, Derek insists on doing all the clean-up. He leads me upstairs to make sure I don't get dizzy and fall or something and says good night at the bedroom door. His footsteps grow faint as he descends the steps and returns to the kitchen. I don't feel dizzy, but I do feel tired. I'm taking advantage of this opportunity to go to sleep early.

24
Is It Obvious?

Amira

Derek's face is tantalizingly close. Why don't I kiss him? *Kiss him, Amira. Forget his female fast. Kiss the boy!* I slide my fingers across his eyebrow, his cheekbone, his strong jawline, bring my thumb to that luscious bottom lip. He moans softly. I circle that sexy mouth with my tongue, nibble the bottom lip lightly, then bring my lips to meet his. He tastes like coffee, like the scent of the freshly brewed coffee that just roused me from sleep. Damn. What a fantasy.

I wish I had kissed him last night. I wish I had held him close and run my hands down his sides onto his hips and pressed him into me. I need caffeine, but I think I need to take care of this throbbing between my legs first. Otherwise, I'll be all shaky and unable to get down the stairs without help.

There's a thought. Derek holding me in his arms, carrying me down the steps, laying me on the couch, or... No, that soft, hand-tufted silk rug in the living room. He lays me on the rug, and then...

Yes... I let my fantasies guide my fingers until I cry out in ecstasy.

"Amira?" he calls, a note of panic in his voice. I think I hear him run up the stairs. He knocks rapidly, then opens the door.

I throw the sheet over myself and smile brightly. "Good morning." *Is it obvious I just pleasured myself thinking of you?*

Derek holds the door handle and shifts uncomfortably, then curses under his breath. "I, uh, probably should've waited for you to say come in, huh?" His slightly parted lips slide into a mischievous grin.

A giggle emerges from my throat. Embarrassed, I lower my gaze and can't help noticing my appearance seems to be having an effect on him. Heat rises to my cheeks, and my nipples harden to the point of pain. I try to act casual as I wrap the sheet around myself, swing my legs over the side of the bed, hop out, and stride toward the bathroom. "Is that coffee I smell?"

"Uh-huh," Derek says, following me with his eyes.

"Yum!" I lick my lips. "I'll be right down after I freshen up."

Derek

SHE'S NAKED IN MY BED, COVERED BY THAT FINE LINEN SHEET, smiling like someone who just had a moment they won't forget for a while. Damn. Naked in my bed, morning sunlight revealing all the right curves through that thin fabric covering. Naked in my bed without me.

By the way she's glowing and the way those pert little nipples are protruding through the sheet, I'd say she just pleasured herself in my bed. An image flashes through my mind: Amira touching herself, arching her back in climax, lips parted to receive my tongue or... Oh man.

The woman touched herself in my bed, and now she's striding across the room, wrapped in a sheet. She's not trying to tease me, but my captain is standing at full attention, waiting for Admiral Amira to hand out orders. Fuck.

Fifteen days.

Yesterday I didn't even know she was interested. Thought all I had to battle was my fantasies. Now Amira's giggling and blushing, breathing rapidly. What happened? She hit her head. Something jog loose? Maybe she has a TBI. Is that possible? A serious traumatic brain injury from a bump against a marble countertop? Gonna have to ask one of my colleagues in neurology. Amira is not herself. She can't possibly want me now when she didn't seem to before. Maybe a little, but not like this, not the... What the hell happened?

"You're still here," she says as she emerges from the bathroom even more radiant than when she entered. Thank God she's wearing clothes, not that she's any less alluring in that tight-fitting tank top and yoga shorts.

I'm actually starting to throb. My lower half might be developing a medical condition caused by chronic and intense swelling. I can't take my eyes off her, can't seem to move either.

She comes toward me, places her hand lightly on my chest. "Shall we go downstairs?"

It takes everything within me not to grab her by the hips, slide those shorts off and stroke her skin until she begs for me to fill her. I summon all my strength to keep my hands firmly on the doorknob and the doorjamb, which, I now realize, is why she's standing in front of me. I'm blocking her exit. I want to reach down and lift her onto me so she can feel my lust between her legs. I want to bend down and kiss her, and...

"Derek?"

"Huh?"

"You're breathing kinda heavy. You okay?"

Humiliation fills me. Damn female fast. If this were a normal day, I wouldn't be ashamed. I'd look into her eyes, proud to show her the effect she has on me. And she'd want it too. She'd stroke me and take me into her mouth, taste the pre—

"Coffee?" she asks and places her hand below mine on the doorjamb. "Can we go downstairs?"

I moan and let her slide my hand off the doorjamb, interlace her fingers with mine.

"Come on, you," she says with a giggle.

"Uh-huh," I manage, like a dog following his master.

"Is it really seven a.m. already? What time do you have to be at the hospital?"

"Nine," I breathe as she leads me down the stairs.

"Good. There's time to relax and enjoy each other. I need to find out if the center is open today. If so, I'll have patients to see. And I need to confirm that Lila and Phoebe are out of school. If they are, and I don't have patients, it'll be a good day to see about getting her some clothes."

My faculties are returning to me. Clothes. Money. "I'll leave you some cash, okay?"

"For what?"

"To replace Lila's wardrobe and whatever you might need."

"Derek," she starts.

We reach the kitchen, and I pour us each a cup of coffee, get out the almond milk for the woman and the regular milk for me. I follow her outside onto the patio. The sway of her hips mesmerizes me. How I long to take care of her, ensure her safety and well-being. This I can do, even on the female fast. The rest will have to wait.

Amira

SITTING ACROSS FROM DEREK, SCANNING HIS FACE, I WONDER what's going through his mind. He sips his coffee, extra quiet. I sip mine and try to catch his gaze.

What flipped my switch last night? Was it the actual bump on my head? Or the tenderness he showed in caring for me? Actually, I think it was the vision of us and a baby, combined with the sensation of being in his arms, safe.

For eleven years, I've been the one person ensuring Lila and I were safe, fed, clothed, and sheltered. Derek has unlocked a desire I didn't even know I had—for someone to take care of me. The way he does it and has since that moment at the airport in Hartford... it all came to a head last night. And once it clicked into place, my body went into high gear. I never knew being taken care of was such a turn-on until now. Just thinking about it makes my nipples perk up.

"How much do you think you'll need?" he asks. "Not sure what's in my wallet, but I've got a few thousand stashed around the house."

"Dollars?" Being taken care of is delightful. Being paid for, though... I don't love that.

"So if you'll be okay with, like, a thousand for now, then we'll be safe until the banks open again even if the ATMs are out of cash."

"A thousand dollars," I say, unable to keep the disbelief out of my voice.

"If that's not enough, I can see whether the ATMs are running now, and if so..."

"Enough! What are you even talking about? Why are you trying to give me money?"

"Doubt you can replace a twelve-year-old girl's wardrobe for less than five hundred, and women spend way more."

"Not me. I shop at Goodwill and Salvation Army and this fun indie thrift store in the Bywater. And that's beside the point. You're not giving me spending money like I'm a child."

"Shoes cost an arm and a leg. You don't buy used shoes, do you?"

"We buy shoes new at discount stores. Still, how is this your problem?"

He sighs. "I thought we agreed you'd let me help you until you're back on your feet."

"You're renting a car for me—"

"Only until your insurance pays up. Plus, you insisted on covering the first few days. Remember?"

"The car insurance will take months to process. You're housing me and Lila. I can live with that, but handing me cash?" I shake my head and let out a frustrated grumble. "Let me see if I have to work today, all right?" I reach for my phone, grateful for this return to normalcy, and check the Terrebonne Community Center's website. "Closed until Wednesday."

"So you have time to shop, which means..."

"Actually, what it means is I'll probably end up taking a hundred phone calls today, counseling people down from their various ledges, and being unable to bill for any of it because health insurance doesn't pay for phone sessions."

It's exhausting just thinking about it.

"All the more reason to let me help you. You're staying here at least through November, right? Maybe till the New Year?"

I shake my head. No way is Lila ready for that, but I don't want to throw my daughter under the bus. "Derek, you need to get on with your life."

He sighs. "Come off it. I know what I need: you two with me, safe and sound through the holidays. Please."

I meet his eyes. They're pleading, sincere, radiating desire. Doesn't he understand living together is no way to start a relationship? Greg and I basically did that, and it was a disaster. "The last thing Lila needs is to watch her mother go through a devastating breakup, especially over the holidays."

"Huh?"

"Romance is temporary, but my kid is with me forever."

He recoils. "You're joking, right?"

You can't really be this naive. "Who stays together forever? Fifty percent of marriages end in divorce, and most couples never make it to the justice of the peace."

"Never pegged you as pessimistic. All those chick flicks you watch."

"I'm realistic."

"My parents have been married over fifty years. Grandparents made it to their diamond anniversary. Wesley's parents were together until she died. His sister's been with her man for ten, fifteen years. Don't tell me you can't think of anyone who's been together for the long haul."

"Siri," I say to get my phone AI's attention. "Search the web for answering services in Louisiana."

"I found this. Check it out," Siri responds.

I scan the screen and tap my finger on the first option. A website comes up with information about a local answering service. I smile at Derek. "Now this may help: putting the plan you and I came up with into action."

"Kinda feels like you're dismissing me. Thought we were having a conversation about relationships."

I sigh and think. "Elara and Zaki. I believe they just celebrated nineteen years together in August. And Sage's sister and her husband have been married for like, twenty-five years."

"Sounds pretty real."

"Be that as it may, I'm not ready to commit to living with you before we've even dated. I'm too old and have too many responsibilities to take such a risk."

"You're already living with me."

"Temporarily. Can we please change the subject? I was trying to tell you how much I appreciate you helping me switch gears in my career." Seeing Derek smile eases the tension in my shoulders.

"Glad to be of service. Feel like a swim? I wanna do a few laps before I get ready for work."

"As soon as I do my yoga."

A strange expression crosses his face, a smile mixed with the tightness of being in pain, plus both mischief and sadness in his eyes.

"You okay?" I ask.

"Don't think twice. Just..." He whispers something and shakes his head.

I'm not sure, but I think he said something about how watching me do yoga will make it hard for him to get across the pool even once.

"I guess I'll get started," I say, standing and going to the shady spot beside the pool. "Maybe by the time you're wet, I'll be ready to join you. I mean... uh..." I giggle nervously. Did I actually just talk about him getting wet? Out loud?

Derek

GLIDING THROUGH THE COOL WATER BRINGS MY BODY AND mind into a state of calm. Thank God. I could never perform surgery in that distracted state. Of course, as soon as I get in the shower, I'll make sure to take care of myself the way I'd like to take care of Amira.

At least I can help her financially. It's no replacement for sexual healing, but for now it'll have to do. Besides, she needs money way more than sex at the moment.

She dives in just as I'm finishing my laps. Tempting as hell with the tight clothes clinging even more.

Don't go there again, man. Get yourself together.

I push myself out of the pool, enjoying the flex in my biceps, and grab a towel from the lounge chair. "Hey, I'm going to work in a bit. I'll leave some cash on the counter for you, all right?"

"I already said it's not your problem. Besides," she says, her breath ragged as she swims toward me.

"Don't argue, woman." I towel off and send a pointed look at her.

"Excuse me?"

"Let me help you. Please. It feels good to me."

"Well, it doesn't feel good to me." She comes to a stop at the edge of the pool and looks up at me.

My stomach tightens. "Seriously?"

"I'm an independent woman. I can take care of myself," she says. Her voice has a light tone, but her eyes look intense.

I squat by the water's edge. "So you have all the cash you need to clothe yourself and your daughter and rent a new apartment since you're refusing to stay here."

She purses her lips, takes a deep breath, lets out a growl. What is her problem? Seemed like she was starting to appreciate what I offer. But now? Maybe this is why her ex refused to help her. Lack of appreciation.

I stand and turn to go, but she touches my ankle, setting off a chain reaction of neurons firing throughout my body.

"Derek," she says and looks up at me with tears in those almond-shaped eyes. "I'm sorry. I see you're trying to help, and I appreciate it. I'll pay you back. Promise."

Fuck. She just doesn't get it.

25
Thrift

Amira

TWENTY CRISP ONE-HUNDRED-DOLLAR BILLS LIE ON the kitchen counter with a note. Derek's handwriting is almost illegible, but I think the note says:

> Thanks for letting me help you and Lila. I know you prefer thrifting to the mall, but the mall's most likely to be open today. Thrift stores probably still cleaning after the flood. Have fun.

He signed the note with a smiley face inside the letter D, then:

> P.S. This is NOT a loan.

I know his heart is in the right place, but I can't take two thousand dollars, especially not as a gift. That's insane. We'll find sales, search the discount stores. One thousand dollars is more than enough, and I'm only using it as a last resort.

LILA AND PHOEBE ARE CHILLING ON THE FRONT PORCH when I roll up to the Onirymbas'. It's silly, I know, but my body fills with pride, driving this fancy car.

Lila runs down the steps and meets me at the curb. "Whoa, Mama, is that our new car?"

"Cool," Phoebe says.

"I wish. But we do get to ride around in it for a few days until we find a new one."

"Can we *not* find a new car? Please?" Lila asks.

I laugh. "Hop in, kiddo. Phoebe, you coming with?"

Lila throws her backpack into the back seat and looks expectantly at her friend. Phoebe digs at a crack in the sidewalk with her shoe. "Mom said I need to clean my room and finish my homework."

"Back to school tomorrow," Lila informs me.

"Yes, I heard. Well, we need to do some shopping. Good luck with your homework, Phoebe."

The girls hug, and Phoebe waves as we pull away.

"So... you need some clothes, and I promised you eye shadow. What do you think, Lila? The mall?"

"The most eco-friendly makeup is at the health food store."

"The most eco-friendly makeup?" I ask.

"I've been doing my research. The stuff you get at the department stores isn't good for you."

"What about the pharmacy?"

"The drugstore and department store brands aren't good for your skin. They cause cancer, *and* they're really bad for the environment too. Did you know they kill whole species of bugs just to make the red for your lipstick?"

"Eww." An image of someone smashing bugs on my lips fills my mind. It makes me shudder.

"As if that bug has no other purpose than to color your lips!"

"Where do we get the bug-free, eco-friendly makeup?"

"I already told you, Mama: the health food store. Or we could go to the Aveda salon, because they make really good stuff too."

"What would you prefer?"

"Let's go to the health food store. They have this brand called Pacifica, and it's really pretty, and the colors have names like Angel Wings and Cosmic Love Beam."

"Cosmic Love Beam? When did you become a hippy?"

"I'm just saying, Mama, the names are fun."

"Okay."

At the health food store, Lila leads me right to the makeup section.

"How do you know about this? We don't shop here."

"Phoebe's mom. She gets her nail polish here too. Because you know the stuff at the drugstore usually has formaldehyde and toluene and that's not good for you either. And the polish at most salons is really toxic. They're supposed to leave the doors and windows open because manicurists get really sick from it."

"Oh my goodness. I'm gonna have to ask Elara about this."

"You can, but I know everything about it. She taught me and I've been researching," Lila says, examining the products. She holds up an eye shadow palette with six remarkably tasteful colors. "What do you think about this palette?"

"I think that's beautiful. Do you like it?"

"Uh-huh."

"That was easy."

"Do you think I should get mascara too?"

I take a deep breath. "Sure."

She pulls a purple tube with silver stars and moons on it from the case. "I've read a lot about this one. Cosmic Hemp."

As she plops the items into the basket, I glance at the prices: twenty-five dollars for eye shadow and mascara. A bit more expensive than the drugstore brands but less than the department store lines. And if Lila's right about the health hazards of normal makeup, it's totally worth the cost. I pick up a mascara and lip color for myself.

A FEW HOURS LATER, WE'RE IN THE CHECKOUT LINE AT THE discount store across the street from the mall. Lila's babbling excitedly about where she'll wear each outfit: at school, at her Coalition to Restore Coastal Louisiana meetings, at the next slumber party. She practically has a schedule established for each article of clothing by the time we reach the cashier and plop the clothes and shoes onto the counter.

The cashier fills big paper bags with our new wardrobe. I didn't get as much for myself, but those combat boots were too hard to resist, and I love the adorable fifties-style dresses I found. Since all my steampunk clothes were ruined and I shaved my head, I'm trying a whole new look.

"The total is eight hundred eighty-nine dollars, ma'am."

"Look at that, Lila! We stayed within our budget." I hand the cashier my Visa card, then high-five my daughter.

"I'm sorry, ma'am. Your card was declined."

"What? That can't be right. I haven't reached my limit," I say, doing the math in my head and realizing the car-rental place put the first few days of the car on my card because I wouldn't let Derek cover the full cost like he wanted to. "Oh darn. Maybe I have."

"Mama!" Lila's eyes widen in panic.

Great. Just what I want my daughter to experience while shopping.

"Okay, no worries, hon," I say, pulling the crisp hundred-dollar bills from my wallet. "We have enough cash."

"Really?" Lila asks. "You never have cash."

"Today I do." I slide the money across the counter.

The cashier takes it and runs a counterfeit-testing marker over each bill. How humiliating. Is it because the card was declined? She doesn't trust my money now? Or can she just sense it's not my money? Do I have *can't afford it* written all over my face? Derek may not realize it, but I will be paying him back. I sigh. It was such a fun shopping trip until this moment.

The register spits out our receipt. The cashier hands me my change and releases our bags to us.

I thank her, take the bags, and lead Lila out of the store. "See, hon? No problem."

"Why do you have so much money today?" she asks, catching up with me on the way across the parking lot.

"Why shouldn't I?"

I've been careful to model good financial habits, and now it seems like it's all falling apart. I click the button on the key that makes the car beep and the doors unlock, then follow the sound to the vehicle.

"First the fancy car. Now buying nine hundred dollars in new clothes in one shopping trip. It's not like you, Mama. You never have money."

I groan. "A friend offered to help, and I decided to receive. It's a practice, like meditation or yoga."

"Uh-huh. A friend." She winks. "Derek texted me he gave you $2,000 to go shopping, but we didn't even spend $1,000. Now I can practice this too, right? Because I'd like to receive some pralines from Leah's if they're open and maybe another pair of shoes from—"

"Whoa. He texted you?"

"Yup."

All my parenting, undone in a single text message. Some very unpleasant energy courses through my body. What. The. Hell. Was. He. Thinking.

I take a deep breath, shake it off, grab Lila, kiss the side of her head. "You know what? Pralines are a great idea. No more shoes today though."

"Aww, Mama."

"Not today, Lila."

She gets into the car, and I try to talk myself out of a spiral before joining her.

No need to catastrophize. Derek's misplaced generosity doesn't have to ruin our mother-daughter excursion or my parenting. This is a teachable moment, and once I figure out exactly what to teach her about this...

I take a deep breath and hope some smart idea will pop into my brain. I'm drawing a blank.

Stupid men and their financial power trips. I didn't need his damn help anyway. Why did I take it?

Derek

AFTER A LONG DAY, I WANT NOTHING MORE THAN A BOURBON, a shower, and a fine meal. All those things are available to me, thanks, in part, to Amira and the delicious meal she made last night. As I walk home from the hospital, I anticipate the flavors of leftover chowder on my tongue. More exciting, I get to see Amira.

A few minutes later, I walk into the kitchen and my body sags with disappointment. Why is the money still on the counter? Or... half the money? What's she trying to say?

I find her in the bedroom, watching Lila spin around in a dress with tags attached. She's praising her daughter's taste. Adorable. They are such beautiful creatures. The hurt I felt a moment ago dissipates as I watch them. Now I feel full with love. Amira says something about trying on one of the dresses she bought. I clear my throat to announce my presence before either of them starts removing clothing. "Someone's looking fancy."

Lila smiles but looks horrified at the same time. Amira flashes that look with the flared nostrils and tight lips.

Uh-oh. I screwed up. "You guys eat already?"

"We were waiting for you," Amira says.

"How was the shopping trip?"

"Fun," Lila says. "Until Mama's card got declined."

"Card," I say, more sharply than I intended. "Didn't you have cash, Amira?"

She nods and meets my gaze. "I borrowed a thousand dollars, which I will pay back as soon as possible."

"Why use the card at all?"

"I didn't want to take advantage of your generosity."

The words sound right, kind of, but I have the sense there's a subtext.

Lila rolls her eyes.

I sigh and step away. "It's been a long day. Long surgery. See you downstairs in a bit."

I drag my tired and now irritated self to the guest bathroom.

What is her problem? Pay me back? I'm not a banker; I'm her friend. If not for this damn female fast, I'd be pressing for more. Why does she have to push me away at every possible opportunity? This doesn't feel right.

Before going downstairs, I go back to the bedroom, knock to announce my presence, and pull $500 from my wallet as I enter. Lila gets a funny little smile on her face and looks from her mom to me like she's expecting something exciting.

"Okay, kid. This is only for clothing and school supplies. Got it? Necessities," I say, as I extend the bills to Lila.

Her eyes widen as she takes the cash. "Necessities. Got it," she says, a huge smile brightening her face.

"Wait a minute. Excuse me?" Amira raises her hands in a stopping motion. "We don't take money from…"

"You did," Lila says. "Why can't I practice receiving like you?"

Amira sighs and glares at me.

"Thank you, Derek!" Lila takes a photo of the cash. "I can't wait to show Phoebe."

"Absolutely not!" Amira says. "You wanna keep that cash, little girl, you will *not* be flashing it around to your friends."

"Why?"

Amira growls. "Because it's tacky, for one thing. Show me you have no photo of that cash please. *Now.*"

"God, Mama, chill out." Lila holds up her phone, and Amira examines it, then nods.

"Yeah, I do need to chill out. I'm going to take a little swim. Lila, you have reading to do, right? We'll make dinner in forty-five minutes. Derek, I'd like to speak with you for a few minutes after I change into my swimsuit."

"Uh... sure. I'll wait for you on the patio."

Gives no bullshit, takes no bullshit. She's perfect for you, I hear Wesley say in my head as I stride out of the room. Is this what he meant? If so, I might need to question his judgment.

AMIRA WALKS ONTO THE PATIO IN A NEW SWIMSUIT THAT highlights her figure in all the right places. *Damn.* My mouth goes dry. I take another sip of bourbon and lean back on the lounge chair. She stands over me in a slightly aggressive stance that raises my flagpole. That bathing suit was money well spent.

"What the hell, Derek?"

I raise an eyebrow. "You're welcome. I hope you enjoyed your mother-daughter shopping trip."

"Yes, for that, let me thank you again. But I do not appreciate you undermining my parenting."

"Undermining? How did I undermine your parenting?"

She shakes her head and sighs, hands on her hips. Fuck. She's just getting hotter. "One: you went behind my back to make sure my kid knew you had given me money to spend on her."

"So?"

"I have a certain way I do things. I may not *have* a lot of money, but I make things work, and I've been teaching Lila to be financially responsible since she was about three years old. I don't include her in financial decisions other than: Which pair of shoes do you want, honey?"

"Maybe it's time you do."

Amira looks like she wants to spit venom at me. Fortunately, she presses her lips together in a grim line and fixes her furious eyes on my face.

I can't help but smile. "Has anyone told you how sexy you are when you're angry?"

She deepens her breath, stares, says nothing. Guess this wasn't the time to mention her sex appeal.

Right, Derek. That's called being dismissive. Have you learned nothing from the program?

"So it was bad that I texted your daughter. Is that what you're saying? Because you didn't know. Because I left you out of the loop."

"Exactly."

"But I thought I was bringing her into the loop."

"She's twelve! She doesn't belong in the loop."

"Never pegged you for that old-school *kids should be seen and not heard* bull... uh, mindset."

"You're missing the point. You don't text a kid behind their parents' back or sneak stuff to them."

"My grandma used to do that all the time."

"With hundreds of dollars? I mean, mine did too, with sodas and cookies and the occasional five bucks to go buy an ice cream. Not hundreds of dollars."

"Things cost more now, Amira."

That icy glare of hers returns, and I hold up my hands in surrender. "Okay. Okay. I see your point."

"And you sure as hell don't hand them insane amounts of money because you don't like the way their mother shops for them."

"That's not what I was saying. I was just helping."

"I doubt she sees it that way. And you're not her grandma or her uncle or her... anything."

"I'm not anything? You're saying I'm nothing?"

"No, I didn't mean... You're not nothing. Come on, you know that's not what I meant."

"What did you mean?"

"You're just a friend. A new friend at that."

I clear my throat. My eyes burn. "Sorry." My voice comes out husky, as I struggle with my emotions. "Thought maybe... uh..."

I get up and walk back into the house. Not even hungry now. Too tired and frustrated to swim, and I don't really feel like being around Miss Thing at the moment. After a beat, I find myself in my office, cross-legged on my meditation cushion. The gentle sound of a body gliding through water comes through the windows. I time my breathing to the rhythm of her swim strokes.

26
Synching Up

Amira

THE FRENCH DOORS OPEN JUST AS I'M STEPPING OUT of the pool. Derek strides onto the patio, swim trunks low on his hips, towels in hand. I always forget towels, and he always seems to remember one for me. The warm feeling of being taken care of spreads through my thighs again. I wish my body could get the message that I'm mad at that man right now.

I take the towel from him, my gaze accidentally dropping to his taut navel. I quickly raise my eyes to his face. "Thank you."

He nods. "Listen, I owe you an apology."

My thighs go into happy spasms. I wrap the towel around myself and sit, hoping Derek won't notice my quivering legs.

He sits beside me on the chaise. "You expressed a legit concern about boundaries. And I dismissed you before I really listened. I was out of line. My whole approach was wrong. My life is helping children. I make life-and-death decisions for kids, and most of their parents never question my judgment. But I don't know how to raise kids, Amira. I'm not a parent. I'll never be an uncle. Couple of my cousins have kids, but I don't see them more than once or twice a year. All right? I wasn't trying to undermine you, but I see that I did, and I'm sorry."

"Thank you."

"I didn't think how it would look to Lila or how it might look to her friends or yours or even mine that I'm giving you money. I should have asked. I guess I was trying to make sure you have what you need, and I wanna be the cool guy with Lila."

"Yeah. Well. Cut that shit out. No offense, but she doesn't need a buddy. She needs responsible adults in her life. And... anyway, it's too soon to, you know... act like a step... uh..." How do I say this without offending him more?

"Got it. I'm nothing."

My heart drops. "Oh, Derek." I start to reach for his shoulder but stop myself.

Female fast.

Instead, I look him in the eyes, conveying as much softness as I can through my expression. "I was rude before. I was upset, and I spoke harshly. I apologize."

"The way you described our relationship, Amira. I mean, of course we're friends, but after last night, I thought maybe..."

"But you're on this fast, and... I mean, we just... Well, it's not like anything..." Gosh, I really hurt his feelings. Shit.

"It's cool," he says in a tone that lets me know this situation is anything but cool.

"Derek, you're not nothing. I didn't mean it like that. Please, you know how I feel about you."

"Do I?"

"Kind of. Maybe not. I..." How do I say this? "I'm enjoying the friendship that's growing between us. A lot. And... We've both got things to figure out."

"You do."

"So do you. That's why you're on this fast."

"Right. Well, I'm gonna clear my head," he says, leaving me alone on the chaise.

"I was thinking I'd heat that leftover soup and make the salad I didn't get to make last night."

He nods curtly and dives into the pool. Before I finish toweling off, he pops up from under the water and says, "But I don't have to take that $500 back from her, right? That'd feel real shitty."

I sigh. "And it would hurt her feelings and confuse her further. So no, but, Derek..."

"Understood. Never again, unless you say it's okay."

"And I think you should say something to her. Like, not quite an apology, but..."

His eyebrow quirks up, and he stares at me for a moment, then dives back underwater. He does a full lap below the surface, comes up for air without even looking my way, and goes under and swims another lap fully submerged.

27

Patients

Amira

I'M SO LOST IN THOUGHT, CALCULATING WHEN I'LL BE able to repay the $1,000 dollars Derek gave me, plus the $500 he gave Lila that I nearly miss the exit into Houma. The sameness of Route 90 often puts me in a virtual trance. Now I cut the wheel sharply, maneuver onto the highway off-ramp, and slow down at the stop sign. Traffic here is light, as usual, at least compared to New Orleans. I turn left onto New Orleans Boulevard and drive into the center of town.

If all my patients show up today, I will earn more than enough to repay Derek's generous $1,500 loan, and I'll have enough for a few groceries on top of that. Of course, there's almost always a no-show who doesn't pay. No wonder my budget's a mess. I work in a part of Louisiana where cost of living matches the low incomes, but I live in the most expensive city in the state. And between the wide range of payments I receive from insurance companies and patients, and the fact that I can never count on a set income, how can I plan, save, or prepare?

The answering service is a great idea for a time when I'm seeing more patients. Maybe next month I can swing it. Greg is right; I need to work harder and smarter. True, the mind map revealed I need to find another way to serve patients without doing direct care. Maybe actually seeing patients will spark an idea.

The Terrebonne Community Center looks unaffected by the storm. Even though this isn't the town where the tribes will be resettled, it's about the same distance from the coast and the advantages are clear. Less flooding is a major benefit. I park in a spot marked RESERVED and walk into the old brick schoolhouse turned community center.

Elsa looks up from her post at the reception desk and gasps. Funny, even though I'm still surprised every time I catch my reflection in the mirror, I didn't anticipate such reactions from everyone else. I smile, run my hand over my head, enjoying the sensation.

Elsa recovers her composure and speaks, her Creole accent thick. "Hi there, Ms. MacKenzie."

"Elsa, how are you? Your mama an' them all right after the storm?" I ask.

"We didn't get much here, other than some rain. The folks in Isle de Jean Charles and Pointe-aux-Chênes is another story though."

"I saw that on the news. Another three families displaced from the island. Terrible."

"You know the road got washed out," Elsa reports. "If they didn't have boats, they'd all be stranded."

"Is it dry now?"

"Yes, ma'am. LaForce family's coming at nine thirty."

"Thank you," I say, walking past the bulletin boards to the room I share with the after-school tutor. Morning sunlight makes the white walls and dark wainscoting glow. The twitter of birds filters through the open windows along with a soft breeze, brightening my mood.

I review the schedule, then set up the room for the LaForce family, placing little people, a small sand table, and art supplies in strategic places near and between three chairs. Just as I finish, Brenda LaForce and her seven-year-old, Shaleen, enter. They both look disheveled, which is unusual. Brenda normally takes a lot of pride in her appearance.

"Hi there," I say, trying to sound welcoming and cheerful. "How are you?"

Brenda starts when she sees me, then nods solemnly and looks at her daughter. "Shaleen, you want Mama to stay in here today, or you wanna talk to Miss Amira on your own?"

Shaleen whines and clutches her mother around the waist. Is it my new look or what the family has just been through? Either way, the little girl's behavior tells me I need to take this session slowly. She and her mom need time to settle into the space.

"All right," I say, closing the door and turning on the sound machine so no one will hear us outside the room. "I always enjoy spending time with both of you. Have a seat."

"Almost didn't recognize you, Miss Amira," Brenda says as she guides her daughter to a chair and sits in the one next to her. Shaleen leaves her chair and climbs onto her mother's lap. "Sweetie, you recognize Miss Amira without that long hair?"

Shaleen shakes her head.

"I do look different, Shaleen. I bet you recognize my voice though, right?"

The child nods.

"How've you been this week?" I ask.

"This one's having a hard time, ma'am," Brenda says.

"I'm sorry to hear that," I say.

Neither one is naturally effusive, so I suspect they haven't been talking about the flood at home and don't want to now either. "Can you say more about that?"

"Storm wasn't big. A lot of rain. You know."

"Actually, I was out of town."

"Lucky you."

I nod. "So what happened?"

Shaleen sinks her knees to the floor and buries her face in her mother's lap.

Brenda strokes her child's hair. "Dog wouldn't come in. Swam a long time. Didn't make it." A tear rolls down Brenda's cheek.

"Oh no. Brenda, Shaleen, I'm awfully sorry!"

Shaleen looks up. She makes eye contact for about a second, then buries her face again.

"We tried to be real comforting, soothing, like you showed us. Didn't seem to help. This one crawled into bed with us. Hasn't left. Every night, she's tossing and turning."

Of course Shaleen is tossing and turning and acting like a toddler. She just watched floodwaters rise, threaten her home, and kill her dog. Her mom is visibly worried also, which makes perfect sense. This family has been through a lot in a short time. I jot a quick note about Shaleen's behavior change in her file.

I ask the child a few questions, carefully avoiding the subject of the dog. The last thing she needs is for me to trigger a trauma response when she's in this state. The girl doesn't respond until I question her mother about her own dreams. After Brenda admits to having nightmares, I ask Shaleen if she was scared during the storm, and she looks at me and nods.

If the child were in a better state, I'd see if she wanted to make a picture or play with one of the toys. But she's not, so I focus on having a gentle chat with Brenda that Shaleen can overhear. It will help both of them. Brenda needs help processing her feelings about the event, and Shaleen will feel reassured knowing that her mom is being cared for. If we're lucky, the girl will open up a bit by the end of the session.

"Did the water reach the inside of your home?" I ask.

"We were trapped inside with the water real high, but it didn't come in the house. Thank God we elevated it after Katrina."

"What a relief!"

"My gardens though... All the kale and tomatoes and winter squash mildewed and rotted."

"I'm sorry. Your gardens mean so much to you." Their vegetable garden is important to them financially as well as emotionally.

She nods and kisses the top of Shaleen's head. "But if this doesn't remind us of what really matters, I don't know what can."

I smile, catching her gaze. "It's family, isn't it?"

"Sure is," she says, I think more for her daughter's benefit than mine.

"How's the rest of the family, Brenda?" I ask, thinking about the twelve-year-old stoic they call Sloop and Brenda's burly man's man of a husband.

"Sloop's coming in after us."

"Good. You two don't mind if I make a picture while we talk, do you? I have these new sparkly crayons I wanna try. Brenda, you're welcome to make a picture too."

"I'd love to," she says, getting the hint.

Forty minutes later, the pair leave with pictures of safe spaces in hand. Although Brenda made the picture to encourage Shaleen to do so, the activity seemed to soothe her nerves as well. She drew a picture of a garden, something she may not be able to have much longer if she and her family try to stick it out in Pointe-aux-Chênes. But since neither she nor her husband nor her children have ever lived anywhere else, that's hard for them to envision.

I slide the sand table and toys against the wall, then notice Brenda's son Raymond standing in the doorway, as if he's unsure what to do. I welcome him, using his nickname. "Hey, Sloop."

He's tall and thin with a walk that makes it seem like he's riding a horse. He does a double take when he sees me, then flops into the chair across from me without saying a word. Sloop is a little precocious, and in the past year he's adopted a tough-guy facade.

"You back in school yet?" I ask.

"Yup," he says.

Our sessions often start like this, with me asking simple questions and him responding with one-word answers.

"How's school been?"

"Boring."

"I bet it's nothing compared to the excitement of that flood. Did you like that?"

He shrugs.

"Have you seen those people on YouTube who go out of their way to take videos of storms and tornadoes?"

He shakes his head no.

"People actually go to the storms to take photos and videos."

"Cool."

"How did you feel during the storm? Scared? Excited? A little bit of both?"

"Both," he says, looking directly at me. Good. He's engaging, so I know we can go a little further.

"That makes sense. I can see how you might feel scared because you don't know what's going to happen. You don't know if everybody will be safe. But you might feel excited because you don't know what's going to happen. There's a sense of adventure there. Did I get that?"

"You got it."

"What else happened?"

"Dog died."

"I'm sorry, Sloop. What happened?"

"Drowned."

"Oh no! She was your dog, wasn't she?"

"Had her from a puppy," he says, his voice cracking. "Sorry."

"You don't have to apologize for being upset. Never in here, never with me."

His lip quivers.

"You had her from a puppy. Who trained her?"

"I did."

"You did a good job training her, didn't you," I say.

"Not good enough," he says and breaks down, wrapping his lanky arms around himself.

I hand him the box of tissues. He takes one and blows his nose.

"I called her and called her. Pumpkin just wouldn't come. Just went out there swimming."

"What do you think she was after?"

"I don't know."

"Do you think she was afraid? Confused?"

He shrugs.

"Do you ever feel afraid and confused?"

He nods with his whole upper body, rocks back and forth, hunching over, sobbing. "Feel that way a lot."

"Sometimes, when we're feeling confused and frightened, we do things that don't make sense to anybody else."

"But why didn't she come?" he asks.

"I don't know, Sloop. What do you think?"

He shrugs.

"What do you remember about that day?"

"It was dark. The wind was loud and the rain on the roof... We couldn't hardly hear ourselves talking to each other inside."

"So it was hard to hear over the storm," I reflect.

"It was, and..." Sloop looks at me, his face opening as realization dawns on him. "Maybe she couldn't hear me over the storm."

I nod. "I bet Pumpkin wanted to come but was confused by all the sounds."

It's possible this understanding will help alleviate the guilt Sloop feels. But I'm going to dig a little deeper to help him process the helplessness and trauma of watching someone he loved die.

"So it was loud with the rain on the roof and the wind. And it was dark. Was it nighttime or was the sky dark from clouds?"

"Clouds. And there was lightning striking nearby."

"How did that feel?"

"It was too close. It would flash and then boom right after. That's what spooked Pumpkin. She was going crazy on the porch, looking for something. The water was rising so fast. I tried to get her inside, but she wouldn't come. Tried to lift her. She's squirrelly and heavy and she jumped out of my arms, tried to go down the stairs. Good six feet from the porch to the ground. By then the water was about four feet. I wanted to go after her, but Daddy said no way. Said the current would carry me."

"And then what happened?"

"He made me come inside. I watched through the window till I couldn't see her no more. She swam against the current at first, then it carried her away. Wednesday, the Aucoins found her in their yard, couple of miles down the road."

"Oh, Sloop. I'm so sorry."

He looks up at me, his eyes rimmed red.

"What happened after the Aucoins found her?"

"Daddy and me drove over and put her in the back of the truck."

"And then?"

"Brought her to the vet, and they took care of her. Her eyes were the worst part," Sloop says, shaking his head as if to clear the memory. "And the smell."

Sloop goes on to tell me about his little sister's behavior. He's disturbed by her whining and sucking her thumb. He tells me that Shaleen used to take naps curled up against the dog's belly.

Envisioning the scene, I understand the little girl's reaction even more. "It sounds like both you and your sister are feeling very sad about Pumpkin."

Sloop nods, sniffling again. "Darn it."

"It's okay, Sloop. You know what?"

"What?"

"I'd be worried about you if you weren't feeling sad right now."

"Huh?"

"You've been through a lot, and you lost someone you love so much. Of course you're sad. Of course you need to cry. That's a healthy response."

He looks at me, raising an eyebrow. "It's healthy?"

"Mm. Feelings are part of being human. You're sad now. That's okay. You will be happy again sometime, but for now, it's okay to feel sad. It's okay to cry. You understand? It's holding our feelings in that makes us start acting out."

By the end of the session, Sloop seems to accept that it's okay for him to feel sad and confused. I make a note in the file about grief rituals. I might mention something in my next session with Brenda. This family might be willing to try a grief ritual, and it could be an excellent tool for healing.

Before my next patient arrives, I take a minute to meditate. A knock sounds on the door at the same time as my phone vibrates, and a message from Derek flashes across the screen:

Thinking I'll say something to Lila at dinner tonight. Like: *I shouldn't have gone behind your mom's back. I was trying to help but crossed her parenting boundaries.* How's that?

Good, I think, but I'll have to read it more carefully and respond to Derek later.

I open the door, and Ruby Boudreaux, a seventeen-year-old radical activist with half her head shaved and multiple piercings, glances at my head, nods, and strides in like she's on a runway. "Nice look, Miss Amira."

"Thanks. You too, Ruby."

Today's outfit is brilliant purple and black with feathers and sequins. She stands out in this part of Louisiana and has been itching to get to New Orleans for the past couple of years. I think she could hold her own at New Orleans U, maybe even at Loyola, if she can drop the conspiracy theories. Before she even reaches the chair, she's talking about the political ramifications of the flood. Staying in her head helps her process the trauma without getting overwhelmed by it.

"People got no place to go on the island when they lose their homes. Houses keep disappearing. But the Army Corps built them new fishing piers all along the road out to the Isle. How come they can build that but can't rebuild someone's house?"

"That's a good question."

"Everyone's real charged up about whether to stay or move to that new community up here."

"What do you feel about it?

"We don't wanna be forced to move by any government."

"I don't blame you. Do you think the government's forcing people out?"

"Some people say it is."

"Do you believe them?"

At this point, I could remind Ruby that the community leaders worked with nonprofits and the federal government for many years to make this resettlement happen, to preserve the culture while bringing people to safety. But my role here isn't to teach politics. It's to help this girl deal with the traumatic experience she had when her home flooded. Besides, the issue is so complex.

We unpack Ruby's thoughts about community and personal freedom for a while before she starts to express her feelings, the fears she holds for her grandparents and elderly neighbors. Typically, teens focus on their friends, who—neurologically—they correlate to the future. But Ruby isn't a typical teen by a long shot. I wonder what she'll do when faced with the decision to move away from her family and community for college.

After Ruby strides out, Christian saunters in. His emotional burdens are all over his face, and at fifteen, his hair is already thinning from his nervous habit of pulling it out. He was having nightmares a week ago before he flunked his math test. Now he says he's not sleeping at all. Instead, he stays up mapping escape routes.

There can't be many. None of the homes on Isle de Jean Charles are very large, and there's only one road leading into and out of the town.

I write "increased hypervigilance" in his file and listen to him describe what happened to him and his dad during the flood.

Of all my patients, he may be the one who's most traumatized. It's not that what happened to him was worse, but his thoughts about what happened and the sense of complete aloneness he feels that makes the flood more traumatic. Ruby's focusing on her grandparents and elderly neighbors. The LaForce family is tight-knit and all channeling their grief into the loss of Pumpkin. Christian lost his mom to cancer several years ago, and his dad shut down emotionally and never quite opened back up. I worry about this kid.

I bring the toys and art supplies out again for session number five with the large, rambunctious Courteaux family. Both parents and all four kids have big personalities, which makes for lots of friction. Adding trauma to the mix makes this family dynamic nightmarish at times.

Of course, the session runs over, which means I'm unlikely to get home by three-fifteen. Shoot.

As we finish, I confirm our next appointment and try to maintain my calm, cheerful demeanor while asserting the fact that this session is over. I really need to go. But the toddler is distracted by the little people playhouse, which gives the eldest child a reason to scold and the mom a reason to chastise and on and on.

I need to find a different time of day to meet with this family. They are lovely people. They need my help, or someone's help, maybe not mine. Lila needs me too, though she may not want to admit that anymore. I hate to leave, but I have got to go.

28
RePrioritize

Amira

SINCE THE SESSION WITH THE COURTEAUX FAMILY RAN late, I am going to be late to pick up my kid unless I make good time getting back from Houma. Of course, because I need to hurry, the traffic on the highway is unbearably slow. What is going on?

Lila texts me, and the fancy rental car asks if I want it to read the message. Of course I do.

"Can you pick me up early? I don't feel good," the mechanical voice says.

Shit. "Siri, call Lila."

"Hi, Mama. Are you coming now?"

"Sweetie, I'm on the highway."

"Mama, please!"

"Lila, I'm too far away. I'm sorry. What's going on?"

It seems like everyone ahead of me is driving around something. I follow the line of cars veering into the breakdown lane to get around a big piece of tire. Wait. It's moving. That's not a Mack truck tire.

"Oh my goodness! Honey, there's a baby alligator in the highway!"

"Awww. Poor thing! Can you rescue it?"

"Are you crazy? I'm not the crocodile hunter."

"But it's a baby."

"Lila, you know as well as I, even baby alligators can bite your hand off. Poor little guy. It must've escaped the Barataria preserve. Anyway, I'm driving as fast as I can, but I guess you'd better walk to Derek's. I'm sorry."

Lila grumbles into the phone. "I can't walk seven blocks like this."

My heart thuds. "Like what? What happened? Are you injured?"

"I'm bleeding," she hisses.

"Bleeding. What happened?"

"Shhh. I don't have my earbuds, and people can hear you."

"Lila," I say in a lower tone. "What's going on? Why are you bleeding?"

I wish I could look at her face right now, see her affect. "Honey? Talk to me please."

I hear the sound of tween boys laughing. "I've gotta go," Lila says. "God, they're such jerks." She hangs up.

Is she being made fun of at school? Are they bullying her? Why is she bleeding? There's still hope I can get to school in time if I just pick up the pace. I thought I was getting better at setting boundaries, but how do you tell a five-year-old and their mother you have to stop when they're finally talking about the problem?

Forty-five minutes later, I tell Siri to text Lila: "Are you still at school?"

At Derek's.

I drive onto Nashville Street with its manicured lawns and lush flower beds. As I pull into the driveway at Derek's house, my body starts to relax. Home-*ish*. Not our home, but a clean, safe place to stay until we find a new apartment. True, it would have been even better if I was able to pick her up or even if I could have been here when she got home, but at least it's not like she's sitting outside the school waiting for me like so many other times. As soon as I walk in, I hear the TV.

"Hey," I say. "Did you do your homework?"

"Well, you weren't home," she says, not looking at me.

"What does that have to do with anything?" I ask. "You know the rules."

"Different house, different rules, right? Besides, if you're not following the rules why do I have to?"

I take a deep breath and let it out slowly. What's going on here? Is she acting out because we're in an unfamiliar situation? Is she getting unpleasantly fresh because of the age? Does this have something to do with the experience in the storm? Is this her trauma response? Dammit. I'm much better at this with other people's children.

"Let's have a snack, hon. Are you hungry?"

She holds up a bag of potato chips, makes an extra loud crunching sound.

"Well, I hope you saved some for me," I say, plopping down on the couch, wrapping my arm around her shoulder and kissing the top of her head.

"Mom," she grumbles, pulling away. My cuddly girl? Pulling away? This is not good.

"Lila, what's going on? What happened today? Hey. Weren't you wearing that white outfit when you went to school? Oh! Oh no."

Her face crumples. "Uh-huh. My new pants are ruined, and all the boys made fun of me when they saw the blood on the chair, and..."

"I'm sorry, honey." I try again to embrace her, and this time she lets me, sort of. "We'll get the stain out of your pants. And, if we can't, just this once, we'll go buy you the same pair."

"It was the last one in the store," she cries.

"Then we'll look online. Oh, Lila. What a drag to get your first period at school."

"I have to deal with this every month now?"

"Welcome to womanhood."

"It really sucked that you couldn't pick me up. I had to walk home with my backpack behind me. I'm pretty sure every car that passed me slowed down to stare."

"I'm sorry. I'm trying to be better about setting boundaries with my patients. You know you're more important to me than anyone or anything. And in the midst of listening to a little kid who just lost their dog in a flood and has been having nightmares every night since, isn't eating..."

"Yeah, Mama, I get it. They're suffering."

My heart sinks. "Honey, I will do better. I promise. What are you watching anyway?"

"Buffy the Vampire Slayer."

"How long until it's over?"

"I don't know."

She's playing on my guilt. It's working. I feel more guilty than I did when I walked in the door. And I know if I act from that feeling, it will backfire. I take a deep breath and squat between her and the television. "I know you've had a bad day, and I'm truly sorry. But you need to do your homework. Is that clear? When your homework is finished, we can watch the rest of this show together or another show."

She scowls at me.

"I understand you're upset with me. That's fine, but it's not a reason to be irresponsible."

"You were irresponsible."

"Not even close. I had trouble managing my responsibilities to you and to my patients at the same time. I didn't choose to not show up for work or for you simply because I felt some kinda way. I was there, and now I'm here. You have a responsibility to finish your schoolwork. You can feel whatever you feel. But you don't get to not show up. Is that clear?"

"Yes, Mama," she grumbles.

"Good. I'll be sitting here making some phone calls and billing insurance companies. Where will you be doing your homework?"

"By the pool."

"Great. Once you show me all your completed homework, then we can watch something together or look for apartments online if you want."

"Can I just go to Phoebe's?"

"Actually, I think it's important for us to have some mother-daughter time right now."

"Until Derek gets home."

I sigh. When *is* Derek getting home? It's Wednesday. Did he say he had a surgery today? Derek's a big boy. He can take care of himself. Lila needs my attention.

"I'll let him know you and I are spending the evening alone. Okay? Now, turn this off please," I say, pointing to the television. In theory, I could turn it off, really make a statement about who's in charge. But I don't like to parent that way. Even if I did want to, I couldn't figure out how to turn off the TV. I don't see a power button on the set, and that remote control looks more intimidating than the alligator I saw on the highway today.

Lila presses a series of buttons on the remote until the screen goes dark, then grabs her book bag and leaves the room.

Billing. I didn't put that on my mind map. I spend hours billing insurance companies every week. Maybe I could hire a service for that. Maybe that would cost less than an answering service, and having someone else do my billing would definitely save time.

I walk into the living room with a big bowl of hot, organic buttered popcorn and the six-pack of sodas Lila insisted we get from the health food store. She sprawls across the couch and presses a series of buttons on the remote. Derek's big-screen television beeps and plays some sort of tune. I don't understand what she's doing. Thank God she inherited these helpful tech traits from her father.

"See, Mama? Easy as pie," she says, pointing to the TV just as the logo to our video streaming service appears on the screen. It's like magic.

"So you just hooked up the television to the internet?" I ask, confused.

She shovels a handful of popcorn into her mouth. "It's not difficult, Mama."

"Maybe not for you. Popcorn is more my speed," I say, settling onto the couch.

Lila cuddles up next to me and reaches for a soda.

I crack open one of the sodas, take a sip, pull a face.

She laughs. "It's not that bad."

"I'm sure the popcorn will help it taste better." I miss the sweet taste of the classic cola I'm used to buying.

"Come on! It's just 'cause this one is sweetened with stevia. I like it, but maybe next time we should get the one made with cane sugar."

"Why didn't we get that one this time? Are you trying to torture me?"

The opening music and credits run for our all-time favorite romantic comedy. The faces of Meg Ryan and Tom Hanks fill the screen. My body melts into the sofa.

My phone vibrates, and Sage's face pops up on the screen.

"Oh, Lila, pause it for one sec please. She texted earlier she needs a favor. This will be quick."

Lila sighs but makes the movie stop anyway.

"Hi, there!"

"Mimi, how are you?"

"Good. How are you feeling?"

"Exhaustion set in after the show, but I'm recovering. Listen, I have a favor to ask, now that you're all safe and sound."

"Sure."

"You know the gallery down there on Royal had their open-ing the same night that we did in New Haven and the show was supposed to be up for the month. I haven't been able to reach anybody since the floods. I didn't wanna ask you before, but now that you're resettled, would you mind—"

"You want me to go check on things? See what I can find out?"

"That would be great."

"I'd be happy to."

"How are things with Derek?"

"Things?"

"Well, I mean, seems like you two got pretty close during that crisis. And Wesley said you're living with him?"

My heart starts pounding. "Just until we find a new place. Besides, he's doing a kind of fast."

Sage chuckles. "Wes told me about that. Good for him. If you look at his Instagram…"

"I have."

"Have you seen the change? It used to be, like, food and booze and women and travel. In the past few months it's morphed. Inspiring quotes and serene photos. Meditation. He's even got a photo of you and Lila after he shaved your head."

"I know. Isn't that fun?"

Now something else is throbbing. He put a photo of me on Instagram. Instant turn-on.

I take a deep breath, re-center. "Listen, Li and I were just watching a movie, but I'd love to chat with you. How about I call you after I check out the gallery? I'll go this week. K?"

"You're the best. I love you, and I love Lila. Give her a huge hug and kiss for me."

I end the call and point to the screen. "Ready?"

Just as Lila restarts the movie, the front door opens.

"Hello?" Derek calls.

Lila grumbles under her breath.

"We're in here," I call.

Derek strides in, looking incredibly fine in a pumpkin-colored button-down with mother-of-pearl buttons. He loosens his tie and sits next to me on the couch. "Hi," he says, his voice bright.

"Hi." I can't help but match his tone. Ever since Monday I've been in this weird state. Around him, I feel so light and free.

Lila nudges me with her foot. Right. Mother-daughter time. I squeeze her foot, which I hope will reassure her I haven't forgotten.

"How was your day? Did you eat? Lila and I were starving, so I made veggie kabobs and rice. That stove-top grill you have is supercool, by the way. And I saved you some."

Derek laughs. "Slow down, woman. You wanna show me where this is."

"It's on the stove, Derek," Lila says, not hiding her annoyance. Derek looks wounded.

I squeeze Lila's foot again this time in warning, then stand. I throw a pointed look at my daughter, then turn my attention to Derek. "Let me get you a plate, okay? Lila and I are watching a chick flick."

Derek follows me into the moonlit kitchen. As soon as we're alone, he whispers, "Did I do something?"

I shake my head. Lila would be mortified if I told him she's being hormonal and bled through her clothes. "My kid just needs some time alone with me. And Sage just called. We haven't managed our mother-daughter night yet."

"Oh," he says, and something in his tone tells me he understands but feels disappointed. "So you don't want me to say anything?"

"About what?"

"The text. I was going to tell Lila I was out of line during dinner but you ate."

"Shoot! Derek, I was going into session when your text came, and the rest of the day has been a blur. I meant to read it carefully and respond. I'm sorry."

"Don't think twice," he says, but his mouth is curled in a way that tells me I just hurt his feelings again. If not for this damn fast he's on, I'd hold him and comfort him and let him know he's okay. I care about him. Lila likes him. But he is on a damn fast, so all I can do is talk and hand him the plate I fixed him. I hope it's enough.

"She and I really need some time alone. Okay? You understand, right? The kid comes first, always. I really do appreciate your effort though. Maybe tomorrow over breakfast?"

Derek stands by the stove, holding the plate I offered. He removes the plastic wrap and takes a bite of a mushroom. "Mmm! Delicious. Thank you."

I run my fingers down his arm, wanting way more. "My pleasure. I hope we're not cramping your style, taking over the living room like this."

He shakes his head, presses his lips together like he's trying to be cool with it but isn't. "My home is yours. A little alone time will be good for me too."

"Thanks for understanding," I say over my shoulder as I return to the living room. He's trying to be cool with me and Lila taking mother-daughter time, but he isn't. And that is exactly why we can't stay through the New Year. If Derek and I are going to have any kind of romance, he needs to get right with my priorities.

29
Not Quite Ready

Derek

SHE RUNS HER FINGERS DOWN MY ARM, BUT SHE MAY AS well slide her hand down my pants. I'm on fire, and not only can't I satisfy my natural urge to take the woman right here and now, but also I can't even eat my damn dinner with her. I get that they need alone time. And, of course, her kid comes first. Always. I'm fully on board with that. I was trying to support that, to show them both I understand their needs, their priorities.

Just wish my body could get the message and understand why I can't have Amira right now, why she can't sit with me while I eat my dinner and look into my eyes and touch me some more and love up on me.

Wonder if I should be concerned about Lila's attitude tonight. She feeling some kinda way about me? She knows I just bought her a whole new wardrobe. Does she understand her own father wouldn't? I handed her a wad of cash, for Pete's sake. Doesn't that mean anything? Is entitlement a family trait?

Fuck. This isn't like me. I'm not petty. I don't give to be appreciated. I give because I like to help. And who am I jealous of? Amira's child? I'm not the jealous type. Am I? Who knows? I never let anyone get close enough to me after Riley to find out.

I was taking the high road when I said a little alone time would be good for me too. Actually, I guess it will. After I finish this fantastic meal—and what does she mean she's not a gourmet cook? She's phenomenal—I will shower and meditate and write in my journal. And I need to look at flights out to Santa Barbara. The men's retreat is in ten days, and I don't even have a plane ticket.

Am I ready for this program to end? I'm not sure. My body's ready. My body's screaming *end this damn fast so I can pounce on Amira.* And my heart aches to be closer to her. But am I *ready* for an actual relationship with a woman? I want Amira. But these thoughts, these petty, jealous thoughts. This need for her approval... Maybe I have a lot more work to do.

30
Shoe Budget

Derek

THE OATMEAL BUBBLES IN THE POT. I GIVE IT A QUICK stir, set the breakfast table for three, return to the stove, and finish the task. These women have me using coconut oil instead of butter. And I've got them enjoying my special addition of maple syrup, cinnamon, and ginger. Don't mind altering my recipe a bit for these two. To my surprise, I actually prefer the oatmeal with coconut oil.

"Yum," Lila says, coming into the kitchen.

I'm glad she's here first, and I'm nervous. Should I broach the subject before Amira comes down or at the table when we're all together? Don't want Lila to feel ganged up on, but I don't want Amira to feel undermined again. I'm not the parent. When I think about it, my parents broached most important matters together.

I set the orange juice on the table, pour another cup of coffee for myself and one for Amira, just as she strolls into the room.

"Good morning," she says, kissing her daughter on the head and smiling at me.

When we're all at the table, I take a deep breath and look from Amira to Lila. Here goes. "Listen, Lila, I need to clear the air about something."

"Okay?" She meets my eyes with curiosity.

"I was out of line the other day, texting you about money and then giving you cash without checking in with your mom first."

Lila looks from her mom to me. Amira nods at me as if to encourage me to finish.

"Your mom's got your back. I know that. You know that. I was trying to be helpful and fun, but the way I did it wasn't cool. I crossed some boundaries with your mom, and I'm sorry for that. Now, what's done is done. The money's yours, and you and your mom can decide how you spend it. But I won't be giving you more spending money unless your mom and I discuss it first and she agrees that it's a good idea for whatever reason. We clear?"

"Uh-huh." Lila digs into her oatmeal.

"Thanks, Derek. Lila, let's find a time to do more school shopping. You can spend the money then."

"I can get those shoes!"

The matching smiles that brighten the faces of both mother and daughter melt my heart.

"Maybe. This will be a good opportunity for you to do some budgeting of your own. We'll figure that out before we go."

That went better than I hoped. Way better. Maybe we're figuring this money thing out.

31
Brainstorm

Amira

"Can we go shopping today, Mama?" Lila asks from the back seat. "Ooh, watch out!"

I jam on the brakes to avoid hitting the older couple before they step in front of the car. Of course, they're staring at their phones and a map.

"See girls? This is why we don't text and walk."

"We know," Lila grumbles. "So can we go today?"

"I think this weekend will be better."

"Can Phoebe come?"

"If her parents agree."

The girls squeal and lapse into excited chatter as if I'm not here.

Driving through the French Quarter is impossible on a good day. Now that the city is starting to reopen to tourists, traffic is a mess, so I let the girls out in front of the library and watch them mount the steps into the atrocious modern building. Then I park in the lot down the block and walk down Tulane Avenue toward the French Quarter.

As I turn onto Burgundy Street, a memory flashes before my eyes: two-year-old Lila meeting two-year-old Phoebe in the library children's room. They fall into easy play on the colorful rug while Elara and I, both sleep-deprived and bleary-eyed, introduce ourselves.

Ten years later, they're visiting that same library to write a report for school about its latest art exhibit. The work depicts a future that Elara and I could not have envisioned for our children, a future in a world that's falling apart.

And as that world falls apart, society does as well, one family at a time. How often have I suggested that the Courteaux family bring their two-, three-, and five-year-old to the library story hour, just to give themselves a break from their little bundles of energy? They say their library is too far away to make regular visits. I did persuade them to stay for the story time happening in the community center after I left. Of course, that meant the two older children would be bored and trapped and have nothing to do but look at their screens.

I sigh and turn onto Toulouse Street. These narrow streets give me claustrophobia, so I focus on what I see: the way the brick sidewalks are laid out in a herringbone pattern, the Creole Cottages with their low roofs and stucco walls painted in soothing muted colors.

All the Courteaux kids were coughing the other day. I hope the parents will bring the family to the doctor for asthma screenings. Do they have black mold growing in their house? If so, it's opening them up to permanent lung damage and permanent brain damage. That could make their highly energetic children even more difficult to manage and give the parents fewer mental resources to deal with the constant stress of life. Jacque and Stella Courteaux need a respite.

The library story time was such a respite for me and for Elara. In those early years, it was one of the few times in the week that Lila got to play with other children her age. Greg and I always read books to her. But there was something special about hearing a story as part of a group and being read to by her special friend the librarian. Wouldn't it be wonderful if a program like that could serve double duty? What would happen if a library story time program also became a mental and physical wellbeing screening program? The city doesn't have anything like this right now. Does the state? Maybe the state of Louisiana doesn't have the resources to run a program like that.

32
Churning Things Up

Derek

THE SMELL OF SUGAR HITS ME AS SOON AS I OPEN THE door to Leah's Pralines. "We make everything proudly by hand and from scratch," a sign proclaims.

Lila loves pecan brittle. She's a great kid; someone I'd be proud to call my stepdaughter. With Halloween coming, I want this girl, and more importantly her mother, to know I want them in my life. These two talk about Leah's all the time like it's some Holy Grail. They love the pralines, the dark chocolate turtles, and mostly the pecan brittle. Not my taste, but I'm not the one I'm shopping for.

On the other side of a glass window, a large mixer churns something that looks like caramel. The young lady behind the counter offers me a sample. I place the confection on my tongue, and that's when I hear it. A husky female voice: "Derek?"

Every muscle in my body goes tense. I turn slowly.

"Derek, it is you," she rasps.

Standing before me, tall, gorgeous, with her wavy blond hair draped over one shoulder, characteristically wearing too much makeup, body trim as ever, Riley strikes a pose.

My mouth does something of its own accord. I don't try to force a smile, but it's almost an autonomic response, isn't it? See a familiar face; the lips curve up.

"Riley," I say.

"What are you doing here?" she asks.

"Buying pralines and brittle."

"I mean in New Orleans."

"Right. I moved here a while back. What about you?"

"I'm here with my husband. We've always wanted to experience Halloween in New Orleans."

"Have you," I say, wondering what number husband this is. Has she managed to keep one and cheat on him? Or does she keep going through them? Ice runs through my veins as I stare into her bloodshot eyes. "Where is the man?"

"He's meeting me at Arnaud's."

"That's the place for oysters."

"It's so nice to see you," she says.

"Is it?"

"Oh, Derek, don't be like that. I miss you."

"Huh."

"Anyway, we're living in Brookline now. But New Orleans at Halloween, well, it's on the bucket list, and..."

"Of course you have a bucket list."

I don't know what to do to get rid of her or why she's chattering away as if we're old friends. I place my order, let the woman behind the counter know I'm in a hurry, which I wasn't until about three minutes ago. When she hands me the order, I interrupt Riley's rambling. "Enjoy yourself."

I leave the store and start down the street. A moment later, Riley's yelling my name outside.

"Derek, please! Wait!"

I keep walking, hoping she'll think I don't hear her, but Riley keeps calling. For some reason, I slow and let her catch up. She reaches me, places a trembling hand on my arm. She's always had nerves of steel and a solid build from tennis. Why's she trembling?

"You left your wallet on the counter," she says, handing it to me.

"This is a change of pace: you giving me my money instead of trying to take it from me," I say, then almost regret the words.

She laughs, a note of sadness in her voice. "Derek, that was so long ago. I'm over all that now."

"You on medication?"

She taps my arm playfully, gives my bicep a squeeze. "You've still got it."

"Oh, Jesus Christ, Riley. Now that you're married to someone else, you want me?"

Her face turns serious. "Listen, I knew you'd moved down here. You don't answer my calls."

"Blocked your number years ago."

"Oh." Her face falls. "Well, maybe I deserved it, but I never stopped loving you."

"Huh. I was under the impression you never started. Listen, it's been fun, but I've gotta run."

I walk toward my car. I've got a few more errands, but all I want to do now is go home and shower.

"I'm sick, Derek!"

"No shit," I say, but something in her voice tells me that was a mistake.

"Really, Derek." She catches up with me again. "I came down here to tell you, to make amends."

33
Visions

Amira

As I turn onto Royal Street with its slate sidewalks and cheerful shops, the vision of a library story time screening program expands in my mind. What if I created a nonprofit birth-to-five screening program for the state's public libraries? So many children and families could benefit. There would be no stigma attached to the assessment process; families wouldn't even have to know they were being screened. But if the social worker noticed the signs of family upheaval, signs of mental or physical illness, they could offer resources.

Thinking about this idea fills my body with energy. I think this program could be possible, and I think I could create it.

The door to the art gallery is wide open, and no one seems to notice or care when I enter. A crew of four scrubs the mildew off the walls. Sage's artwork seems unaffected except for one piece. Darn it. It's a six-foot-tall print of the tornado piece that upset me when I saw the original in New Haven. Due to its height, it extends closer to the floor, and judging by the placement of the mildew stains, the water must have risen about five inches above the bottom of the artwork. I snap photos of each piece of art and shoot several images of the damaged tornado piece.

"Excuse me, what are you doing?"

I turn toward the sound of the voice, where an older gentleman removes a respirator mask and rises from the floor.

"I'm taking photos for the artist. She can't make it down from Connecticut and hasn't been able to reach the owners."

"That would be me. You know Sage?"

"All my life."

"Shit. Tell her we're doing the best we can down here. I'll call her in the next week to talk about extending her show."

"Sure thing. I live here too. She knows we've been under it."

"No doubt. How's your mama an' them?"

"They live up north, so they're fine. Thanks for asking. Yours?"

"All right. Minimal damage this time. Take as many pictures as she wants. You don't mind, I'll get back to work on this mold."

"Of course. What should I tell her about the tornado piece?"

He shakes his head. "It's a damn powerful image. Hate that it was destroyed like this."

"I know."

"But our insurance'll cover it, so we'll pay her direct and wait for reimbursement. She wants to send another augmented print, we'd love to have it."

I snap a few more photos and text them to Sage, along with the message from the gallery owner. She texts back a request for more close-ups of the damaged piece. I hope I'm getting what she needs. I'm struggling to focus because my mind keeps racing back to the nonprofit idea.

If I run a program and hire newly minted licensed clinical social workers, I could have the best of both worlds: helping families, maybe even developing relationships with them, without providing direct service myself. Plus I'd be providing on-the-job training for young therapists.

Just thinking about this idea makes me feel like a success. Now I'm going to celebrate with Leah's pecan brittle for all of us: me, the girls, Elara and Zaki, and for Derek to take on his trip tomorrow.

I bid goodbye to the gallery owner and step into the sunlight and fresh air. I turn toward St. Louis Street, and that's when I see them.

34

Letting Go

Derek

I LOOK RILEY DEAD IN THE EYE. SICK? MAKE AMENDS?
Is she serious?

"I know I hurt you. What I did was wrong. I lied over and over, betrayed your trust in so many ways for so many years. Now I'm on my fifth husband and trying not to screw it up. It's easier when I have so little energy, believe it or not. I have ovarian cancer like my mom did."

Ovarian cancer kills swiftly. My body goes numb. "Prognosis?"

"Always the doctor first." She chuckles with no trace of cruelty. "I've got about a month left."

I nod, dazed. "Any kids?"

"Just Scott and me. Dad passed a few years ago. I made amends with my sister, my other three ex-husbands. I needed to find you. I don't want you living another day, thinking I still blame you for the problems in our marriage. You weren't perfect.

No one is, but I really screwed up. And I made matters worse during the divorce. I'm sorry, Derek, and I hope you can find it in your heart to forgive me, for your sake as well as mine."

At the moment, seems like the only thing I can do is breathe. So, I'm breathing. Watching her face. Breathing. Now I see the cheekbones are a little too prominent. The collarbones too obvious. She's not trim from tennis. She's skin and bones from chemo and a killer disease. The makeup on her face covers the jaundice that's evident on her hands and neck.

"Riley," I say, my voice breaking and surprising even me. "It means a lot you coming down here to find me. And I do forgive you. But how'd you know where I'd be? Leah's, of all places."

"That was just dumb luck. I was going to call the hospital and find out when your shift ended, see if I could wait for you outside."

"You've always been a little outside the box, Ri."

"I think you mean crazy, and yeah. You're right. It's part of my charm. Can I hug you?"

I open my arms, and she walks into them. I haven't touched this woman in over ten years. Used to be a spark between us. That's long gone. In its place is familiarity and compassion. She squeezes me, and I kiss the top of her head, whisper a blessing into her hair, then release the hug.

We look into each other's eyes. I don't think either of us has words for this moment. She touches her fingers to her lips, and I place my hand on my heart and watch her walk away.

35

Trust

Amira

THE SIMPLE FACT IS: MEN CANNOT BE TRUSTED. I FEAR for Sage but hope that Wesley is an exception to the rule. My father proved it. My brother proved it. My ex-husband proved it. And now Derek is proving it.

Just when I finally trusted someone, there he goes, supposedly on his female fast, hugging a woman in the middle of Saint Louis Street. Kissing the top of her head. Looking into her eyes.

Here I am, heading to Leah's to buy treats for him, and he's being romantic with a woman—exactly what he said he wouldn't do.

I should have known. In fact, I did know; I knew it the moment I met him—the man's too charming. He was too charming; he is too charming. What else is there to know? I don't need anyone to tell me what I intuited from the start, and my intuition is always correct. My chest hurts like someone stabbed it, and my body trembles.

I don't think we will stay with him through the holidays. I'll find a place this weekend. His financial help is nice, but I don't need a man. And if I'm going to be with one, it's going to be one I can trust, and if I can't trust him, I'm just not interested. That's all there is to it. I don't care how gorgeous he is or how safe he makes me feel when he speaks. I'm glad nothing happened between us. It's a huge relief.

Derek and his lover part. She walks toward me apparently clueless. And why *would* he tell her about me? We never really started anything. He just said some nice words, helped me out a bit.

He goes in the opposite direction, thank God. I walk past her, overwhelmed by a cloud of expensive, cloying perfume, and stride into Leah's. I still have something to celebrate, so I order treats for everyone except that man. After this, I'm going to the bank.

36
Toxic Residue

Derek

𝕴'M STILL PROCESSING THE RUN-IN WITH RILEY AS I PULL into the driveway. As soon I see Amira on the patio, I want to tell her everything, how shocking it was to see my ex and how unclean I felt until she told me she was sick, and all the emotions that churned up. I want to tell Amira, but I can't. It's humiliating.

Besides, she doesn't need to hear about my issues any more than she already has. She keeps saying she's burned out from vicarious trauma, listening to other people's suffering all day. I don't blame her. I wouldn't want her job, though she does it heroically.

Now here I come with my little ex-wife problems. It's not actually a problem though, more of an emotional experience that I *will* get over. The blood pulses in my ears, loud as a drum beat.

Amira

DEREK STANDS ON THE OTHER SIDE OF THE SLIDING GLASS doors, smiling, a package in his hand.

I don't get up from the deck chair but refocus my gaze on the iPad in front of me. Billing services don't cost as much as I thought they would. I scan the same line of information three times before I realize I'm not taking in the words.

Derek joins me on the deck chair as if we're friends. The nerve.

"Did we have plans?" I ask, keeping my voice cool. It irritates me that I actually feel excited to see him, the liar.

"We didn't. Did I catch you in the middle of something?"

"Actually, yes."

"Oh... sorry. I guess I forgot my manners. Thought maybe it'd be okay to interrupt."

"We're not in Boston. We're in a city with a small-town feel, and people in New Orleans often see each other doing things."

"Okay," he says, sounding confused. "Umm, so you're... working. Can I interrupt?"

"Derek, you know, I just..." I try to retrain my attention on my iPad.

"Hey, do we need to talk?"

"I'm not sure it's worth my time."

"Huh? What happened?"

"How's your female fast going? Did you decide to end it early?"

"Um, no. Why would you ask?"

"It was supposed to end after your retreat this weekend, right? Must have been hard to keep it going though, so many pretty women in New Orleans."

"I've managed. Been hard to resist one woman in particular though," he says.

He places a hand lightly on my leg, and my body blossoms. Darn it.

I feel his gaze on me, but I avoid returning it. I don't wanna fall prey to his sweet talk anymore, and if I look into his eyes, I am far more likely to do that.

"Kinda seems like we're about to have our first argument. Where's Lila? Don't want her to overhear."

"Are you questioning my parenting now, after what you've done?"

"I thought we were over the *giving Lila money* issue."

"She has long, wavy blond hair, and I saw her kissing you in the street just two hours ago. I guess you decided to end this fast early."

He takes a deep breath and lets it out slowly like he's trying to stay calm. "Nope, I've been working wicked hard at it because there's been one temptation staring me in the face since that fateful flight home from Hartford."

"It's funny, because I would think you were talking about me, if I hadn't just seen…"

"Amira, you are the one," he says and tries to cup my face in his palms.

I back away. "I know what I saw, Derek."

He stares at me a moment, a wounded look on his face, lips curled into a pout. "Why don't you believe me? I thought you trusted me."

The sad face, the soft voice. I'm not falling for his manipulations. He tries again to touch me, this time reaching for my shoulder.

I stand and move out of reach. "I did trust you, and I was wrong. That was a mistake on my part."

"It wasn't a mistake. I haven't betrayed your trust."

"Then what were you doing with that woman?"

A sweat breaks on his forehead. "I don't have to explain myself to you."

"If you wanna talk to me, you do."

"I'm not stooping to this."

"To what, Derek? The truth? To honesty and transparency? You're not gonna stoop to that? Are you too good for honesty and transparency? Because those are the foundations of any kind of relationship with me, not just romantic, but friendship, and even a working relationship. I wish you the best of luck."

"Whoa." He holds up his hands. "Amira, please calm down. Let's talk about this."

"There's nothing to talk about. I'm asking you to tell me what you were up to, and you're refusing. I have no further questions."

Derek stares at me, open-mouthed, for a long moment, then lowers his eyes in something that looks like disappointment. "Wow. Why'd I even bother with this fast? You females are all alike."

I laugh. "From the man with the black book."

"There is no black book. But you women sure do have a playbook. All this 'No, Derek, it's too much!' Just a front."

"A front? For what?"

He sings the opening lines of Kanye's "Gold Digger." What a jerk. Money's the last thing on my mind, and he knows it.

"Thought you were different, Amira. Thought you had substance, but I guess you just know how to dig deeper than most."

"Wow."

"You wanted my cash all along, didn't you? Just like Riley. But you manipulated me in a different way. You got me thinking I had to persuade you to let me help you." He says it like he's some detective on a mystery show, putting the final pieces of the murder together. Except in this case, he's the murderer, and the victim is our relationship.

"You know what?" I pull the cash that I retrieved from the bank out of my wallet and throw it at him. "I've had it with you and your fake generosity. We're getting out of here ASAP. And take my picture off your Instagram page. My child and I will not be part of your female trap."

"You like being canceled?" He taps his phone hard like he's trying to injure it, then holds it up for me to see. "You got it!"

Lila and I no longer grace his Instagram feed.

My heart pounds an insane and unpleasant rhythm. This does not feel good.

Where the hell will we go? I'll figure it out. I don't have to leave tonight, do I? Thank God Lila's sleeping at Phoebe's tonight.

37
Gold Digger

Derek

THE BOX OF PRALINES AND BRITTLE HEAVY IN MY HAND, I stand and slump toward the kitchen, playing "Gold Digger" on my phone and ignoring the money she just threw on the patio.

Fake generosity? How could she assume, after everything I've done for her, that I would lie? I know I could have told her about Riley's surprise, but why the hell should I? Don't I have any credibility with this woman? I have kept her and her kid safe. I've been supporting them. I haven't laid a seductive hand on her. I even opened up to her, except about this one thing.

Riley's presence in my life was, and became again today, a nightmare, but thank God for it. Something needed to show me what Amira's really capable of.

I stalk up to my bedroom. It smells sweet and light like Amira, and the scent gives me an erection and a stomachache simultaneously.

Get moving, Derek.

The duffel bag is in my closet, along with the clothes I want to pack for the retreat. I throw in everything that makes sense for Santa Barbara's temperate weather, retrieve my shave kit from the guest bathroom, then walk out to my car.

Once I'm halfway down the street, I tell my phone to call Ned.

Amira

A DOOR SLAMS FROM SOMEWHERE INSIDE THE HOUSE.

Yeah, real mature, Derek. You think I'm running after you? Hell no.

Then again, it dawns on me. He could be meditating, trying to cool down. There is the distinct possibility that he's going to come back out here in fifteen minutes or so, apologize, tell me what's up with that woman, and promise to never see her again.

I stand and stretch, do a few sun salutations just to clear my mind, then sit under the magnolia tree in the corner by the pool, set the timer on my phone for fifteen minutes, and meditate.

WHEN THE TIMER DINGS, I FEEL SLIGHTLY BETTER. DEREK has been trying to change his MO. He wants to be trustworthy. He hasn't come out yet, so I decide to give the process a little push.

No surprise, he's not in the kitchen. My guess is he's either meditating in his office or in the living room or maybe in the bedroom where I've been staying. His closet is there, and I know he needs to pack for his trip. I haven't heard water running, so he can't be in the shower.

The living room is empty. His office is empty.

"Derek?" I call softly as I run up the stairs. The bathroom door is wide open, and he's not there. My heartbeat speeds unpleasantly. The only sign of Derek in the bedroom is the open closet door. I peer out the window. My rental car is the only one in the driveway.

He didn't stay to apologize. Did he run to her?

I tap a quick message to him:

Where are you?

The messaging app lets me know he read the text. I stare at the screen and wait for a response.

Finally, the three moving dots turn into words.

Why do you care?

The air leaves my lungs, and I slide down to the floor.

Derek

Ned's raspy voice comes through the line. "Derek, what's up?"

"Dude, you're not gonna believe this. You know that woman I told you about?"

"You mean Amira? The one you've been calling and texting about almost every day for the past three weeks?"

"That one," I say as embarrassment surges through me, tightens my throat. "Oh, hold on."

The touch screen on my dash console shows a text message from Amira:

Where are you?

I stare at the road, slow with the traffic, stop at the light, recall the way the cash floated to the ground after she threw it at me. Since I'm stopped, I tap a response into my phone:

Why do you care?

She doesn't respond. And that's perfect because I'm done with her manipulations.

"So, what's up?" Ned asks.

"Sorry, she was just texting me."

"Things are good then?"

I let out a cynical laugh. "After everything I've done for her, she doesn't trust me."

I tell Ned the whole story, my chest tightening with every word. I should be sharing a nice dinner with Amira.

Instead, I'm driving aimlessly through the city and whining to my accountability buddy.

"How'd it feel when Riley hugged and kissed you?"

"Couldn't wait to go home and shower. I felt dirty being in her presence."

"Guess you're over her."

"Not that it was a question in my mind."

"Then why don't you just tell Amira?"

"Shouldn't she trust me after everything I've done for her?"

"I don't know, man. Should she? Sounds like she's dealt with a bunch of assholes, from her father right down to her ex-husband."

I think about the argument I overheard between her and her ex. Then I think about how I've treated women over the past ten years and cringe. And I sang "Gold Digger" to her before I stormed out. *Fuck.*

"Derek, you're gonna have to take responsibility for all the generational trauma men have perpetrated on women now."

"All of it?"

"We all do. It's our job to heal each other."

"Dude, I know, but..."

"If you give her the chance, she'll heal you as much as you heal her."

"You think so?"

"If there's one thing I've learned from this process, that's it. Of course, this is my second time through, and being an accountability buddy has helped even more than being a participant. You know, my relationship with my sister has changed dramatically.

Clearly not a romantic relationship, but we're having conversations I never dreamed we'd have. Now we're closer than I knew was possible."

"So you're saying treat her like a queen?"

"That's not what I'm talking about. Pedestals keep us separate. You need to get into the emotional weeds with her."

I groan. "Last time I tried going deep was in therapy with Riley, and as soon as we finished our sessions, Riley played with my mind, convinced me her infidelity was my fault."

"You think Amira's like Riley?"

"Don't know anymore."

"From what you've said, I don't think she's like that. I think you should give her a chance, Derek. Don't just sulk."

We end the call, and I get out of the car on Frenchmen Street. It's not fully recovered since the storm. A lot of places remain closed, and it's jarring to see the clubs on this normally vibrant street mostly dark. Music so loud and raucous that it could only be live is coming from The Spotted Cat tonight, and I'm in the mood for a drink.

At the bar, I order a bourbon and sip it slowly as the notes of the brass band penetrate my skin.

A soft voice tickles my ear. "I'll have what you're having."

I turn. Beautiful dark eyes, a full heart-shaped mouth. I smile, say, "Not tonight. Thanks," and return my attention to the musicians.

"You look lonely," she purrs and runs a painted fingernail up my arm.

Without looking at her, I move to another stool.

"Don't be like that, handsome." She comes closer.

What kind of generational trauma is causing this woman to throw herself at me after I've already said no? The program's got me thinking about things differently. About women differently. Three months ago, I would have bought her a drink and seen where the night would take us.

Now I take another sip of the bourbon, let the pleasant sting slide down my throat. My watch says it's ten. If I'm gonna make my four a.m. flight, I'd better get some sleep.

Is Ned right? Damn it. I know he's right. Amira's the most incredible woman I've ever met. No, she's not perfect in every way, but she is so beautifully real. Maybe I should go to her, say something.

I throw back the last of the beverage.

The damage is done. Nothing to do now but hole up in a hotel room until it's time to go to the airport tomorrow morning. Isolation. That's what I deserve.

I slide off the barstool, leave a tip under my glass, and head out.

38

Distraction

Amira

MY REFLECTION IN THE MIRROR IS TRULY HORRIFYING: eyes so puffy I look like a frog. Streaked complexion. Swollen lips. Three hours of crying on the bedroom floor will do that, I guess. I should just go to sleep, but I want to do something to get into a better headspace before bed. With Lila at Phoebe's and Derek out prowling, no doubt with that skinny blonde, I have time to plan for our future. Where do I start? With an apartment or with my business idea?

I splash my face with water, return to the bedroom, and crawl into the soft, cozy bed. It's been nice sleeping in luxury, but I'd better get un-used to it fast. In a few days, I'll be sleeping in a bed within my price range.

Okay, business time.

I need to know if this idea is even viable, and if it is, how the heck to get it up and running. I've never wanted to think about business. But as a therapist in private practice, I suppose I am a businesswoman, just not a very good one.

I pull my iPad from the nightstand and search the web for how to start a nonprofit in Louisiana. A bunch of legal websites pop up, each one with info about articles of incorporation. That's not very helpful. I search *entrepreneurs in Louisiana* and find a site that hasn't been updated in three years and another site that seems to be just for tech startups. Gosh. How do I figure this out? Maybe my old faculty adviser at Tulane can connect me with the right people. And here's something: the New Orleans Business Alliance Health Innovators Challenge. Am I a health innovator? I guess there's one way to find out. I click Apply, then follow the link to Rules.

When did Derek stop following the rules of his fast? How long has this thing been going on with her? Was he ever really into me?

I try to refocus on the rules of this health innovators challenge, but the tears are blurring my vision and—*great*—now they're dripping onto my iPad, making it even harder to read.

How could I misread his signals so badly? I'm a professional therapist, trained to read people, but I can't see what's staring me right in the face.

Focus, Amira. Look at the words.

"Must be a legally formed entity." Well, I'm not that. I'll reach out to the folks at Tulane tomorrow. But I want to make some progress on this now. I think I'll take Derek's advice from before and make a new mind map. I fill a page of my journal with circles filled with words and connected by lines. In a way, it's like writing a poem.

Nonprofit

Focus on ages one to five.

Is he coming back?

Shit. Erase that. Anyway, of course he's coming back. It's his house.

Birth to five: most crucial years

The vision of the baby in my arms flashes through my mind again. Derek's sweet eyes.

Library screening for families

Observe during story time and play groups.

Derek would be a great father.

Sigh. Erase that. Focus, Amira.

Screen for mental health issues.

Screen for physical health issues.

Offer direct service to families with struggling kid(s) or parent(s).

PRIVATE—no stigma

Team of new MSW grads and LCSWs

2 social workers per library

Funded by ???

Didn't Derek say something about the hospital maybe funding it?

Set hours

No direct phone calls from patients.

Start in New Orleans.

Grow throughout Louisiana.

He's leaving tomorrow before I wake, and when he gets back, we'll be gone, and I'll never see him again. Thank God.

Sobs rise from my stomach up through my chest. Again. He shouldn't mean this much to me, but he does. Now he's off with someone else. My head pounds.

What could I have done differently? Nothing. I feel like crap now, but I'll feel better after a good night's sleep. Then I can move forward.

I close the iPad and turn out the lights, hold the pillow tightly, and close my eyes.

39
Write Off

Derek

THE HOTEL POOL IS FULL-LENGTH, SO I CAN DO REAL laps, not like at home. Temperature's on the cool side. If Amira were with me, her little nipples would be poking through her swimsuit. Sexy and cute.

I don't owe her an explanation. But maybe I owe it to myself to give her one.

Be here now, Derek.

I return my focus to the sensations in my muscles that arise with every stroke. Tensing and flexing. Engaging and releasing. Like Amira's muscles engage when she holds a yoga pose. *So hot.*

Changing strokes will help. I switch from the crawl to the butterfly. I've always loved the view of a pool underwater through goggles. A feeling of home. Amira feels like home.

Felt like home, dude. It's over now. You gave in to shame instead of opening up, and you blew it. That's why you will not contact her again. Just leave her be.

I hear Riley's voice in my head:

I didn't want you living another day, thinking I still blame you...

Why would I want Amira to go another day thinking I'd blow a chance with her just to fool around with another woman? Thinking I don't value her. Thinking she doesn't deserve honesty, transparency, and fidelity. Doesn't deserve respect. Why would I want to send her that message? And I insulted her integrity on top of all that—called her a gold digger, a dishonest woman scheming for my money. I'm an asshole. No wonder she wrote me off.

40
Love

Amira

TOSSING AND TURNING. LISTENING. NO SOUNDS IN THE driveway. No sounds of the door opening or footfalls on the stairs. No water running in the shower.

It's eleven p.m. Doesn't his flight leave at four a.m.? Shouldn't he be home by now?

I drove him into her arms. That's why he's not home.

Maybe he came home, and I was asleep when he arrived.

I throw the sheets back, slip on a T-shirt and yoga shorts, and pad downstairs. The living room is empty. No sign of him in his office, kitchen, patio. No sign of him in the guest bathroom. I look out the window at the driveway. No Tesla. My rental car is still the only one there.

We had a fight. A big one. And he was a total jerk. If he apologized, I would have welcomed him back, I think. Instead, he's otherwise engaged.

What is it about men that makes them cheat? What is it about me?

I crawl back into bed and FaceTime my brother.

Josh answers on the first ring, his tan complexion and dark red curls filling the screen on my phone. A pale glow lights his face. Behind him it's dark.

"Hey, sis. What happened to your hair?"

I run a hand over my head and open my mouth to make a smart retort. Instead, I choke out sobs.

"Uh-oh. What's happening?"

"Why do you do it? Why do men cheat?"

He pulls a face. "Nice to see you, too. And you're what? Ruminating on your ex-husband after eleven years of divorce because...?"

"No," I say, defensive. "It's Derek."

"Who's Derek? You're dating someone?"

"Not dating. He's been doing a female fast."

"A what?"

"Google it."

"Hang on... Okay, wow. He's dieting, and you're upset?"

I fill Josh in on the details and progression of my situationship with Derek. "It seemed like we were moving toward a relationship. I thought he shared my feelings, until I caught him downtown hugging some blonde. I don't get it. He seemed so into me."

"How do you know he isn't?"

"I know what I saw." Damn it, my nose is running.

"You sure? Maybe the guy was clearing unfinished business with someone."

"No. He never dates anyone more than three times."

"Sounds like a real winner."

"Shut up." I sniffle, blow my nose. "He is. Derek saves lives. He's kind and sweet, and he doesn't want shallow sex anymore. He wants something real."

"Hmmm. I don't know, sis. Impulse control issues?"

"Why did you cheat on Celeste?"

"I take it she told you, huh?"

"No, but last time we talked, you said you broke up. That's how you end every relationship."

"Harsh!"

"True."

Josh sighs. "I hate that you're right."

"So, why do it?" I ask. "Why not use your words? Say, 'I don't want you anymore.'"

"It just happens."

"Every time, Josh. It's a pretty shitty M.O."

"Thanks for the attack, Amira."

"Sorry." I sigh, choke out another sob, try to speak, sob more. Finally, I pull myself together enough to inhale a shaky breath and sputter, "I need to understand, and right now, you're the representative of all men who cheat."

He growls.

"What is wrong with your species?"

"You know, kid, the only reason I haven't hung up on you is because you're my sister, and you're a fucking basket case right now."

"Love you, too."

"I could ask you why women are so damn high-maintenance."

I snort. "By high-maintenance, I assume you mean recognizing her worth and expecting to be treated well?"

"Hey, this fast he's doing looks interesting."

"He says he's rising from the sewer of toxic masculinity. I thought—"

"Really? Rising from the sewer... he says that?" Josh's judgement is not subtle.

"I was being poetic, Josh."

"Good, because any guy who's that full of himself—"

"Today he called me a gold digger."

"Ouch."

"Do you know how hard it was for me to accept help from him?"

I laugh. "I can imagine. You hate receiving gifts."

"That's not true!"

"Mmmm."

"Of course, I like gifts!"

He purses his lips like he's trying not to say something.

"Really? Is it that bad?"

"You're just weird about accepting gifts and money. Last year, you made Celeste cry at Christmas."

"What? She never told me that. We've been friends for twenty-five years."

"Which is why she went out of her way to get you that beautiful handmade bowl, and you acted like she committed a crime. Afterward, she asked what's wrong with our family, and we had a big fight about it."

"Oh. I had no idea I was coming across that way."

"If this dude's helping you, paying for things, offering you more, more, more, and you're acting like he's wrong for giving, maybe he feels unappreciated. Some women actually like that shit."

Pain stabs my heart, and a pit forms in my stomach. "What do I do, Josh?"

"You're still at his house, and he left?"

"Yeah. To meet that woman."

"If that's the case, why is he letting you stay there?"

"Because he likes to take care of me."

Josh raises his eyebrows. "Mm-hmm."

"Oh."

"And you think he's putting eggs in other baskets? Things aren't always what they seem."

"It could've been a misunderstanding, I guess."

"Occasionally, you are wrong."

He's baiting me, but I don't have time for that shit. Derek is getting on a plane in less than twelve hours. "How do I make up to him, Josh? Derek is the first guy I've actually loved." My breath catches in my throat. "Oh my God."

There's a clattering sound on Josh's end as he goes out of view. The screen is dark except for a few bright dots. "Sorry, sis. Dropped the phone." He comes back into view. "Love, huh?"

I love him. That's why I'm falling apart right now. "Yeah," I say with an exhale.

"That's a big deal."

Josh props the phone at an angle, and I can see him chopping something with a big chef's knife.

"Where are you?"

"In the backyard, grilling tofu and veggies."

"At... what time is it there?"

"Nine-ish. Long day at work. Listen, sis, you want him? Apologize. Make it abundantly clear you see and appreciate everything Derek's done for you. From where I'm sitting, it doesn't sound like you appreciate him. And if I were him, I might look for an exit."

"Oh." I thank Josh and end the call. I need to figure this out, and fast. Derek can't leave without knowing I love him. I love Derek. But love isn't enough. I need to apologize. How? Words won't be enough.

I run downstairs and onto the patio, strip down to nothing, and dive into the pool.

In my mind, I repeat the single word *appreciation* like a mantra with every stroke. After several laps, my thoughts turn more solid.

How do I express appreciation? No, that's not the right question.

I know how to tell someone I appreciate them: cards, meals, flowers, blah, blah, blah. My problem is actually feeling it. How do I shove my damn pride out of the way so I can experience gratitude? I don't wanna fake it till I make it. I want to express genuine appreciation for Derek. That's what he deserves. Not some cardboard approximation.

What's behind my pride? Fear. Fear of what? Failure. Fear of not being good enough. Fear that the only reason people give me stuff or help me is because I'm incapable. Goddamn it, why couldn't I have figured this out earlier?

Negative self-talk isn't helpful. I'm on the right track. Keep going. Meditate. Do some yoga. Call Sage.

But what if it's too late? Derek's last text wasn't exactly friendly.

Can I blame him?

41

Real & Imagined Storms

Derek

WHO AM I KIDDING? I CAN'T SLEEP. THE BED IS comfortable enough, better than my couch anyway. The problem is that I very quickly grew accustomed to sleeping with Amira nearby. Knowing that tomorrow I'll wake up and she won't be there to have coffee... that when I get back from the retreat, she'll be gone and I'll never see her again... Knowing that she'll think she did something wrong and I didn't care enough to give things a try... I think I'm gonna be sick.

I leap from the bed and run into the bathroom. Nothing comes up though. I'm just dry-heaving. Dry-heaving over a woman. No. Not over *a* woman, over *the* woman. The only woman. Fuck.

Would it be wrong to call her? I send a video chat request to Wesley.

"Hey. What's wrong?" he asks as soon as his face pops up on the screen. He rubs sleep from his eyes.

"How can you tell something's wrong?"

"You're calling at midnight... from the bathroom? My God, you look like a mess."

I try to speak, but my throat tightens, as if I'm being strangled. It's hard to breathe.

"Derek?"

I gasp and choke the words out. "I lost her."

"What happened?"

"Huge argument. Now I'm in a hotel. She's probably still in my house. It's over. I have no right to talk to her again, but I wanna at least say I'm sorry. Would that be awful?"

"Shit. From what Sage said and the texts you've been sending, I thought you were perfect for each other."

I share my side of the story. "Thing is, I don't know if I can trust her about money. And she made damn sure to let me know she doesn't trust me."

Sage's face pops into the screen, also looking very tired. "Hey, sorry, I couldn't help overhearing."

"Aww, man. I didn't mean to wake you, Sage." I sniffle. "I'm sorry. I'll let you go."

"Hang on! Can I say something, Derek?"

"Sure."

"When Amira decided to divorce Greg because he was cheating on her for the God-knows-how-many-eth time with the God-knows-how-many-eth woman, her lawyer wanted her to go after his money."

"What money?"

"Greg grew up in a very wealthy home. Amira's lawyer assumed, possibly rightly, that Greg had money secreted away."

I think about the argument Amira and Greg had over helping her and Lila move. What a cheap SOB.

"He's distantly related to the MacKenzie family that gave Wesley and me the Brilliance Awards. His part of the family isn't involved with the foundation, but it's that family's money."

"Whoa."

"They were like railroad magnates or something back in the day. The point is though, Amira could have really gone after Greg, but she didn't. She doesn't have to work as hard as she does. But she's so bound and determined to take care of herself and Lila that she wouldn't even ask the father of her child to support her with alimony. She gets child support and that's it."

"You're joking."

"I am not joking. Whatever issues Amira may have, going after people's money isn't one of them. It's that she sabotages herself because of... whatever. I don't know. I'm not the psychologist, but I can just tell you, whatever you think about her being untrustworthy with money, it's not true."

"You're saying I really did have to persuade her to accept help."

"Oh yeah. She wasn't bullshitting you. In fact, wanna hear something funny? Well, it's not funny actually. We have this mutual friend, Celeste, who was in a relationship with Amira's brother for years. Last Christmas, Celeste had a beautiful ceramic bowl handmade just for Amira, the kind of thing she loves and would never buy for herself. Apparently, when Celeste gave it to her, Amira was so rude Celeste walked away feeling like she had done something wrong, when all she had done was buy Amira a beautiful gift. Oh shoot..."

Sage slides the phone back to Wesley, then pops her face in the screen again. "Sorry, Derek. I've gotta get up for the hundredth time tonight. Good luck!"

Amira

ASIDE FROM MY MOM, THERE'S NO WOMAN I TRUST MORE than Sage. I know it's late back east, but she's pregnant. She probably has to pee anyway. Her face pops up on the screen. She's on the move as she answers the call.

"Hey, did I catch you in the middle of something?" I ask, trying to keep my voice calm.

"Actually," she says, walking into what looks like the bathroom, "I was just talking to Derek."

Hearing his name puts me over the edge. I bawl into the phone.

"Oh, Mimi. Talk to me."

"Hang on." I pause to wipe away the snot dripping down my face.

"I haven't seen you this upset about a guy ever, not even during your divorce."

"Because I never loved a man like I love Derek," I wail. "And he thinks I'm a gold digger."

"I gave him some perspective on that."

"You did?"

"He's not doing great, Mimi."

"Really?"

"Maybe about the same as you."

"So really bad."

"Hmmm. You wanna tell me what happened?" The sound of a toilet flushing comes through the phone. "Or... maybe let's not focus on what happened. What are you thinking now?"

"I've been doing a lot of soul searching. I talked to Josh, and he helped me see I just suck at showing appreciation and that can be really off-putting, and I was afraid to trust Derek. I mean, I did see him with this woman."

"Yeah, honey, that's not what you think."

"Really?"

"I promise you. I just overheard him tell Wesley about it. But that's a story you need to hear from Derek."

Elara's voice pops into my head: *real and imagined storms.* Have I brewed an imagined storm in my mind?

"How do I make up to him, Sage? I've been racking my brain, and I see I keep letting fear and pride get in the way. But how do I stop? I'm afraid of looking like I can't handle anything. Afraid of being that stereotypical pathetic single mom."

"We know that's not you, or most single moms for that matter."

"I know. It's a bullshit stereotype made up by patriarchal... Don't get me started."

"Try to breathe," Sage says, then takes a deep, audible breath.

I follow her lead and remember, again, how calm I get when I make a conscious effort to give my brain space. "It's kinda scary being with someone who comes from money. Greg's family—"

"I know, Mimi. Greg's family were assholes."

"And Derek..."

"Derek doesn't come from money. He's earned what he has."

"Right, but he grew up in that swanky suburb of Boston..."

"Did he tell you how they ended up living there?"

I shake my head.

"The landlord knew his grandmother, and as a form of kindness and personal activism, chose to rent his parents the house for way below market rate so that little Derek, who was just four at the time, could go to a good school and have a better chance at success. That's how the Forets ended up next door to Wesley's family."

"Oh."

"Anyway, Greg isn't Derek, and their families couldn't be more different. I don't think anyone looking at you and Derek would think you were trying to manipulate him."

"That's what he said though."

"He was really hurting, and you need to let him tell you about that. Sounds like you've done some work thinking about what held you back from trusting him. All I can tell you is if you are ready to be real, vulnerable, and completely honest with him, I think you need to get out of bed, get dressed, and go find him at the Hilton near the airport. Skip your usual primping."

"But I'm a mess. My eyes are…"

"It doesn't matter. If you guys work things out, he's gonna see Amira with frog eyes again."

"That's not very persuasive."

"Maybe you can suffer a little embarrassment for love."

A sense of strength surges through me. "Yeah. I can do that."

Sage opens the door to the bathroom, then curses. "How can I possibly have to pee again? Please don't tell me the constant peeing actually gets worse in the third trimester."

"It does," I assure her.

She rolls her eyes.

We end the call, and I throw the covers off myself, dig a pair of skinny jeans from my suitcase, and slip into a bra and yoga top. Sage is right; it's okay if I look like hell, but there's no way on this earth I am going to apologize to that man with bad breath. I brush my teeth and head into the night.

Derek

Wesley reappears on the screen.

"You got yourself one fine woman there, Wes."

His face lights up. "I know. I can't wait to marry her."

For the first time all night, I smile too, happy for my lifelong friend. Then the tears start flowing.

"Oh brother, I am sorry," he says. "I haven't seen you in this much pain since Riley, or maybe ever. This seems worse, and I know the feeling. Remember the state I was in last summer?"

"Yes, I do, and I know I've apologized for this before, but now that I'm going through it, I understand even more how much of an asshole I was when I told you to forget her."

"It's okay. I'm just glad I can be here for you. I love you, Derek."

"Aww, come on, you're gonna make me cry more." I sniffle, then flash back to playing that song as I stormed off. "I called her a gold digger."

"Yeah, sometimes we do stupid shit, say stupid shit, think stupid shit, and believe stupid shit when we're in pain and afraid."

"Fine. That's my excuse. What's hers? She's a therapist."

Wesley laughs. "Therapists are people too. My dad's a therapist, and I've seen him do some really stupid shit. She's not gonna be perfect. She's gonna screw up from time to time."

"Hmmm."

"Do you know why you couldn't tell her what happened?"

I sigh. "I've figured out it was shame. That's my Achilles' heel."

"Then just go be as real with her as she has been with you, or even more real. Maybe you guys can work this out."

"You think?"

"If nothing else, give her the apology you know she deserves. If it doesn't work out and you wanna be able to have an honest, lasting relationship, you're gonna need to learn to apologize."

"That's never been my strong suit."

"Go try. Worst case, maybe you both will feel better and be able to part without animosity. Best case, maybe you guys make up. Maybe this is the beginning. You go do your retreat, and then you come back and start the romance you've both been waiting for."

Hearing those words, envisioning Amira and me together, my body fills with energy.

"Derek, the night I met Sage, I knew I would marry her. You described a similar experience meeting Amira. I think that means maybe you really have a chance."

Now I'm smiling through tears, breathing again. "I'm gonna get dressed, go home, and let her know I see her and that I should've been straight with her. I should've trusted her. No wonder she didn't trust me; I wasn't trusting her."

"There you go, buddy. Good luck! Listen, I love you! Let me know what happens, okay?"

I flash a thumbs-up and end the call.

42

Crossed Paths

Derek

My driveway is empty. What the hell? Wesley said Sage said she was here. Damn it. What do I do now? I get out of the car and pace, trying to clear my mind.

Think, Derek. What's the objective?

To apologize.

So don't give up.

I get back in the car, where I left my phone, and call Amira. Before I have a chance to fret, she answers. "Hi, what room are you in?"

"I'm outside."

"The hotel?"

"My house. Where are you?"

"I'm at the airport Hilton."

"Fuck. Stay there."

"No, Derek, wait. I'm sorry."

"I'm sorry too, Amira. I need to tell you..."

"I should have trusted you."

"True, but I can see why you didn't. And I was stubborn."

"Are you on your way back to the hotel?" she asks.

"I'm pulling out of the driveway."

"Wait. I have a better idea. Meet me at City Park."

"How do I get there?"

"I'll send you a map."

I stop, wait for the text, click the screen, and look at the directions that appear.

"Got it. On my way."

"Derek, why did you go to a hotel tonight?"

"Because for half a second I wanted to get away from you, and I didn't wanna displace you, not when I was on my way out of town anyway."

"Wow," she says, an unfamiliar type of softness in her voice. "Even in anger, you were taking care of me."

"Of course."

"No. Not of course. A lot of people would have kicked me out and stayed in their own house. You just go above and beyond, and I..." Her voice breaks. I hear a car door slam and an engine start. She sniffles.

"You okay?"

"I don't know. I'm in the car now. I suck at showing appreciation, Derek. I-I get all wrapped up in pride and fear, and... God, I'm just so sorry I fought every attempt you made to help me, to take care of me and Lila. And I should have trusted you..."

"Listen," I say, turning onto a busy boulevard. "Wait. Is this South Carrolton? Shit. I think I made a wrong turn."

"Do you see a bus stop in front of a tan building with a big red oval sign that says RAISING CANE'S?"

"Uh... oh yup, there it is."

"You're on the right street."

"How's your drive?"

"Boring. I'm on I-10. Do you wanna talk now?"

"Don't wanna get off the phone with you."

She sighs. My heart pounds. Hope that sigh was a good sign.

Her voice tentative, she asks, "What happened today? Who was that woman I saw you with downtown?"

My chest and abs tighten. I know this sensation. No need to fight it.

Okay, Shame, I feel you, and you've had your say and fucked things up. Now you get to take a back seat while I talk to the woman I love.

But do I own it up front? Or tell her afterward? Thank God we're on the phone so I don't have to look at her when I say this.

"It was my ex-wife."

"Riley?"

"You remember her name?"

"Of course. Are you reuniting?"

I half choke, half snort. "Hell no! Woman, are you crazy? I want you so badly I can hardly stand straight."

A cute little Amira-squeak comes through the speakers. I wish I could take her hand right now, kiss it, hold it in both of mine. Should I wait to tell her my story until we're in person?

I've gone too long without explaining my past.

"You want the story now? Or should I wait till we meet at City Park?"

"Go ahead and start please."

"You know I was married. I was so in love with Riley, so in love with her. But, you know, surgical residencies are demanding. Hundred-hour weeks. Sleeping in the hospital night after night. Coming home exhausted. You kinda can't get the blood out of your mind. And the pressure to learn, to do it right 'cause somebody could die if you fuck it up... Riley didn't understand, or pretended not to... Fact is, she never respected me. But I didn't realize that until it was too late."

"So what happened?"

"I'm turning onto Esplanade now, driving into the park. Do I just park on the street?"

"Yeah. Keep talking. I'll be there soon."

I park on the right side of a wide boulevard lined with tall, leafy trees and get out of the car, pressing the phone to my ear.

A majestic building lies straight ahead. It looks closed.

What does Amira have up her sleeve?

"All those nights I was working my ass off, Riley was taking someone new into our bed. She had a string of men on rotation, long-term affairs, but at least three different guys. One of them, a colleague of mine. She kept asking when I'd start making bank. I was thinking: Could we have kids? She kept saying she didn't wanna get pregnant, and I thought she was waiting for me to finish my residency and start earning more money. Then one night I came home, and there they were. I started piecing things together that I had been trying to ignore, trying to pretend I didn't see. Then we went through this divorce, because she didn't feel sorry at all. She justified it. She tried to blame me for being upset, like I had no right to feel anything about what she was doing because I wasn't home. She blamed me for not being home, for working a hundred hours a week, saving lives and building a career. She said I deserved to be cheated on."

"What did she do for a living?"

"Really, nothing. We met in college. She was smart. She coulda done anything, but she had no drive. Riley went from one job to another, always hating her boss, always hating her coworkers, always bored. She shopped. And she resented me because I didn't tell her to just quit. I didn't say: 'Just live off me; I'll support you.' Can't imagine what she thought: that I would just pay for her to be fucking all these other guys?"

"Oh, Derek. That's horrible."

"So when she came to New Orleans to find me and then accidentally on purpose ran into me at Leah's, I felt sick. Couldn't wait to get away from her. I left the shop and she followed me out."

"That was today?"

"It was."

Amira pulls up behind me and steps out of the vehicle. Puffy eyes, streaks of mascara on her cheeks, tight jeans and a tank top—even when it's obvious she's been crying, she makes me aroused. More than anything, though, I just want to hold her right now, to feel the warmth of her body against mine. As sexy as she always is, what's turning me on more at this moment is that as soon as I see her, it feels like I'm home.

The night air brings a floral scent and hardens her nipples. She shivers, the perfect excuse to unbutton my shirt and slip it around her, not just to be chivalrous but to hide those distracting little nubs from my sight.

Amira

DEREK'S SHIRT BRINGS WARMTH AND HIS SWEET, MASCULINE scent. His eyes are puffy like mine, and his voice cracks as he continues his story. Hearing about Derek's marriage and nasty divorce puts so much in perspective.

I often think about how men wound women, but I sometimes forget that women wound men too. He alluded to this a while ago when he told me about his dating history. Now I really get it, and my heart softens. I want to squeeze his hand as he talks, but I'm not ready, not yet.

"I said nasty things to Riley, just to get her to go away. Then she told me she'd come to make amends. She's only got about a month to live."

"You believe her?"

"I'm a doctor, Amira. As soon as she said it, I started really looking at her. All the evidence was there."

"So what does this mean for you?"

"Nothing, really."

"Then why didn't you just tell me when I asked?"

"At first, because I didn't wanna be another person burdening you with their problems, especially when your patients deal with so much worse."

"Derek!"

"But if that was my real motivation for keeping it to myself, I wouldn't have gotten angry. In hindsight, I see it was shame. I guess, deep in my heart, I thought Riley was right—that I deserved what I got because I was a bad husband. During this female fast, it became clear to me that even though I blamed Riley all these years, when I look at my behavior toward women... She didn't treat women that way; I did. I treated women like commodities both to protect myself from them and to protect them from me, the big bad neglectful husband. Riley was always disappointed in me. I never felt good enough."

"Good enough. Oh, Derek."

"Not good enough as a husband or as a man. Seeing her brought all that up, but she made sure to let me know she had been wrong to blame me. I was processing that when I got home.

Then when you thought I was lying to you, it triggered that sense of shame. Not your fault in any way. It's a trigger of mine. Oh shit, I just realized something else."

"What's that?"

"Riley wanted my money, or the promise of it. That was what made me acceptable. When you didn't want my money, I didn't know how to handle it, especially since you seemed to need it so much."

My throat tightens and my lower abdomen clenches. I close my eyes and envision light filling my body with the in-breath and all the pride and fear leaving with the exhale.

"You okay? Your nostrils are flaring."

I open my eyes. "Fun fact—that statement about me needing your money just triggered my unresolved issues around pride and money."

Derek winces and curses under his breath, like he did so many times after complimenting me.

I can't help but laugh. "You're doing it again."

He looks into my eyes, and it's like a helpless little boy is gazing out at me. "I'm sorry, Amira. That's the last thing I wanted to do."

"It's okay. Let's celebrate the fact that this time I didn't act or speak from that triggered place."

He holds up his hand for a high-five, and I respond. For a moment, I do nothing but bask in the sensation of our palms touching. The look in his eyes shifts, softens, and relaxes. He lowers his hand without releasing mine. "Can I ask a question?"

"Of course."

"How did what I said trigger your stuff about pride and money?"

I groan. "I guess I've always had trouble accepting things from people. Every visit with my dad was punctuated by an argument between him and my mom about money. There never seemed to be enough, and I just thought I could end their arguments if I took care of myself. I started cleaning house when I was thirteen and then cashiering at the health food store in our neighborhood once I was old enough."

"That's a lot for a young kid to handle. And did it work?"

"Of course not. Me working didn't change my dad's stinginess. Then I went to college and accidentally got pregnant, and I've got old-fashioned values. Greg wanted to do right by me; we got married. His family accused me of getting pregnant so I could trap him, and I guess I've just been trying to prove myself ever since then. When we split, the law made me take child support, but I didn't fight for alimony even though I could have. I just felt better taking care of myself."

Derek changes his grip on my hand to intertwine our fingers, then he pulls me a little closer. "You're very brave and incredibly good at taking care of yourself and Lila. I hope my attempts to help you haven't given you the impression I think you're not capable."

"Well..."

"Because that's wrong. These are traits I admire in you."

"Oh," I say, genuinely surprised.

"And while I know you don't value me for my money, I really hope you will let me share what I have with you. I enjoy taking care of the people I love. It makes me feel good to offer gifts. Like you, I didn't grow up having. Maybe unlike you, I grew up around kids who always had what they needed and usually had what they wanted. I like being in a position to give. It's a sense of freedom I've earned for myself."

I nod as I take in Derek's words and the sentiment behind them. "That makes sense. In fact, I've always fantasized I might someday have enough to be the generous one. I'm just not there yet."

"But you are generous with your time and your insight and your love and your poetry."

He gazes into my eyes, and I wonder how I ever could have doubted his sincerity. The man has authenticity oozing from his pores.

"So tonight I've been thinking about forgiveness and shame and what I really need to do to move on in my life. To move forward with you, if you'll have me. I can't leave for this retreat with you thinking I don't believe you're the one for me, woman."

"Woman?"

"Alexis Amira Albright MacKenzie, I want you and only you. Female fast be damned, I'm gonna say this now because I know there's no chance another woman's gonna come into my sightline. Not after the fast ends, not ever. I knew on that flight from Hartford you were the one."

My already softened heart just turned to mush. "Come on," I say, pulling at his hand. "I want to show you something."

43

Singing Tree

Amira

HE FOLLOWS ME DOWN THE PAVED PATH, THEN ONTO the grass toward the lake. We stop at a huge live oak tree strung with wind chimes of all sizes. The smallest one is about six inches high. The tallest one is five, maybe six feet high. They glow in the moonlight and blow in the soft breeze.

"This is called the singing tree," I say over the sound of the chimes. "Come here."

I take his hand and guide him under a medium-sized wind chime. The breeze picks up, and the chimes grow louder.

A huge smile spreads across his face as he looks around in awe. "The notes are filling my whole body!"

"Right?"

He shakes his head, the smile on his face growing bigger. "Never felt anything like this."

"Stand right under this one," I say and bring him to the spot directly under the biggest wind chime. "Drop your arms to your sides. Close your eyes. Feel that?"

He does as I command and nods slowly. "The tones go from my head to my feet and back up, like a musical massage."

"Sage's big sister calls it harmonic vibrational healing."

"What's that?"

"The theory says using specific tones on the body affects its vibrations and stimulates healing. I never believed in it until I stood under that wind chime."

"Letting the sound travel through my body and mind feels like a brain cleanse." Derek opens his eyes and walks around the tree, looking at the wind chimes. He settles on another slightly smaller one and stands under it. "Just as powerful, but the sound lands in a different part of my body, a little higher."

Derek

STANDING UNDER THIS TREE, THE VIBRATIONS OF THE human-sized wind chime filling my body uplifts my spirits like nothing else I've experienced. I'm not sure why Amira chose this moment to bring me here. It's dark. There's nobody else around. It's romantic. Is she letting me know she forgives me?

"Derek," she says so quietly I almost don't hear her. She's gazing at the water, leaning against the tree.

"Yes?"

"When we were at Sage's art show and you were trying to impress me with your understanding of her work."

I groan.

She continues, "You brought me to the tornado painting. I felt a host of different emotions in that moment. My somatic awareness was completely heightened. Sage is like family to me, and looking at that painting showed me how close I had come to losing her without even realizing she was in danger. There have been few moments when I felt so scared. I said something about that to you."

"I remember."

"And you said 'She's safe now,' and something happened in my body that's never happened before. Your words filled me with a sense of safety and peace."

I step toward her, wanting closeness.

"I have never been in love with a man."

"Not your ex-husband?"

"It was a crush. We wouldn't have kept dating if I hadn't gotten pregnant. He wanted to do what everybody said was the right thing. I did too. We chose to love each other, but it never went beyond that. The first person I fell in love with was Lila. When she was born and I looked at her little face and held her to me, it was like I had known her all my life. I can't even describe that feeling except to say that the closest thing that I've ever felt to that is the way that I feel when I hear your voice."

My heart stops, then goes wild as if floods with dopamine.

Amira continues. "No matter what's happening at work, in the world, or in my life, when I hear your voice, I feel okay. Until our argument this evening, it didn't occur to me that it was love. But now I know it is. No man, other than a patient, has ever shared something with me that was so real and so raw or made me feel so honored until you just opened up like that."

Her eyes are earnest, gentle. I am drawn to her. The fast is almost over. What am I waiting for? Permission. "Amira," I say as I move in, place my hand on the wide tree trunk behind her.

"Yes, Derek," she answers.

I lower my lips to hers and she meets them with warmth and pressure. This is what I need right now; only this. I don't need to take her to bed. This moment, with her sliding her arms around my waist. I pull her to me, press her body into mine, feel the warmth of her chest, the beat of her heart. This makes everything that happened before worthwhile. I am gone.

A gust blows through the leaves and wind chimes, creating a wall of healing sound around us. I tighten my hold on her as soft rain falls, washing away the past.

⬿⬾

Amira

RAIN FALLS AROUND US BUT SEEMS NOT TO TOUCH US. THE tree must be protecting us. But it wouldn't matter if we were being drenched. Derek's kiss is bringing me to ecstasy. He parts my lips, and I yield to him.

All my muscles tense and relax. The dormant parts of me stiffen and release. I feel more alive than ever. Everything inside me is waking up, lighting up, as if my cells are dancing with the notes on the wind. Fireworks are exploding from every part of me.

The heat of Derek's body penetrates and fills me as if we are merging into a single organism. If there is anything nearby, I've lost sense of it. All I know is him, and me, and the energy we are generating. We might be levitating. We might be dissipating into the air.

I have just found home.

When we slowly separate and regain ourselves, I open my eyes and look into his. Even in the darkness, a light shines in them that wasn't there before.

44

Vital Heart

Derek

KISSING AMIRA LAST NIGHT AND NOT FOLLOWING her into bed was one of the hardest things I've had to do until I said goodbye to her this morning.

She made a point of getting up with me, sharing a cup of coffee, and seeing me off at the airport. She told me about the idea that came to her for a nonprofit, and just as I was getting excited about that, she said she'd found an apartment and would be looking at it this weekend.

I begged her not to. I kissed her hands, her face, those sinful lips. I pleaded with her to stay, to give us a chance. But she has some idea in her head that it's foolish to start a relationship already living together.

I tried to tell her our relationship started the moment we met, and we've been through more in three weeks than most couples go through in their first year together. Isn't that testing ground enough?

She flared her nostrils and narrowed her eyes at me. It's supposed to be her warning look, but it's gotten so it raises my flag. Goddamn. Is there anything she can do to turn my motor off?

I'm not supposed to be thinking about that now though. I'm also not supposed to be staring out the plate-glass window at the expansive view of the wharf and harbor in the distance. I'm supposed to be paying full attention to Ned as he talks about the challenges and celebrations that he experienced over the course of our three-month female fast.

We've been chatting regularly by text and phone and occasionally by video chat. I know his voice, but I'm still getting used to his facial expressions and the way he gestures with his long, thin fingers, like every word is a note on an instrument. He finishes his story, and we all applaud quietly. The retreat leader asks Ned if he's open to feedback. He agrees, and each person in the circle offers an affirmation, a question, or a gentle suggestion. Ned nods in humility, places his hands before his heart like he's praying, and thanks us.

Now it's my turn. I inhale deeply and consider where to begin. "Ned can tell you I've been vigilant. Temptation has arisen in a wicked lot of forms. I resisted. My journal became my best friend, followed closely by my meditation practice and my phone calls to Ned. But on October 4, a woman plowed into me at the airport and my life changed forever. What can I say? I resisted. But fate kept throwing us together." I look at Ned for affirmation.

He's not supposed to say anything, so he nods vigorously. The faces around the circle register skepticism.

"That night, I arrived in New Haven, Connecticut, and discovered her best friend is marrying my best friend. We had flown to the same city for the same event. Four days later, I saw future versions of her and me together. Thought I might be losing my mind, except I remembered a beautiful quote from a Rumi poem my grandmother used to read to me as a child:

> *"Tend to your vital heart*
> *And all you worry about will be solved.*
> *Your donkey is afraid of work.*
> *Tie it up and make it carry many loads*
> *Of patience and gratitude*
> *for a hundred years*
> *Or thirty, or twenty."*

"Back in New Orleans, we had a storm. You may have heard about it. It came down to the woman and her child needed shelter. Where I have a four-bedroom home and no one to fill it, what could I do? I already saw her in my future. Sure, I tried to journal my way out of the visions. I tried to meditate my way into another state of mind. I got quiet and calm, and I tempered my physical arousal. But my heart would not be still. Then she hurt herself and needed my care. That meant we had to touch. It was torture, and she wound up confessing her desire for me. I slipped up and shared my desire for her too. Not like all the times I accidentally winked at her or called her beautiful without thinking about it. No, this was a direct statement that I couldn't take back once I said it and, frankly, didn't want to. Then yesterday we had a misunderstanding and I almost lost her. I couldn't risk it. Felt I had to open up to her about the shame I carry. I told her flat out I see a future with her, and we kissed."

No one is supposed to make a sound, scowl, or cheer me on. Variations of all these reactions travel around the circle of twenty men.

"With my history and knowing the sincerity of my intentions now, I have no regrets about kissing her. Far as I'm concerned, I made it to the end. Thanks for listening. Thanks for your support, especially Ned. Couldn't have done this without you, brother."

I clap him on the back, and he puts his arm around me. We sit arm in arm as the retreat leader asks if I'm open to feedback. I agree, and then sit, stunned, as one man after another acknowledges my resolve, tells me how my story inspired them. A few guys start crying, and before I know it, I'm crying too. This has been a test, what Elara and Zaki call an imagined storm, which in this case was caused by a real storm. I made it through with Amira by my side, and I want nothing more than to ride out all of life's other storms with her.

45

Ain't Nobody

Derek

ANDS ON THE STEERING WHEEL, THAT NEW VERSION of "Ain't Nobody" playing on the stereo, I'm energized. Going home to Amira and Lila. I know what I need to do, though I'm still figuring out in my mind how to do it.

Soon as I enter the house, I know something's off. "Amira?" I call.

"Up here," she yells.

I slip my loafers off and run up the stairs. The duffel bag pounds my hip with each step.

Lila lies on the bed reading while Amira packs her suitcase.

"What's this?" For Lila's sake, I'm trying to keep the panic out of my voice.

"We found a place!" Amira beams at me and opens her arms.

I drop my bag and walk into her embrace, wrap my arms around her, and pull her as close as is physically possible. I nuzzle her ear and whisper, "What if I don't want you to go?"

She pulls away just enough to scan my eyes. Embarrassing as it is, they brim over with tears.

"Love having you two around. I brought you presents from California," I say and pull away from Amira to open my duffel bag. I retrieve a book about the ecology of California and hand it to Lila. She widens her eyes. "Cool! Thanks."

"My pleasure. And for you, Alexis Amira Albright MacKenzie, I have something to help you on your new journey."

She takes the business planning book from me, reads the back cover copy aloud, and flips through the pages. "This is so thoughtful." She wraps her arms around me again and kisses my cheek. "Thank you!"

"Hope it's helpful."

"I'm sure it will be. Hey, Lila, honey, we need to have a private conversation for a bit. You comfy there?"

"Uh-huh," she says, scanning the book I got her.

"We'll go outside then."

Amira takes my hand and leads me out the door, down the stairs, and through the kitchen onto the patio.

I sit on the table and rest one foot on a teak chair, hold my hands out to her.

She takes my hands but resists my pull. "How was the retreat?"

"Fantastic. Decided I'm doing it again."

Her eyes widen. "What?"

"Kidding! Kind of. I'm not participating in the fast, but I will be an accountability buddy, help some other guy through."

"Amazing." She laughs. "You might see my brother there. I told him about the program, and I think he's realizing he has some growing to do too. Anyway," she continues, talking a mile a minute, "how are you? Thirsty? I always get dehydrated when I fly."

My heart pounds. I spent the past four days getting clear about what I can and want to offer this woman, and her tone of voice makes me think she's about to cut this relationship off before it's had a chance to really start.

"Do you want some water?" she asks.

"I want you."

She smiles. "Good. And I know you have this whole idea about how we're supposed to move forward, but the thing is I have a child to consider."

"You serious, woman?"

She gives me that look. Uh-oh. "I mean, Amira. Come off it. I know you're a package deal, and I love the package. I *want* the package. I want to help you raise that girl or to support you while you raise her... whatever you want. If it makes you happy, I want it."

"What will make me happy is to establish some normalcy for Lila and with Lila. Moving in with you would be a big step even without her in my life. With her, it's gargantuan. I'm scared."

"Of me?"

She shakes her head. "Of what might happen."

"Amira."

"It's not just you and me that have to adjust. She has to adjust. I keep thinking if we live together, Lila will be traumatized by watching her mother go through a devastating breakup."

"You said that once before. You really think that's our destiny?"

"I don't know. Probably not, but—"

"Say it is. You think either of us would let her get traumatized?"

"No, but—"

"You've ended us before we started."

"You're right. I just… The way she's been acting lately, I think she's not sure where she fits into this configuration."

"So we show her."

"Are we even sure what this configuration is?"

I nod, but she keeps lecturing, pacing back and forth in front of me.

"When I said goodbye to Lila on October 4, I was a single woman with a child. The next time she saw me—five days later, mind you—I was living with a man and it was probably obvious to her even before it was clear to me that I had feelings for you."

"And that I was falling hard for you. Come here. I wanna kiss you."

She stops pacing, faces me, raises her eyebrows. "I'm trying to make a point right now."

"Uh-huh." I take her hands and pull her to me, not letting her resist this time. When she's close enough, I take hold of her hips. My God, I've been wanting to do that for so long. "Come to me." I pull her closer until our lips meet.

A soft moan escapes her and makes me swell. I explore her mouth with my tongue, slide my hands under her rear, and press her into me. She moans again.

"You like that, honey?"

"Yes," she moans into my mouth. "I like feeling you against me, ready for more."

"I am ready for so much more. In every way."

She responds with a passionate kiss and rubs her hands down my arms, my back, my neck. Her hands seem to be everywhere as she strokes each muscle. She holds my head in place but releases her grip once I slip my mouth from hers onto her chin, her neck, her collarbones, just above her heart. I want more, but for now this will have to do. I pull away, gasping for air. "We don't stop now, I won't be able to stop at all."

"I feel you," she says.

"One last time: please stay."

"Here's what I need: I need to reconnect with my child alone. I need to date you like normal people do. I need to take things slow. This being-in-love thing is new and weird and exciting and scary. And I'm doing it while parenting and exploring the possibility of starting a new business."

"Now that you lay it out like that, I see it's a lot."

"Thank you. What would make me happy is not just your admiration and your love and respect but your patience."

"Will you let me help you if I see a need I can fill?"

"Are you talking about money?"

"Maybe."

"I will ask you if I need financial assistance."

"How will you pay rent on this place?"

"One. It's a great deal. Two. Greg came through with more child support. Three. It's not like I don't work."

"I'm sorry. Your finances aren't even my business. Still, it would make me happy to help you when I can."

"Let's take that on a case-by-case basis."

"How long do I have to wait to live with you?"

"I don't know. Let's see how things go over the next month or so."

I groan. "I'm finally free to be with you."

"And who says you can't? Lila has a sleepover this weekend. I expect my boyfriend to take me on a proper date and seduce me the good old-fashioned way."

The woman just called me her boyfriend and told me to seduce her. I'm going to spend every spare moment of this week planning for our date.

46

Sensations

Amira

Chaka Khan and I belt out the chorus of "I Feel for You," and despite the way I'm bouncing and grooving with the beat, I manage to hit the high note almost effortlessly. If Lila was here, she'd either be making fun of me or singing along. As it is, I get to dance nude around our new apartment in anticipation of my date with the man I love.

The carpeting feels soft under my feet, though nothing like the kind of soft of the hand-woven silk rugs in Derek's bedroom and living room.

Thirty minutes before he arrives. I would have thought that with only two new dresses to choose from, it'd be easier to make a selection. But I can't decide which look to play with: the 1950s pinup girl or the 1980s faux innocent. I guess I'll take inspiration from the music and go with the 1980s shimmery eggplant sheath and a pair of stilettos. The eggplant color is good for fall and brightens my complexion. Derek looks good in fall colors too. Maybe we'll match. I hope I don't regret the heels. I slip some flats into my purse just in case.

The chunky acrylic hoops and bracelets I inherited from Mom's jewelry box complement the dress. I'm trying the new eye shadow and mascara Lila persuaded me to buy. I glide a shade of rose gold called Unicorn over my lids, finish with mascara and the new lip gloss. The doorbell rings. He's here!

I text him that I'll be right there, slip into the stilettos, grab my purse, and run to the door. "Hi!"

Derek doesn't even try to hide the fact that he's scanning me from head to toe. He smiles appreciatively. "You look stunning!"

I take the sight of him in: flowy black trousers, a dark paisley-patterned shirt with shell buttons, no tie. A tuft of hair peeks above the collar, giving me ideas about what I might do later, or... Why not now? I lick my lips.

"Would you like to see my apartment?"

He toes his shoes off at the door and follows me inside. The tour doesn't last long. How could it with only two bedrooms, a small den, a living room, and eat-in kitchen? The bathroom is functional but nothing spectacular. I do happen to love the subway tiles in the shower and on the walls though.

"Nice place," he says.

"It feels good for now," I say, realizing I've been caressing his back unintentionally.

He purrs. "That feels good."

"Yeah? What are we doing tonight?"

"Uhhh... Dinner reservations in an hour. Thought we'd stroll through Audubon Park first, check out some clubs after. Dance like we did the night we—"

We're on each other before he can finish the sentence.

The night we met, he was going to say, I'm sure, but I don't care because I want him now. Now. In my hallway.

He feasts on my mouth. I'm tingling everywhere good. I back up to the wall, and he comes with me, never taking his mouth from mine, but now he's moving his mouth onto my cheeks, my eyes, my ears, my neck. I moan. He lingers on my neck. I stroke his chest, want that chest hair in my fingers, undo his shirt buttons one by one. He slides his mouth onto my collarbone, my shoulder, slipping the strap of my dress off. He reaches his hands behind me, feeling for the zipper, slides it down.

My body shudders with pleasure as his fingers reach my sacrum. His mouth continues its journey from my shoulder down my upper arm, then back to my collarbone, my décolleté, my cleavage. I gasp, slip his shirt off, pull the tank top up and over his head. At last I can slip my fingers through that gorgeous chest hair. I tease it, revel in its softness, massage his pectoral muscles, slide my hands over every inch of his torso, feeling the well-defined muscles between his ribs and on his waist.

My dress is loose by my hips, and he slides it down farther, lowering his head to kiss each pert nipple, to suckle gently. The sensations flowing through my body right now are almost too much to bear. I grab his biceps, just to feel him in my hands, and push him down.

He gets the hint, kissing and nipping at my stomach, my magic triangle, and finally, bringing his tongue to flick my pearl. He flicks it, encircles it, then sucks lightly on it, gently pulling the pearl into his mouth. All my lips swell and pulsate. I need him everywhere in me, on me, and around me. His hands cup my cheeks to spread my legs farther apart and rest them on his shoulders.

"You must be kidding," I pant.

"This okay?"

"Incredible!"

He fills me with his tongue, then with a finger as well. He comes up for air, just long enough to say, "You taste phenomenal." Then he dives in for more, moans as he finds my G-spot. I'm beside myself. I slide down the wall, weak, but he catches me and slides me upright.

I can reach his belt buckle now, and I work it furiously until it's open, then undo his pants and push them to the floor.

"I want you inside me. Now."

Derek steps out of his pants and presses me hard against the wall. I lift my leg high enough to prop the stiletto against the hall table. He growls and brings himself to my temple. I take his tip between my fingers, caress the head, then move his hard, thick unit in circles around my opening. He's wet. I'm a virtual river. He's hot. I'm throbbing.

He groans until I bring him to the doorway and let him in, opening as he slides inside, then squeezing tight and holding him there. "You fit me perfectly."

We find a groove like two waves moving in synchrony, cresting and falling, rising and rolling. My eyes loll back. I've never tasted erotic bliss like this. He keeps moving with me, pressing and backing off, thrusting and releasing, all while kissing my neck, my chest, my mouth. He strokes me in all the right places while I explore every inch of him I can reach. I want to memorize each sinew and joint, each muscle fiber and tuft of hair. I stroke between his legs, the insides of his thighs, his hips, his lower back.

A wave of energy courses slowly up my spine now, sending offshoots of ecstasy from each vertebra. It makes me writhe against the wall, lift my arms over my head. Derek's groaning and shuddering, and just as I feel him release inside me, I also feel the energy shoot out the top of my head. I gasp and scream in ecstasy, then collapse against him. We sink to the floor and lie there holding each other, laughing, looking into each other's eyes.

Derek

AMIRA IN MY ARMS—FANTASY MADE REAL. I'M TEMPTED TO stay like this, wrapped in each other on the floor of her dark hallway. But the woman requested a date, and she's right. We need to do something normal couples do. "Maybe a quick shower before we leave?"

"Mm-hmm," she coos as she strokes my body.

"You keep doing that, though, and we'll never leave this apartment. Be lucky to get off the carpet."

She giggles. "Let's go then. I wanna see you on the dance floor."

"We'll get there eventually. I'm gonna need sustenance if you plan to give me a workout tonight." I wink at her.

"Oh, I do!"

47

Worthy

Derek

OUR ROMP IN THE HALLWAY NECESSITATES A SHORTENED walk in Audubon Park. But I plan to return here with her. A colleague told me about a beautiful stone pavilion by a pond, and I want to find that place with her, maybe, eventually with a ring in my pocket. But I heard her concerns about moving too quickly. Just because I'm crazy enough to see a future for us and want to hasten its coming, doesn't mean I shouldn't honor her need for safety.

"Oh, Derek, have you seen this?"

"What?"

"Do we have time? Look! It's a little meditation garden." She pulls me off the main path into what looks like someone's backyard.

"Sure this is okay?"

"The owner of that house created this for the public. Sometimes I come here to meditate after dropping Lila off at Phoebe's. See the fountain? Isn't this sweet? Come sit with me a moment."

I consult my watch. "We've got about five minutes. Okay?"

She nods and leads me to a swinging bench suspended from an Asian-style trellis.

"Meditate with me?"

"Sure." I set the timer on my watch for four minutes.

We sit side by side on the swinging bench and close our eyes. I deepen my breathing, allow air to move slowly through my lungs. The word *shame* flashes in my mind. I let it go like a cloud in the sky and keep breathing. I don't feel ashamed anymore, but I know that word appeared to remind me of something important I need to address with her. Let that thought go. Keep breathing. My muscles relax with the breath. Time seems to stop until my watch dings at us. Open my eyes, squeeze her hand. Look into hers. Kiss her cheek.

"Wonderful idea, woman. Thank you."

She breaks the peaceful look on her face with a smirk. "You have got to stop calling me that."

"What? Woman? Why?"

She sighs. "Because I have a name."

"Alexis Amira Albright MacKenzie." *Foret, eventually, if I'm lucky.* "Your name is beautiful but doesn't come close to doing you justice. To me, for me, you are The Woman. The Only Woman I see. When I call you *woman*, it's not to dishonor your identity but to demonstrate the esteem I hold for you."

"Hmmm," she says as she rises and leads me back to the main path. We walk at a faster pace toward the park's exit.

"How was your meditation?" I ask.

"Lovely. Yours?"

"Wonderful. Something came up I want to share with you though."

She scans my face. "Judging by the tone of your voice and your affect, I'd say it's serious."

"I need to come clean about something."

Amira's hand tenses in mine.

I slide my hand down her back. "Nothing to worry about. Don't brew up storms in your mind."

"Okay," she says slowly.

"It's just… I've been thinking about why I couldn't let this idea of you and Lila living with me go."

"Yeah?"

We reach the car, and I open the door for her, help her into the seat and close the door. By the time I get to the driver's side, she's opened the door for me and is looking at me with anticipation. I start the engine and drive west on Saint Charles Avenue.

"When I realized I wanted to start our life together as soon as possible and came home from the retreat and found you packing, that shame rose up again."

"You thought it was your fault we were moving out?"

"Thought I had failed again before we even got started."

"Oh no."

"Somewhere deep down, I thought if I could just get you to stay, it'd prove I was okay. Worthy of your love."

She leans across the console, kisses my cheek, whispers in my ear. "Hear this, Michael Derek Foret. You are one hundred percent worthy of my love. And you have it. Understand?"

I nod. That expansive feeling fills my chest cavity again, like a million cells of light are flowing from my heart outward.

Amira

THE BASS IS PUMPING IN THIS CLUB. SINCE WE GOT ON THE dance floor, Derek has managed to keep one hand on me the entire time. Now I press my hand into his chest, feel the beat of his heart. Which rhythm do I move to? I let him guide my hips and movements around the floor.

The opening notes of "Still Not a Player" come through the speakers. Derek and I look at each other and sing, "I don't wanna be a player no more." Then he takes over. He knows it's one of my favorite songs, and watching him go between singing and rapping along opens my heart even wider and makes my thighs burn.

What this song has always meant to me was fun. But the lyrics are real to him. He wanted to shed his player ways before we met, and meeting me just gave him a more concrete reason to change his mindset and his behavior. Maybe I was right not to trust him initially. I sensed his ability to charm a woman right out of her clothes. Now I'd be crazy not to trust him. No man has ever shown more care or respect.

He takes my hand and twirls me around, then brings me close. Our hips move in sync.

"How about Thanksgiving?"

"You wanna celebrate Thanksgiving together?" I ask, envisioning him at my mother's dining table.

"With our parents, in our house?"

"Derek... that's only three weeks away."

"Christmas?"

"Hmmm."

"Have I mentioned patience is a virtue I do not possess?"

"Then I guess you best keep dancing. Keep your mind in the here and now."

48

Christmas

Derek

LILA HELPS ME PUT THE FINISHING TOUCHES ON THE garland adorning the stairs, adding ornaments the three of us made together last week.

She looks up at me. "What do you think, Derek?"

"Phenomenal. The old folks will be impressed."

Amira runs down the stairs. "They're here. I just saw the Uber pull up."

"Do the honors, Lila?"

Amira and I hang back while Lila opens the door wide.

The sounds of Amira's mother squealing and my mother laughing carry through the open door.

"Lila, help your grandmother up the stairs."

"Are you crazy, Amira? I'm fine. Lila, you stay where you are so I can look at you."

"Now don't you get any ideas, Michael Derek," my father grumbles from the back of the pack. "I've been helping your mother up the steps for fifty some years. Still got a handle on that."

"Yes, you do, Daddy."

The elders enter my home and pause in the foyer, admiring the changes in the space since their Thanksgiving visit with clucks and coos. We exchange hugs all around. When I embrace Amira's mother, I whisper in her ear, "You ready, Tania?"

"Oh, I've been ready!"

"Ready for what, Mom?" Amira asks.

"Hmm? Amira, I don't know what you heard. Where can I put my bags down?"

"In here, Grandma." Lila leads her upstairs. "Mr. and Mrs. Foret, you're staying up here, too, in the other guest room."

"I just put fresh sheets and towels on each of your beds," Amira calls after them. She tries to follow, but Tania shoos her away.

"Isn't it nice of Derek to invite you to stay here so you don't have to sleep at our cramped apartment, Mom?"

"Derek knows I'm forever grateful."

"Don't think twice, Tania."

Amira turns toward me, looking confused. "How would you know she's grateful without her saying so? My mother must have woken up on the wrong side of the bed."

"Travel can take it out of a person." I wrap my arms around her.

"Can you believe she's the one who taught me manners? Maybe something's wrong. She's never like... Wait, you're shaking. Are you sick?"

I force a sniffle. "Maybe a little something. No big deal."

She stands on her tiptoes and kisses my forehead. "You don't feel feverish."

"Told you, I'm all right, woman."

"Woman." She snorts, then changes the subject. "It's great to see your parents again! I've been emailing your mom my ideas for the nonprofit."

"Really?"

"She worked in a library. What better person to bounce ideas off? I just can't wait to show everyone my new business plan."

"That's what you're thinking about on Christmas Eve? Your business plan?"

She looks sheepish. "I haven't yet mastered the skill of compartmentalizing."

"And here I was wondering what's in those presents under the tree."

"You oughta know." She laughs. "You bought most of them."

"I'm not complaining." I beeline to the huge decorated tree in the living room. "Gives me the right to sneak a peek before Christmas morning."

"It does not," she says, laughing and tugging at the back of my shirt.

"Watch out, woman. Keep that up and I may need to wrestle you onto the couch and..."

She gasps. "Your parents are here!"

"As are your mother and child. What would everybody say about two people in love getting down on the couch?"

I watch her face for signs of a reaction. The pink blooming on her cheeks satisfies my desire.

Amira

With everyone settled around the table, I'm eager to bring out the Christmas Eve dinner that Derek and I worked so hard to create. There's Althea's Andouille Corn Chowder and a vegan oyster mushroom stew for me and Lila. Homemade cranberry sauce with maple syrup. Roasted chestnuts. My grandmother's recipe for black-eyed peas, purported to bring prosperity in the coming year. Sautéed collard greens tossed with "bacon" we made from shiitake mushrooms. And a turkey that Lila scowls at every time she sees it. The turkey isn't ready yet though.

"Shall we start with appetizers while we wait for the bird?" I offer.

"Actually, I'd like to start with something else," Derek's dad says.

"Really, Daddy? What's that?"

"Got a little song for y'all, if that's all right."

My mother brings her hands to her cheeks in that flirtatious way she has. "That sounds delightful, Reginald! You sing?"

"Play the trombone and trumpet actually. Can't grow up in New Orleans without learning an instrument."

Reginald stands and moves slowly toward the music room/office. "Care to join me, son?"

Derek shrugs. "Why not?" He follows his father.

Lila giggles and I shoot her my *fierce mom* look. "Manners," I say under my breath.

"Sorry," she says, lowering her gaze but struggling to keep the smile off her face.

Father and son emerge with their horns, and Reginald blows a note, then instead of staying in the dining room, they stroll past us into the living room. My mother and Althea get up and follow them with Lila close behind, carrying her iPad. How did she slip that past me to the dinner table?

Reginald blows the same note, then a voice sings, "Ow, ooh, ooh, ooh. Yeah, yeah, yeah."

When I finally make my way into the room, I see everyone standing by the huge Christmas tree in a horseshoe, the way we used to stand in my college a cappella group. Lila holds her iPad so I can see Wesley and Sage on the screen. They wave at me.

Reginald blows a couple more notes, and the moment Derek opens his mouth I know what's going to come out: the opening line from "Still Not a Player."

With its crude lyrics, I'm surprised he's singing it in front of his parents and my child, but then he lifts his trombone to his lips and changes the song. His father follows along.

I know this song. I haven't heard it in years. It's Thalia's and Fat Joe's riff on Big Pun's classic. What's it called? I don't remember, but I'm blown away, listening to Derek and his dad play the notes in the lower register while our mothers sing the high notes normally played on a keyboard. Wesley fills in with a stunning and beautiful baritone voice. Did my mother and Derek's eighty-something-year-old parents learn this song for this occasion? For me? What a wonderful Christmas present.

My heart breaks wide open, and just when I think this moment can't get better, Lila busts out with a new take on the lyrics that speaks directly to my soul:

"What did we
Do to deserve this man so
Special in our life?
So many days and nights
Came and went while you sat
and hoped for mister right.
Then he came for you."

My mother and Althea sing the part about Derek's fine qualities and how we drive each other wild, and then the three women sing:

"Because he wants you. He wants you."

Lila solos again:

"Mommy, no one else
"Has ever loved you like he does."

Derek lowers his horn to do the rap part about how I'm there for him and how I've got the keys to his heart.

And Lila sings:

"Tell him what you feel.
'Cause he's feeling something real."

Then Derek raps:

"I'm feeling each day
Woman I must say,
That I need you,
And I want you, Bae."

"Whoo," his father interjects, then raps about how Derek used to be in the clubs with different chicks, et cetera.

The song keeps getting better and better. I'm getting chills everywhere, looking into each loved one's face, each one shining with earnestness, love, care.

Then, as if in slow motion, Derek lays his trombone on the floor and raps the line about eloping and having a baby.

"Oh my God," I say, finally realizing what's happening.

He pulls a velvet box from his pocket, kneels in front of me, and sings, "I don't wanna be a player no more."

My hand flies to my mouth. My wide eyes fill with tears. "Derek?"

Tears fill his eyes too as he sings,

"Hey, I want you. Yeah, I need you, Bae."

I glance up at Lila, and she nods enthusiastically as she and her grandmother continue singing the backup vocals.

"Amira." Derek catches my attention. "Marry me?"

He opens the box to reveal the most beautiful diamond ring I have ever seen in my life. "We could elope or have a huge wedding under the singing tree, whatever makes you happy, honey. But I want you and your family. I want us. All right?"

"All right? Hell, yes!" I laugh, keeping my eyes fixed on his beautiful face, even as he slips the engagement ring on my finger. There's a weight to it, not surprising given the size of the stone, and that weight feels just right for the commitment we're entering into.

He stands and takes me into his arms. Our lips meet for a long, sumptuous moment. I'm vaguely aware of clapping behind us. Then he brings my face to his chest and my tears start flowing.

"Derek." I sniffle. "I'm gonna riff a bit for you now, okay?"

"Please do."

I step back, try to pull myself together, and speak what's in my heart:

"A lifetime spent
waiting and watching
for the one,
wanting
so desperately
to be loved and to love
finally

giving up,
then...
From a storm
Both real and imagined,
You emerged,
Rescued me
And my child
You converged
Our three
Selves
Into a family.
Beloved, you're
The one
who showed me
how to love
Who brought me
To higher heights
Than any dove.
Now I'm flying
So high
'Cause I know
you'll always be
By my side."

Our parents, Sage, and Wesley whoop and cheer, and Derek brings me into a tight embrace.

Lila bounces up to us and squeezes me and Derek tighter together. "It's about time you said yes, Mama."

"Really? How did you know he was asking?"

"It's all over his face. The man's in l-o-v-e, and you are too. You're kinda gross about it, actually, but cute. Like Elara and Zaki are cute."

"So you approve?" I ask.

Lila rolls her eyes. "Seriously, don't tell me you need me to spell it out for you. We worked hard on that song. That should say everything you need to know."

"You're right, Li." I squeeze her extra tight, then break our embrace to hug and thank each of the parents and blow kisses to our friends on-screen. "I can't believe you all put this together for us!"

"Let's get to that fine dinner you made, and we'll tell you how we pulled it off," Althea says. "Those were some complicated rhythms we had to learn and practicing from different parts of the country? Thank goodness we're all tech savvy."

"For old folk," Reginald adds.

Wes and Sage congratulate us and end the call. Lila, my little angel, puts the iPad out of sight and joins us in the dining room.

While our parents and Lila settle into easy banter at the dinner table, Derek follows me into the kitchen. I hand him a soup tureen, but instead of rushing to feed everyone, he pauses by the stove and speaks softly in that soothing way of his. "You gonna recite poetry like that for me every day for the next sixty years?"

"As long as the words flow."

"Beautiful, you are the poetry, whether the words are flowing through you or not. All I need is your presence."

"I hope to offer more than that," I say, as I lift the other tureen from the counter. "I hope to be your harbor in the storms of life, just like you've been mine."

Derek winks. "I'm counting on it."

Also By Tara L. Roi

Thank you for reading HARBOR. Please post a review where you purchased it or on your social media channels.

The *LOVE & DISASTER TRILOGY* continues…

Betrayal set their relationship and their lives ablaze.
Desperate for a second chance, Josh is determined to become the man Celeste deserves. All Celeste wants is to escape wildfire country and the man she wishes she could stop loving. *Can love help them rise from the ashes?*
Read Celeste & Josh's story in HOPE: LOVE & DISASTER BOOK 3.

Did you miss Book 1 in the Trilogy?
Doctor Wesley Williams has a reputation for breaking hearts, and artist Sage DesChamps is too busy building her career to risk devastation. But when work and disaster trap them together, they can't ignore their attraction or the feeling they belong together. *Can love born in a tornado survive?*
Read Sage & Wesley's story in HAVEN: LOVE & DISASTER BOOK 1.

A standalone Steamy Romance set in Coastal Delaware.
In a small town on the Delaware Bay, Claire is a single mom starting over. Brian is a young widower who moved to town to escape his loss and grow his career. They're on a mission to save threatened wildlife. *Will they be united by shared passion or divided by fear?*
Fall in love with Claire & Brian in FOR THE BIRDS

Acknowledgements

This book would lack that NOLA spice if not for Eric Epstein and Karen Gilvarg, who opened their home in New Orleans so I could stay in a quiet, charming place while I researched. They connected me with people who shared their experiences, wisdom, and expertise on the city and on life in a climate disrupted community. Many thanks to Ken Caron, Maurya Glaude, Reggie Ferreira, Jeannette Dubinin, and Lyneisha Jackson.

Bennet and Sharon Lovett-Graff loaned me their home in Vermont for a weekend of revisions and nature walks.

As I am not a Gen X Black man and never have been one, I appreciated the personal and cultural insight Mike Freeze offered during the research phase. Mike also provided a sensitivity read to ensure I hadn't misrepresented the (extremely singular) experience of Derek. Of course, I wrote about one fictional man, and I interviewed only two real men (one prefers anonymity). Derek's experience is not intended to represent the experience of all Black men in America, nor did the information I gathered from Mike suffice to cover the breadth and depth of my character. It was a springboard. The documentary film Black Men in White Coats provided helpful information about the experiences of Black male doctors in the United States.

I am deeply grateful to Doctor Edmund Burke, who reviewed the hospital scenes for accuracy.

And to MacKenzie Coffman for the countless hours she devoted to helping me make this book the best it could be.

The writing quality is better thanks to the expert eyes of the New Haven Writers Group and the Connecticut Novelists Group: Greg Greenberg, Drew McDermott, Susan Nathiel, Scott Woods, Ken Levine, Corrina Lawson, Matthew F. Light, and Marcus Milan. Special thanks to my beta readers Beth Lapin, Beth Miller, and Amber Sumner. Thanks also to Annie & Abigail at Victory Editing for their developmental editing and proofreading.

Author's Note

HARBOR was inspired by what I learned at a conference at Columbia University in 2019. The topic, managed retreat, centered on how to prepare and help people living in coastal areas to migrate to safer, less flood-prone locations.

At that time, while people around the world were escaping disruptive weather events that destroyed their homelands, families in Isle de Jean Charles, Louisiana were struggling to hold onto the narrow peninsula where their families had lived for generations. Those forced out by destructive storms, subsidence, and sea-level rise became known as the first "climate refugees" of the United States. (Area residents do not welcome this label.)

I visited Isle de Jean Charles during a research trip to Louisiana in April 2021. I stood in awe of the Isle's beauty and the resilience evidenced by the care taken with the few remaining homes and gardens. In September 2021, I completed the first draft of HARBOR, then heard the news: Hurricane Ida obliterated Isle de Jean Charles.

Now, as people seek refuge from the annual wildfires in California, the USA has a new group of "climate refugees."

In Book 3 of the Love & Disaster Trilogy, you'll meet characters dealing with the new normal in California and working to create a wildfire prevention tool.

Because of Climate Change, we will face more frequent, more extreme weather events in the coming years. Adaptation and preparedness are key. That's why I support The Partnership for Inclusive Disaster Strategies, an organization that helps people with disabilities prepare. Please consider joining me. You'll find info at linktr.ee/TaraLRoi.

FIND DISCUSSION QUESTIONS AT WWW.TARALROI.COM

About Tara L. Roí

Whether she's indulging her creativity, hanging with loved ones, or enjoying a long nature walk, Tara L. Roí is often thinking up meet cutes. You can find her online chatting about romance novels and the writing process. To set up a reading or other author event, reach out at TaraLRoi.com. Get her newsletter, LOVE NOTES FROM TARA, at xoxoTara.substack.com.